Vanishing Points

Vanishing Points

THEA ASTLEY

G. P. PUTNAM'S SONS   NEW YORK

G. P. Putnam's Sons
Publishers Since 1838
200 Madison Avenue
New York, NY 10016

First American Edition 1992

Library of Congress Cataloging-in-Publication Data

Astley, Thea.
  Vanishing points / Thea Astley.—1st American ed.
    p.   cm.
  ISBN 0-399-13770-X
  I. Title.
PR9619.3.A75V3   1992
823—dc20   92-15302   CIP

Printed in the United States of America
1   2   3   4   5   6   7   8   9   10

This book is printed on acid-free paper.

Contents

The Genteel Poverty Bus Company

Ah! que le monde est grand à la clarté des lampes!
Aux yeux du souvenir que le monde est petit!

'Le Voyage' by Charles Baudelaire

Ah! How large the world is by lamplight!
How small in memory!

ONE

*F*rom where he sat on the terrace outside Laforgue's escape hatch, he noted how the uphill sweep of paddock became a rough wedge of unslashed grass between eucalypt hedgings and moved to an unnatural vanishing point as if landscape had taken over and exaggerated the principles of perspective. He found this jarring, as he was sure he would find almost everything else about this weekend gathering. Already, after barely an hour, he was beginning to wonder why he had come, as he weighed up the value of slipping quietly back to the pigpen (not that he wasn't used to the primitive) room allotted, repacking his bag and driving off into coastal blue to the fleshpots of Surfers Paradise. 'Interpretation of the art,' the brochure had said, badly typed, occasionally misspelled but urgent with *Kulturgeist*, 'must be in those surroundings that supplement the art itself.' Jee—sus! 'The dynamics of the written word understood in a setting where nature enhances symbol and metaphor.'

The real world before him ran with sunlight, butter-soft. The air was melting wax.

'To interpret the symbolic or figurative and the reality from which the metaphor is drawn, the weekend proposes to devote itself to a reading of Wordsworth's Prelude. There will be breaks for discussion.'

From the house behind him voices came in splintered syllables. He heard his name called—Mac! Mac!—a burst of Vivaldi raised to painful level—and then a window slammed shut.

There were other visitors coming up the drive now from their parked station wagon. *Just the chosen, old man*, Laforgue had promised with the sly grin Mac remembered from staff meetings. *The elect. It's a nostalgia trip, a* memento vivendi.

You've got the construction wrong, he had said, hoping his acerbity was concealed by twelve hundred miles of phone cable. *The what?* ignorant Laforgue had asked.

The construction. Oh never mind. Yes. Okay. Count me in.

He shrank back, edging his deckchair behind fronds of treefern and watched them haul their bags out of the hatchback. He was aware of blondness and baldness and then he heard the assured quackings of James Binnaway's voice uttering with what Mac decided was a cultivated eagerness as the pair of them disappeared up the veranda steps. Was that Binnaway's wife or some new post-graduate student being groomed for succession?

Escapees. They were all escapees. He recalled those aching gaps when between terms the holidays were deposited like dung, like that badly typed brochure that had landed in his northern mailbox only three weeks before. He was inclined to disbelieve Laforgue and assessed that every academy within chequebook range had been accosted—that was the only word—by this specious bit of preciosity. There were fees for the weekend (moderate) and guests were asked to bring their own liquor. He had noted that information regarding sleeping and bathing arrangements were vague in a trendy way as if bodily functions were not a concern during a spiritual retreat.

What could you expect from a host who had a large notice affixed to his entry gates: *If you are not Julian Meunier Laforgue, BACK OFF!*

He had almost done so. After all, who could rationally face the prospect of guests taking turns to read aloud to other delighted guests?

The project, the wide-ranging advertising, was a failure.

Laforgue had confessed to six other visitors. *Just as well, old man. We're stretched for bathrooms!*

Mac stretched his skinny legs and leaned back, six feet odd of amused resentment. The trick-field narrowed to a triangle. Across the lawn, the bush driveway. To his left, the facade of the rocking old farm house, trapped in a puddle of sunlight across whose far end waded his host, a large crumpled man followed by bald Binnaway, ex-teaching colleague. Binnaway appeared to be dragged on an invisible leash. Their voices linked, separated, linked, and as they emerged from the sunlight to the green shadows of the garden, he felt their gaze seeking him out as he huddled into canvas, feigning sleep. Through blinkers he watched them examine his posture—that tipped hat brim! those long slack legs!—and then turn away.

He removed his glasses and gave them a polish. Without them the landscape melded entirely into a stew of greens. He wondered about the number of variations that slid from the palest of greys to a purplish blue. The world swam drunken before straining eyes useless as counters. Sun scorched his too white skin that never tanned and glistened in the sandy hair straggle that hung limp across his forehead. Already his prominent nose had become bright red. Despite everything he felt gloriously alien under the trees, cut off in his deckchair, catching at stray poetics that pestered like flies. Every now and then he jotted down a phrase and examined it with curiosity and surprise.

BACK OFF!

Why hadn't he?

Laforgue had giggled foolishly when challenged. *Meant to take it down you know. But it's a dead-end road. I've been driven mad by weekend tourists thinking they can cut straight through.*

You'll lose a lot of friends that way, Mac had suggested, smiling.

Not the right ones! Hopeful Laforgue!

The weekend had not begun and already he was lamenting its start, longing for its passing.

Summers, he wrote on the back of the brochure he had taken crumpled from his trouser pocket, *stretch their elastic across the year ends of youth. In age they lose their pliancy and flop about and droop.*

'Jesus,' he murmured reading it aloud. He continued creating appalling couplets, working on the back of the guest list he had not read yet that had been handed to him on arrival. Six others apart from himself he had been told and the massively crumpled Laforgue.

Laforgue was zestful if not culturally formidable, his enthusiasms ignoring follies in a way that was almost ludicrous.

I will not laugh, he told himself. I will accept, behave and sacrifice myself to the tacit humour of the whole thing.

He read the guest list aloud:

Julian Laforgue, host. James Binnaway, Marie Binnaway, Professor and Mrs Stager (Stager? My God! What was this?), Macintosh Hope, Estelle Pellatier (And my God, again! Four years? Five? The bus! What kind of a game was Laforgue playing at?), Christopher Sweers.

He read his own name aloud. Tasted it. Macintosh Hope.

Laforgue would have some explaining to do. A joke in the poorest taste.

'You like this?' a silky voice behind him asked. 'You like it here?'

Mac blinked with sun and shock. Perhaps he had dozed for half a moment. Longer. The colours of the landscape were losing their distinct clarity. The light was edging away from his feet, retreating into shrubbery.

'Sweers,' the man said coming round beside his deckchair, extending a hand.

'Hope.' He reached out, struggled to rise and was defeated by gravity. 'Yes. No.' He grinned. 'Who can tell at this point? It's rather early in proceedings, isn't it?'

Sweers was a short, plump man with thick glasses, a smudge of a nose and a rosebud mouth. His hair was a high surf of grey curl. He nodded towards the house. 'Early high tea,' he announced, giving the last word a satiric inflection. 'After that we meet Wordsworth full on. Estelle is calling for volunteers for the first readings. Can I put you down?'

Sweers waggled a clipboard, an officious pen, his fingers twitching for timetables.

'Not immediately,' Mac said. 'I don't think straight off. I have,' he lied, coughing elaborately, 'a bit of a throat. Maybe tomorrow, eh? First off the starting blocks then.'

Sweers' face assumed the wasted look of one who had attended a lifetime of unwilling assemblages. He watched Mac struggle out of his chair, moving back slightly to avoid helping him. He waved a free hand in listless fashion, a superannuated choir-master. Mac looked desperately around for Binnaway who, he accused mentally, might have come to rescue him, had obligations as an old sparring partner in the turmoil of common room coffee breaks. There he was, the centre of a people-knot on the veranda. They were all staring in his direction.

'I think,' he began, chucking words backward to Sweers. And then he couldn't think what he thought. He strode off rapidly, crumpling his papers and shoving them deeply into his pocket, while he organised his face into smiles.

*   *   *

It had been difficult to corner Binnaway. 'Nostalgia,' Binnaway explained when challenged. 'Purely nostalgia, old man. I thought you'd like a get together. I had no end of bother tracking them down.'

'You missed Gamble.'

'Oh yes. Poor old Gamble. The others told me about him. Sorry.'

'No need to be sorry,' Mac hissed. 'I think this is unpardonable.'

He recalled the general shudders when they all met in Laforgue's dilapidated sitting-room. Pellatier had gone white, even under the portwine birth mark. The only perkiness came from Professor Stager's wife.

'No longer Dickie,' Beryl Dickie had said, tucking a comfily posses-sive arm into that of Professor Stager. Her eyes glinted with a victor's triumph at Estelle Pellatier and Mac. 'Joe's over here on study leave.'

'Yes,' Professor Stager had agreed too heartily. 'Yes. I'm working from the University of Queensland for a while. Julian most kindly ...' He paused and went pink. 'Betsy and I got divorced you know, oh two years back. She's living with our daughter in Florida. What a trip that was, eh Mac! What a trip!'

Mac fought for poise. 'Then the trip did achieve something, I suppose.' He wouldn't enlarge on what. He avoided Estelle Pellatier's anxious eye. 'I've given all that away now. I'm doing a Thoreau outside Charco.'

Everyone was uneasy. Thank *you*, Julian. Thank *you*, James. Marie Binnaway sensed trouble. She began urging them away from the makeshift bar towards the dining-room. *Be calm*, Mac kept telling himself. *Aloof. Suave.* What was the bloody attitude required?

At least, he consoled himself that night as he lay on the folding bed in some kind of cubbyhole at the back of the house, I can leave in the morning. Or tonight? The temptation nudged his body into a responsive jerk. Dinner had been cold cuts and salad that appeared dead. That was the only word. Like the reading and discussion that followed. One thing, he thought, about readings is that they give the impression you're living longer: the hours fly like weeks. The unutterable sadness of the lot of them playing an intellectual cricket of sorts filled him with tears. And after that came anger. Mr Sweers had opened discussion with a Jamesian sentence that he forgot to complete some eighty words down the track. Mac had shifted his long legs into another position and said more to the poster-lurid wall, the bushwhacker knick-knacks, with which the sitting-room was cluttered, 'Christopher, I'm gasping for your predicate.'

Binnaway had giggled while the others looked appalled. Later he had cornered Binnaway outside the sitting-room and under the cover of full-bore baroque had whispered his intention of leaving. Binnaway's neat features registered displeasure.

'You can't. You can't possibly. Poor old Julian. He's gone to no end of bother.'

'Minimal.'

'And it would be frightfully rude.'

'Oh?'

'Well,' Binnaway said confused, 'rude to Julian.'

Should this matter, Mac wondered, knowing Laforgue to have been the phoenix survivor of a dozen similar ventures. The place, the hillscape surrounding, had no tug. It was his own error, having tried to furnish a momentary drab and empty room in his living. Inevitably he thought of the north and knew he was still in love, in love with landscape, weather and the enter-stage-right odd-balls who had peopled his days. At sixty, give or take a few years, he had a right to choose, a right to return to the love object, even if he had come south to view things from a distance, from the urbanities of concert hall and theatre, from galleries and well-stocked libraries. He watched Binnaway's accusing eye and said, 'I'm leaving in the morning. Sorry. Tell them I'm dying.'

'We're all dying.'

'Yes,' Mac agreed and added with the sort of sharpness that had made him contentious in common rooms, 'but there's no need to hasten the process.'

He lay then, on this lumpy mattress, oppressed by the intimacy of window-thrusting branches in a way he had never been at Charco and listened in the late-night dark to breathing sounds and small whimpers from other rooms along the corridor. Across the way a tap played erratic water-beats in the communal bathroom, entered his brain and carved itself there reminding him of Wets and monsoonal boisterousness and the shouting of rainforest creeks; and on an impulse, no longer able to tolerate entrapment, he switched on his bedside lamp, rose, dressed, scribbled an apologetic note that he left on the sidetable, shoved clothing into his bag and crept down the hallway and out to his van in an excess of moonlight. He let the van roll down the driveway under its own impulse before switching on the ignition, observing in his driving mirror the tumbling sprawl of house sinking gradually into its own forest carapace. 'Prelude,' he said aloud as the engine caught and he rattled round the first of the murderous curves.

TWO

After academe, after a stint as personnel manager in a soft drink factory (For laughs! he had explained to everyone), and before he had come to rest on a lonely beach outside Charco Harbour, he had organised rackety bus tours to points north in the Cape.

The organisation had taken him half a year. The idiocies of forming his own small company, obtaining permits, a suitable minibus with four-wheel-drive, and office premises in Charco Harbour gave him a spurious sense of living after the fustiness of Romantic poets. The minutiae of running a business, even such a harebrained operation as his would inevitably turn out to be, energised. Sometimes in the middle of drafting advertisements, he paused, pondering the wording of letterhead and handbills, asking why he was actually doing it. Protest, his inner man answered promptly. You've always been a stirrer. What had begun as a fantasy some years before when his car had died north of Townsville and he had been forced to continue his journey on a bus belting out endless pop music, was assuming a shape.

Whether it was a money-making shape was a matter of indifference to him. It was a shape that contained purpose, amusement and the possibility of meeting others of like taste. He had sweated over that last assumption for he was by nature a solitary, perfectly content with the cadences of water, pavilions of leaf, satisfied with the small exchanges of living when he went to replenish stores, exchange library books. Common room rout had always depleted him. He needed books. He needed music. But if those things were absent he could content himself with the conversation of silence.

He sat back in his weatherboard office, the front room of a rented cottage, staring out his window at the heat quiver in Charlotte Street.

A name? A name? He wanted a name.

Bus tours in silence. No electronic aids. He thought about that. In a world accustomed to living against din, he would attract a rare but thankful few.

Or should he promote his own interests? Could he capture custom whose taste was congruent with his? A bus beating up the Peninsula Road to the strains of Mozart, Palestrina, Allegri? Minimal charges for people who couldn't afford much but wanted travel without the barbaric racket of the nineties? He began to smile to himself. Genteel. Ironic but affirmative. He had it! The Genteel Poverty Bus Company. Oh my God, that was it!

The decision made he had his small bus fitted out with a modest sound system. He had his own large stock of classical tapes. He had cards and letterhead printed. He had the name painted on his office window. There were itineraries to plan, welcomes to achieve from outback stations on proposed routes. The fantasy was being fleshed. The fleshing became the fantasy.

Custom came, but slowly. The first trip out he had five passengers, two of whom were crew-cut teenage boys with mean eyes and idiot giggles.

He drove out through Laura and north up the Cape as far as Iron Range and Portland Roads. They stayed overnight in guest rooms on cattle stations or camped in the tents Mac had strapped to the bus rack. The road was terrible and he played them Bach or Mozart all the way. Not all the way. Twenty miles out of Laura, the teenage kids forced him to pull up in the gravel by the roadside and threatened to break his tapedeck. An older passenger intervened. 'Put us off,' the kids snarled. 'Put us off for Chrissake and we'll walk, then. But give us our money back. Jesus! What a stupid old fart you are!'

'I can't do that,' Mac said. 'I can't in conscience drop you off here in the middle of nowhere.'

There was a stodgy silence from the other passengers. He felt he had no support.

'We were going this way, anyhow,' the taller of the two kids said. 'We're expected at the Bay.'

'What bay?' Mac asked.

'Shelburne, if it's any of your fucking business.'

They became two small figures in his windscreen mirror drifting slowly along the Peninsula Road, their backpacks distorting their diminishing shapes. He had lost heart for the rest of the journey and played the tapedeck only when requested. The remaining three had not, as they told him over beers in a shanty grog shop back near Coen, expected such a cultural assault. 'More like "Sounds of Music",' Mrs Tracksuit had suggested kindly. 'Or "Oklahoma". You know.' 'I know,' Mac had replied. 'I'll have to get those for the next run, won't I?' 'Doesn't help us much,' Mr Tracksuit grumbled. 'Still … And yes I will have another beer, mate.' The third member of the party who was a retired public servant looking for action (Sexual? Mac speculated) had barely uttered a word since the bus rattled out of Charco. His impenetrable silence persisted for the rest of the journey.

As they came back past Violet Vale Station Mac gave them the Sibelius second, and feigned deafness to murmurs and neural anaesthesia to taps on his driving shoulder.

The passengers fell out of the bus in Charlotte Street with tiny cries of protest.

Where else, he had asked them in gentle self-defence, could you have a week of touring, all found, for one hundred dollars?

He decided that his next advertisement in the Reeftown and southern papers should indicate a little more than 'music provided'.

He needed someone to manage the office in his absence and prepare the next platoon to go over the top. (Grin. Grin.)

On impulse he wrote to Binnaway who should, he estimated, be taking study leave and outlined the project. A week went by, two weeks. Then the mail brought him a single sheet response with the word HAREBRAINED printed large. There was nothing else. Mac turned the message over and recycled the paper by typing a reply on the back. 'I don't think you fully understand,' he wrote. 'This is something I can see you come to grips with. Use it as an academic ploy: folk phonemes of the outback. Portmanteau derivatives of the Cape. I'm sure you'll think of something.' He posted it off and waited another week. The reply came in the flesh. Binnaway appeared at his office doorway in the early afternoon of mid-week. 'I have left Marie,' he said by way of explanation. 'Do you mind if we don't discuss it any further?'

On the third and fourth trips up the Cape the bus was filled.

'Financially viable!' Binnaway gloated.

He had made radical alterations to the advertising ploy:

We're trendy, the advertisement ran. *We're cultural snobs. We're selective. But we're cheap.*

The phone shrilled insistently for days. They were booked out within a week. The ten takers were a mixture of Sydney Opera House first-nighters, difficult to please Americans and a Swedish couple on their honeymoon. This time the bus rattled south to Georgetown and north-west as far as Normanton. He varied his Mozart programme with Schubert and Brahms on the forward journey. On the way back he unloaded them onto the Gulflander at Normanton and picked them up after a one-night diversion at Croydon. Through hundreds of miles of claypan and saltbush the minibus bucketed, orchestras blazing, baritones in full-voiced renditions of the *Winterreise*. The muted English countrysides of Delius and Vaughan Williams created a sense of disjunction if not unease. The Yanks were nigglers. They kept pestering for Samuel Barber. The Swedish honeymooners had expected Abba.

When the accounts came in from the places where they had stayed overnight and dined, they found they had not broken even. Binnaway argued for raising the charge. Mac protested that as amateurs they could not do this. Things had not run altogether smoothly. Two back country pubs had failed to record the telephone bookings or slyly ignored them and there had been reluctant doubling up in rooms. Three of the station properties had forgotten their projected arrival altogether and had made shift with shearers' quarters. Four members of the party developed gastrointestinal disorders.

Word spread through the first-nighters. 'Just a touch too *primitif*,' they reported. 'The merest touch.'

The project staggered on through the remainder of the winter season with groups of five or six at most. Mac decided his itineraries needed variation and examined the possibility of driving north to the tip of the Cape before the Wet set in. But this was a long run with backtracking over the same country. The applicants were becoming markedly older, pensioners attracted by the cheapest six nights away they had ever heard of. Camp-outs were difficult for arthritic limbs. The creak of hip would join the querulous plaint of croakers whose deafness prevented them from hearing the lark ascending.

Binnaway fell back laughing. 'God! Let's lock up and we'll suss out the Cape without passengers. I've still got six months' leave. Marie will never find me.'

'Does she want to?'

'She's a tenacious woman.'

*   *   *

It was right at the tip of the Cape on the eastern shores that they encountered the hermit living in a converted bunker left over the from the Second World War with only a blue heeler for company. After trudging across the sandhills towards a faint smoke signal, they expected to find an Aboriginal group who had made camp along the beach. Instead, the crazy yelpings of the heeler followed by the scowling face of its owner startled them both. The old codger ambled towards them, then stood his ground at fifty paces, his mouth munching almost forgotten syllables. Binnaway launched into florid apologies for intrusion until a sharp nudge from Mac who understood the imperatives of chosen isolation silenced him.

'How about a cuppa?' Mac said without preamble. The old man's eyes brightened and his head jerked backwards to the bunker in invitation. A swayback veranda was clinging to the front and the old man watched them silently as they stumbled up the driftwood steps. There was only one chair, one table, a quart teapot and a bottle of overproof rum standing beside an enamel mug. The dog had quietened down now and was circling their heels suspiciously.

'If you've run out of petrol,' the old codger said finally, 'then you're out of luck. Same goes for food.' He grinned unexpectedly and the humour on his features was glazed with salt air and sun. Although he was naked except for dirty ragged shorts he managed the dignity of host seated there behind his massive teapot. 'But you can share what I got, eh? You'll have to take turns with the mug. I've just got the bare essentials.' He cackled over this and out of politeness they cackled with him.

Mac could glimpse part of the interior of the bunker through the narrow doorway. The room appeared to be stacked with canvases. They were nailed to walls, propped against shelving, piled in heaps on the concrete floor. He opened his mouth to comment, repressed the impulse and watched as the old man tossed the dregs of his mug onto the ground, rinsed it briefly with hot water from a billy on the outdoor fireplace and then filled it with tea the colour of toffee. 'Milk?' he asked.

'Please.'

The old man added powdered white from a tin, stirred and then tossed in a dash of rum. 'There's sugar in the tin there,' he said handing the mug across and Mac stirred the lumpy grains into the brew, sipped and groaned with pleasure. The old man grinned. 'Only one spoon.'

In front of the bunker the sea expanded in lurching blue speckled by the grey ghosts of small islands out on the reef. Wind blew off the water and combed the dune-grass, the banana leaves round the old man's water tank. There was no other sound.

Binnaway asked foolishly, 'You ever get lonely here?'

The old man turned his eyes from Mac and looked at Binnaway with something like contempt.

'Lonely? That's a bloody silly question, isn't it?' I wouldn't be here if I was going to be lonely, would I? I like it this way. I like it.'

'But supplies?' Binnaway was persistent. 'You must have to get a few things in.'

The old man turned his head away and looked across the water.

'You don't need much at my age. I get down to Charco once in a while and stock up. Got a van in the shed back there. Paint,' he added. 'Need paints.'

He smiled cagily as if he had said too much. His eyes flickered towards the bunker and flickered back to Binnaway. 'I have everything I need.'

'Everything you want, eh?'

'I said need.'

Chopping semantics in that temperature, in that latitude! Mac finished his mug of tea and handed it across to Binnaway hoping to plug the idiot's mouth. He had to restrain a mateship hand that wanted desperately to pat the old man on the shoulder, to say, *I understand, feller.* He let slip the words, 'I'd like a place like . . .' then stopped. Sudden envy hit him like a fever, like love. *You don't need anyone,* his wife had raged in their last year together. *You certainly don't need me. I'm sorry,* he had said looking at her baffled wounded face. *I'm sorry. You're right. The fault's in me. Not you. Me.*

God! she had breathed. *God!*

He found himself nodding, nodding. 'What more *could* you want?' he asked himself softly hoping only the old man heard and not the tea-swilling Binnaway and found the old man had turned on him a smile that filled out the creases on the aged face and set a gleam in the muddy eyes. 'We're sorry to break in on you like this. We're just up here taking a look around.' He rose abruptly, gestured to Binnaway to stay put and trudged back over the dunes to where they had parked the van. Ten minutes later he was back with a gunnysack crammed with half their own supplies and a bundle of week-old newspapers.

He dumped the bag on the table. 'Travellers' gifts,' he said. 'Maybe you can use this. Sorry there's no paint.'

The old man pulled open a corner of the sack and sat there looking at the tins of corned meat and jam, the cooking oil, the whisky bottle.

'I don't need charity,' he almost snapped. 'Not charity, mind.'

'It's not that,' Mac said, understanding. 'Just a few things to see you through till your next trip down.' He pulled a can opener from his shorts pocket. 'Thought you might like to try this gadget. It's the latest.' He went to the end of the veranda and plucked out a discarded can from a stack under the banana trees and using the untouched end of it showed the old man how the opener worked. 'See,' he said, 'clean as a whistle. Handy for when you're painting.'

'You like to see them?' the old man asked. 'See my paintings?'

His voice had become cautious. He looked almost sly.

'Sure,' Mac said. 'If that's all right.' He gave Binnaway a keep-your-mouth-closed glare and the old man ushered them into his cell-like sleeping room where paintings on bits of fibro, cardboard, three-ply filled every space except that occupied by the stretcher. There were paintings stacked underneath that too.

'I'll just bring a few outside, eh?' the old man said. 'Where you can see them better.'

Binnaway and Mac backed out through the narrow doorway and waited and after a moment or two the old man came out with a pile of canvases under each arm and began stacking them along the wall of the bunker so that they were assessed by the full eye of the late morning sun that found them terrible. Not bad enough to be good. Not primitive enough to capture the pretentious eye of those syco-phants at gallery openings, poised with a glass of cheap champagne in one hand and a chequebook in the other. The colours rushed forward, crude primaries applied straight from the tube, recounting the same piece of coastline over and over. Yet when Mac examined them more closely, he realised the old man had set them up in a certain progres-sion. It was the same beach, the same small headland, the unutterable ache of blue. Walking back past them he noticed the tide out in one, at full flow in another (the sand margin was almost non-existent); trees changed from leafy greenery to tattered dried fronds; in one painting there was a large log of driftwood, in another the plastic detritus of some passing yachtsman scummed the waterline. The last painting along the wall showed footprints leading up from the sea to vanish at the margin into the shack. There was a statement, a story, even if it were a prolongation of mundanities. Mac managed the right sort of puzzled lies as understanding pressed in.

Then Binnaway stupidly asked, 'Do you sell any when you go down to Charco?'

Mac could have punched him.

'They're not for sale,' the old man said. 'They're my diary.'

'Your what?' obtuse Binnaway asked.

'My days,' the old man said impatiently. 'They're my days.'

'I wish they were my days too,' Mac said. 'I really do.'

'You know what I mean, then?' the old man asked eagerly. 'I've got some other stuff in there. It's different though. Earlier. When I thought

I wanted to, well, talk about something else. Poetry sort of. It's not much good. Never felt it said what I was trying to say.'

He was gone for quite some time. From the veranda they could hear ferreting sounds, the dragging of cardboard, oaths, sneezes. Mac wondered how the old man coped with illness. Fatalistically, he supposed. He suspected there were other hermits like him scattered along the sun-blasted edges of the Pacific. People who had no need of each other. No need at all. They were content to let the landscape absorb their bodies when the time came without the blessing, the technical valedictions of doctor or nurse. He thought briefly of another he had met once in Charco who holed up farther down the coast in a shack filled with air. He was younger than this old man and spent his days fishing the waters of a small lagoon that brimmed twice daily with the sea. His shack was shrouded in mango trees and at night the fruit dropped small bombs of juice on the rusty tin roof. 'If ever you get tired of this,' Mac had once suggested, 'I'll buy your place.' 'That'll be the day,' the man had said. 'My God, that'll be the day.'

There was no point in alerting others to the predicament of these solitaries. They held their isolation round them with the pleasure of those who have achieved bubbles of the most iridescent hues, their sole achievement that they had rejected the world and survived. Why spoil that?

The old man was back on the veranda with three paintings that he propped up against the table legs. He went back along the wall and shuffled his diary into place like cards. Binnaway was staring bemused. They were small boards, no more than two feet by three, and were covered, each of them, with what could only be a madman's maze of sudden yellows and reds or blues and violets or greens and purples. In contrast to the other paintings these were drawn with meticulous care, so that when one looked more carefully, more closely, along these mazes of gold, green or blue one could see minuscule figures tramping, looking for exit or final absorption by the intricate barriers of paint. And at the heart of each maze there was a pinpoint of silver that dazzled in the bright sun off the sea. The paintings had even been signed. Earlier the three men had exchanged names over the ritual of tea and the old man had said simply, 'Just call me Snowy.' Now Mac struggled to work out the surname which had been knitted into the intricacies of the labyrinths.

'Don't worry about that,' the old man said, guessing. 'Names don't matter up here.'

'Oh I do like these,' Mac said. 'I really like them.'

'You do?' the old man asked. 'Well, I'm a bit of an ironist.' He gestured with his head at the stacked bundle of landscape clones. His use of the word gave Mac a sharp tug. He inspected those muddy blue eyes and thought he detected amusement.

'If you'd looked,' the old man said, 'more closely at those others you would have found the smallest of differences. Really.' He grinned gappily. 'Day by day by day. Just the smallest. They all add up. You want one of these?' He nodded at the three by the table.

'Could I buy one?' Mac asked tentatively.

The old man merely looked at Mac.

'Sorry,' Mac said. 'Yes. I'd love one.'

'Take your pick,' the old man said.

Mac moved without hesitation to the densely worked jungle of greens and purples. It seemed to hold the peace for which he had been searching. The silver point at its centre was subsumed—that was the word—by mutable growth entirely indifferent to its culminating point.

'This then. This.' He picked it up and held it at arm's length. 'Oh yes,' he said. 'Oh yes.' Then uncertain, 'Are you sure?'

'It's my favourite too,' the old man said. 'Happy it's found a friend.'

He hauled himself up from his chair and walked with them a few yards into the wind and the heat. 'That's the trouble with you city buggers. Restless.' He eyed them sharply and raised one gnarled hand, not to be shaken but in farewell, and as they fought their way back to the track through the tuggings of grass they heard his voice coming after them, the word thanks being touseled out of shape by moving air.

Back in the van Binnaway turned an outraged and glazing eye on Mac as he struggled with the gears. 'You've got to be crazy! Thanks to your bloody generosity we'll have to drive straight back. No prolonging this little excursion now.'

There are other forms of rape, Mac knew. 'Why don't you just shut up?' he asked kindly. 'You shit-mean bastard.' He felt close to tears.

He discovered the words 'No wonder your wife left' springing to and dying at tongue's tip. He flicked the tapedeck on and accusatorily the words of *Der Griese Kopf* filled the cabin like conscience.

*   *   *

After all, Mac finally took over the air-drunk shack near Charco.

In the aimless days that followed the closure of the bus company, he found that the previous owner had at last discovered 'that day'. The neglected little property had been on the market for months. He bought it for next to nothing, knocked down an inner wall, covered all apertures with flyscreen and gave up his days to reading or fishing in the lagoon that cut across the seaward boundary of the place. The old man's painting hung above his bed and was a paradigm for each day's excursion into silence.

Which burst on him in a flood of dew and leaf; the heat rose with the sun, ticking like a clock on the iron roof, and faded into evenings spent wrestling with a primus and kerosene lamps. Outside the flyscreen moths in their hundreds drummed and powdered the mesh with a white and velvet dust. Day flowed into day into week into month into year. Sometimes in the evening Mac drove his van into Charco and spent an evening in the bar of the Sovereign drinking beer with old timers off the prawn boats, and fossickers who were still grubbing the tributaries of the Palmer and had come into town for supplies.

What more do I need? he asked himself occasionally and had to admit there was little else to make his days replete. At the end of the first year he went down to Brisbane to stock up on books and tapes. Out of some kind of nagging concern he made inquiries about his once-wife and discovered that she had moved to the Gold Coast and was managing a small chain of fashion boutiques with great monetary success. It seemed suitable. She had always been interested in surfaces, the externals of things.

He had dinner with James Binnaway who was presently deceiving his wife with a tutor from another department and was in the preliminary stages of infatuation and ecstasy.

'Does Marie know?'

'Women always know. They *sense*.'

'Don't you care?'

Binnaway shovelled more prawns into his mouth and chewed vigorously before replying. 'I can't answer that question. It's a metaphysical one, something like "How are you?" Have you got a couple of hours, I always say. Marie has her own friends, the stray lover, midweek tennis, committees. God, what more does she want? Here's this tiny part of me happily involved. You think she should begrudge me that? Listen, Mac, come back south. You don't know what you're missing stuck up there in the scrub. Brisbane's starting to take off. There are decent restaurants at last. Concerts. Theatre. You must miss people, for God's sake!'

Mac sighed. 'No,' he said. 'No, I don't. I've had enough people to last me a lifetime.'

'You always were a prickly cuss,' Binnaway said good-naturedly. 'Remember that time ...'

And they both remembered a staff meeting when Mac had mentally absented himself from curricula nonsense by reading De Quincey's *Recollections of the Lake Poets* while argument and debate on pass levels roiled about his ears. 'And what,' the head of the department had asked, irritated beyond bearing by a senior staff member's total indifference, 'do you think of that, Doctor Hope?' 'I try *never* to think of it,' Mac had replied looking up mildly from his book, one finger carefully marking the place.

Ah! That had been the beginning of it. Constant bickerings, excessive carping about the timetabling, the lateness of tutorial assignments, the dwindling attendances at lectures. Abruptly he had handed in his resignation—it was close to the awaited time at least—taken overdue long-service leave on reduced pay and had vanished. 'We'll miss you, old chap,' Binnaway had admitted at a farewell drinks session at the Regatta Hotel. 'We'll miss your forked tongue. In the nicest sense, that is.'

Laforgue who was the only other staff member there smiled fatly into his gin and tonic. 'Things won't be the same. Not the same. You'll think of us, Mac, and your eyes will brim with elderly tears and ...'

'I'll try *never* to think ...' Mac repeated his *mot* amid appreciative laughter.

And there at last he was, not even having to try never to think.

They had kept in touch, in an unfeverish way. Letters arrived at various spots along the Queensland coast and remained unanswered for months. There had been the bus. My God, the bus! There had been capitulation when he went south for Laforgue's weekend, more out of curiosity than to satisfy a need. And now here he was, cut off in forest on a strip of beach on the southern side of Charco Harbour, an old man, he said aloud, pottering about his garden, in a dry month, waiting for—not rain, he knew; but lately, waiting.

There was not the isolation he had supposed. Southern dropouts were beginning to infest the beaches. He had been badgered by groups of them in the last year, some moving on, some staying, not far enough from his shack to make their presence bearable. They borrowed kerosene, food, books, tapes. He didn't mind that. He didn't even mind that they never returned the things they borrowed. He simply resented the intrusions at odd hours, the interruptions to reading, listening, even to thinking. If he took a walk he would come back and find them there sprawled in a familiar fashion about his tiny living-room, making free with his possessions. The mildest of protests brought the reply, 'Spread the wealth, man.'

'Of course,' Mac had agreed politely, his voice softening in inverse ratio to his inner rage. 'But do you mind if I do the spreading?'

Day into week into month into year.

Laforgue's culture spot had made him restless, not for further intercourse with humans but for less.

On impulse, and rejecting reason that kept intruding on his movements, he emptied his shack, stacking books into boxes; made bundles of bedding, clothes, kitchenware; locked the shack and drove out to Helenvale where he pitched camp in a rainforest glade on the property of a friend. It was time to assess.

He could not assess.

Restlessly he drove in to the Lion's Den Hotel and sat, a solitary out of the range of drink-gabble, trying not to listen to the tall yarns festering like weeds about him. He tried not to listen. He listened. Either way he was unassuaged.

I need an island, Mac thought, an Ishmael like me. I'm not fit for human conjunction.

Or I'm beyond it.

*   *   *

'You like this?' the man had asked.

Years before Mac had boated across sulky Gulf waters to an island with a bloody history of settlement and destruction. For a while he had nurtured a fantasy of replication, of refounding Sweers Island complete with pigmy hotel, representational as far as researchers could estimate, standing on a rise and at a strategic axis point from houselets built along the shoreline, together with a replica customs house where he, as manager of the whole shebang, might waste time and money in historic game-playing.

As with all dreams, this had ruptured, despite its saving powers during coffee breaks in the interminable marking of semester examinations.

Yet now. *Now.*

He had achieved something: a thirty-year lease on an islet in reef waters where he could nourish his mania for solitude, achieved in the way of those happy accidents that clutter living. Another isolate at the Lion's Den, estimating Mac from the far end of the bar, had finally approached, planking down his glass on the table amongst the mango tree litter. Mac's irritation was mollified by the urbanity of the stranger but the smooth plump planes of that fleshy face, too white for the climate they were moving in, held their own cautionary warning, for merely to watch those planes crease into patterns of attention, interest and caring while the eyes remained watchful, chilled. He was carelessly well-dressed for those parts. There was silk and the glint of gold on a hairy wrist. Curious, Mac allowed himself to be talked to, found himself talking back, admitting things against his better judgement. A manipulator, Mac decided, who made no attempt to conceal his intentions. Rich and with the indifference of the rich, given to bouts of alternate meanness and generosity, a behavioural diametric that appeared also to be the prerogative of the rich. How could it be, he wondered, that this stranger who was offering the solution of ultimate escape had ever himself been moved by light on water, water against sky, by the cliché of cabbage palms against sunsets, by the sweet deadliness of silence and ocean chatter? Impossible? Possible?

The stranger's admissions had their own authenticity. He had come north by whim, he explained, to exploit and develop. He had found the resort market becoming depressed. (Mac repressed his *Deo gratias.*) The trouble was, he admitted disarmingly to Mac in the mosquito-filled shade under the mango trees, that he had never had to struggle for anything. At eighteen he had moved into his father's share brokerage where he was the new whiz kid with a genius for money, the fatso with the knack! He smiled at Mac. 'I never lose. Never.' The loathing of underpaid computer hacks who worked for the firm and the envy of accounts clerks were ripples that slapped against his well-launched boat as little harmful as the glutinous reef waters rippling in from the equator to lay line after line of humble lace on receptive shores.

'My first mistake,' the man said. 'Call it misjudgement.'

Mac decided not to call it anything.

'You really want to pull out? At a loss?'

'I never pull out,' the man said, 'at a loss. You have to understand. I balance this against that. Look, I made a mistake. The island's too small for what I have in mind.'

'You think big,' Mac commented, unable to control irony.

'I think big. Correct. The lease still has thirty years to run. If it's solitude you want, you'll get it. Believe me.'

He hadn't quite believed this.

Despite the shonkiness of the proposition, the shaky sounds of words exchanged over half a dozen beers, there had eventually been lawyers, an exchange of contracts and the former owner had departed the country on an Hawaiian bound plane leaving Mac at Reeftown airport with a memory of a sweaty handshake, an expensive travelling grip and a face beaming (with relief?) at him from behind a newly nourished beard.

'Outcast of the islands,' were the man's last words and Mac trundled them with him as he drove out of Reeftown south down the coast to take possession.

THREE

*T*hey had decided to give it another month before admitting defeat.

Binnaway persuaded Mac that they should advertise in southern papers and before a fortnight was out a letter came from Brisbane making a booking.

We are a mature group, the letter said, *not so elderly as to create a problem, and sufficiently active to cope with any problems that might arise. The group would like to travel as far as Weipa on the west coast, and then go on, if possible, to the tip of the Cape. We are quite prepared to backtrack, having made inquiries about the condition of the roads in that part of the country, and ask only that if possible you can take us as well to some of the ghost towns in the area such as Maytown or Palmerville.*

They remained his sincerely, Estelle Pellatier.

Mac read the letter aloud to Binnaway who was acquiring tropical sloth in addition to his disaffection with the whole project.

'Oh Christ! I bet she's a school teacher. Upper primary. Can't you just see her!'

'Come on,' Mac pleaded. 'One last try. You'll be off soon. The academy calls. And anyway, if it's the last, you can come along and help.'

Binnaway grunted. He was tired of sharing Mac's small flat on the fringe of Charco. He had had enough of sleeping on a shakedown in the living-room. There was no air-conditioning. He was developing tinea under the armpits and on the soles of his feet. He was tired of sweating it out with table-fans that rattled, became mono-directional on a whim and did little more than stir the air. Marie had written, forgiving him. *The bitch*, he had said to Mac. *The selfish bitch! Just as I was getting used to having left, she pulls this!*

'I think,' he said slowly, 'I haven't been much of a help. Frankly I wouldn't blame you if you regarded me as, well, having used this whole thing as a kind of buffer between Marie and me. Maybe I have. Anyway, as you say, my leave is up next month. Back to the salt mines.'

Mac looked at him and wondered if the discontent scrawled all over his friend's face were the result of years of thankless work or the acrid flavour of marriage. An unnatural relationship, he had always called it. Sometimes poetry tickled him with notions of being in love, the chivalric idea of service, but he thrust them back and drowned in imagery instead. He had discovered that being on one's own was a delight and that solitariness had its own rules, that making each day a ritual quickly became a religion. If his colleagues had had the gravity to listen he would have explained that what they saw as idiosyncrasies and eccentric mannerisms were merely the rites of his *missa solemnis*.

'You can go whenever you like, James,' he said. 'We'll catch up again some time.'

Binnaway was gone on the next morning's flight. As Mac drove back to town from the airport he was conscious immediately of a lightening of the heart and he watched the coil of the river as it pursued the road with a sense of release.

*　　*　　*

They were a mixed bag.

As they sat around the office while he briefed them for the trip he speculated on this last run. It *would* be the last, he decided at that moment, for his genteel company. Three women. Two men. The sixth, they told him, had broken a leg. Their explanations trailed unfinished clauses. The American couple couldn't smile enough. Mr Stager ('Professor, actually,' he corrected. 'Wisconsin.') was a six-foot burly ex-Marine, all brick-red skin, a mop of startled white hair and with a wife to match. 'You just call me Betsy,' she ordered. 'Betsy,' Mac obliged diffidently. The two women who sat by the window, loosening shirt necks and fanning with handkerchiefs formed a pair. The younger, Beryl Dickie, a supple blonde who moved as if she were on the catwalk of some expensive salon, was examining the others with blue and brazen eyes as she lit up a cigarette that she handled more as a prop than a palliative. The other woman was an indefinite age, thick-set, soft-voiced, her eyes a cloudy brown under the shadowing of her dark hair. She was disfigured by a birthmark blotching the corner of one eye and clouding the upper curve of cheek. Mac smiled at her. She looked away at that and from near the doorway the last member of the group leaned forward and grinned. He was a youngish man, appallingly thin in his bleached jeans and flapping T-shirt, his hair, which he kept nervously flicking back, a thatch of bright red dangling in sweaty cowlicks over his pasty forehead, flopping onto the rims of his glasses.

'I'm Gamble,' the young man said. 'Bernie Gamble.' He smiled. 'I think your list has my name wrong. There's no "r" on the end.'

'You might well be,' Mac joked, 'taking this on.' The rest of them tittered unsurely. 'But welcome aboard, all of you.'

'We do apologise for our numbers,' Estelle Pellatier said. 'Of course we'll all cover his costs. We discussed it coming up on the plane.'

'No need for that,' Mac said being genteel. 'No need at all.' He bent over his lists, mopping his forehead already dribbling sweat despite the fan, despite the louvres open to the slow curl of the river. Outside in Charlotte Street the pilgrimage of tourists had begun, trailing their disappointment with this hot little nowhere along the waterfront towards Grassy Hill. *No need at all*, he thought, *is a summation of myself.*

He began handing out schedules of times, a list of places they would be visiting and of overnight bivouacs. 'We'll be camping out a couple of nights but there are tents on the bus and sleeping bags so you'll be pretty comfortable, I hope. First-aid kit. Extra water. Petrol. You realise we'll be miles from anywhere a lot of the time, so if there's anyone with special medical needs it might be an idea if they went to the local chemist before we leave. It will be difficult later on.' He paused. 'I'll be frank. It will be impossible later on.'

The group looked at him, each other, smiled and shook their heads. 'It's frontier stuff we're after,' Professor Stager said. 'Isn't that so, Betsy?'

'Right,' Betsy Stager agreed. Her smile would have lit darkened worlds. The beam was overpowering. Why then, Mac wondered, did he feel a peculiar tension in the pit of his abdomen, a tension that rippled electrically with the force of the smile, a shudder, rather than shiver, that exploded outward to his skin as if this particular journey were some kind of testing ground, not in the physical sense but in some unexplored other region he knew nothing about.

*   *   *

'Music everybody?' Mac had asked genially as the bus hauled out of Charco, swung south-west towards Springvale on the way to Laura. There had been a clutter of requests that he cut through smartly by slipping a tape into the machine and allowing Vaughan Williams and a baritone to take over with 'Songs of the Traveller'. 'Stevenson,' he explained when the tape finished, 'letting the lave go by him. I thought that might be a relevant start, eh? To travel hopefully being better than to arrive.' Yet the group had arrived at Laura trailing an atomic explosion of bulldust and had spent the afternoon hiking around the Guguyalangi Galleries, subdued by the rock carvings of Quinkin spirits, the kangaroos, emus, fish, trapped forever on the red rocks of the cliff faces. Over dinner that night in the Laura pub Mac had apologised for not taking them out to Maytown or Palmerville.

'There's nothing left. Maybe the ruins of a blacksmith's shanty. Bits of mining machinery. Remnants of boilers.'

'It's the cemetery I wanted to see,' Beryl Dickie said as if she were aggrieved. 'I really hoped to see that. I hear there are still a hundred or so graves marked. My great-great-grandfather is buried there.'

'Weren't the galleries enough?' Gamble asked. 'The light around the body. Like haloes. Isn't it amazing that ten thousand years ago, say, they were drawing haloes before the mediaeval churches decided to put them on saints?'

'I think,' Estelle Pellatier said, too loudly for the small dining-room, 'that the art of those from whom the country was stolen would matter more than the burial places of those who took it, don't you? Those layers of painting after painting. Generations of paintings. And those paperbark sleeping platforms. The saddest thing.' She put down her fork and looked away from the group into the dark beyond the pub veranda where the voices of Aboriginal women on their way to the outdoor movie came through and mingled with the roar of drinkers at the bar. 'Your great-great-grandfather probably shot dozens of them, Beryl.'

The Stagers looked up from their steaks, bright with—with something, Mac decided.

'You mean,' Stager drawled, 'you folks shot your natives the way we did our Indians? We got more in common than I thought, eh?'

'And don't forget the bases,' Gamble said. 'Don't forget your tracking stations. We've got them in common. High risk factor for us!' He pushed his chair back suddenly and rushed from the table. They could hear the sound of him hawking and vomiting in the dark.

'Jesus!' Professor Stager said. 'Have I started something?' He began to laugh.

Mac tried to steer the conversation onto other ground. The group was failing to cohere. His assumption that they had all been well-known to each other was obviously wrong. He had been misled by the implications of Estelle Pellatier's letter which had suggested longstanding camaraderie. And there was something about the name Pellatier. What was it? He ravelled through his mind, the ragbag of bits and pieces that cluttered from fifty years of reading.

He attempted a joke. 'Maybe you'll wish you had paperbark platforms after tonight,' he said. 'I've tried the beds here.'

In the morning Professor Stager was determined to agree with him. 'We knew it would be rough,' he said. 'But not that rough, eh? The beds are like cots, man, and they're full of lumps. There's no plumbing in the bedrooms. My God!'

Mac wanted to say, You Yanks have an obsession with plumbing, but he smiled and said mildly, 'I thought you wanted the Australian experience. This is it.'

'Well Gahd,' Betsy Stager said, 'you guys certainly deserve a medal. It's okay by us. We're temporary you might say. But how do folks live like this?'

'Keep your voice down,' Estelle Pellatier said with terrible emphasis. The girl waiting table was staring resentfully at the lot of them. She slammed down a teapot so heavily it slopped across the laminex.

'Oh pardon me,' Betsy Stager said. 'I didn't realise I was so *loud.*'

'Americans never do.'

'Well Gahd, Joe. Ya hear what she just said?'

Gamble raised a white and drained face from his bacon and eggs.

'Cut it out,' he said, grinning round the table. 'I want to enjoy this trip. Can't stand fighters. No one expected Hiltons. If they did, they're crazy.'

Beryl Dickie put down her cup with exaggerated refinement. She still maintained radiance that emanated from her skin-tight jeans and dangerously unbuttoned shirt. She put out a slim brown hand and patted Professor Stager's arm. Mrs Stager looked at the hand. 'It's so different, isn't it?' Beryl Dickie was asking them all but particularising one. 'A challenge! We all long for a challenge.' Her eyes, startlingly blue in the morning light, moved round the group above her supple smiling mouth. She patted Stager's arm again. 'I'm determined to get value out of every moment on this trip. *Every* moment.' Her italics pressed the air. She removed her hand slowly and lit up a cigarette.

'*You* might,' Mrs Stager said, 'but I can't stand smoking. You know I can't, Joe.' Her voice took on a peculiar whine. 'Mr Hope, you did assure us that this was to be a smoke-free trip.'

'On the bus,' Mac said, hearing his voice go wimpish. 'On the bus. I can't tell people what to do when they're relaxing over a meal, now can I? That would be an infringement of personal rights, wouldn't it?'

He blinked mildly at them all. 'I smoke myself.'

He drained the last of his tea, pushed his chair back and went out into the morning main street of the little town, the dust still damped down by dew, the scent of the mangoes overpowering from the trees that crowded the old tin pub. He had slept badly himself on the lumpy bed, sweating in the dark as he reviewed the day. The drawings at the rock galleries still crowded his mind as he lay sleepless in the crowding dark. After a while he had given up trying to sleep and had swung his legs out of bed and walked over to the window to see wedges of the main street savaged by moonlight. From the shadows under the mango trees came drunken giggles, the sound of a bottle smashing and then, for one startling moment, Gamble had come walking from dark into light, his red hair flaring as he wandered down the town's one street, a re-run of the totem figure advancing on the jumble of humans and animals at Guguyalangi.

FOUR

*I*magine Macintosh Hope, nudging the climacteric, a man who had cultivated since retirement, all the habits of healthy lifestyle: diet, exercise, the most moderate of attentions to liquor and tobacco and, since the departure of his wife, even sex. All he wanted he told himself was time to watch leaves unfold, observe landscapes solidify and gain meaning and personal history in dawn light only to lose those things again as they were absorbed into the dusk hollows of evening. Years of reading had saturated his spirit with island lust, that perversion that had been the damnation of so many wanderers around the Pacific. In the years before he settled in Charco, long, even, before his failed bus company, he had visited so many places: the Gilberts, the Marquesas, Tahiti, Samoa, the New Hebrides, and found all of them, or parts of all of them turning into plastic Disneyworlds, shrines to the god of hamburger. True, the mountain peaks remained unassailed, the drifting *motus*, the luscious vegetation of hill slopes the developers hadn't yet reached. Even the sewage and oil-spilled ruined waters of those places yielded glimpses of lost elysia. On one sabbatical when he had sworn to the department he could be found swotting it out in the London Museum, he had spent two months on a hillside settlement near Opunohu Baie in a primitive guest cabin, talking night after night with the elderly Swiss owners who had been there fifty years and helping in their gardens by day. He developed a taste for enclosure compounded of broad leaves, pounding sun, the small gossip of hill streams.

He had wanted a place even smaller than that.

He wanted an island so small he could embrace it.

For a mad while he had contemplated buying a *motu* in the lagoon at Raiatea.

The sulky owner of a rip-off tourist shop in Haapiti sneered.

'*Folie! Démence!* Those tiny islands! They are not worth it. You have terrible problems. Getting there. Getting away is worse. And water. Always the water problem. No. No. Forget it. Forget the *motu*. I have lived here fifteen years and I know.'

But he hadn't, couldn't forget.

He inspected atoll after atoll on his trips away. Always there was something wrong. They were either too isolated from what common-sense insisted he would need—the services of doctors or stores—or too close to some lewd assemblage of resorts packed from palm to reef-line with oiled bodies in boutique wear. They lacked water. They lacked interest in their pancake flatness. They were so tiny he could pace their shores in ten minutes. They had little sand. They were three feet above sea-level and six feet below a king-tide. He visited the Carolines, the Solomons and some islets off the coast of Espiritu Santo. He could lease a portion, officials told him grudgingly, but not a whole islet. He abandoned the Pacific and went to the Indian Ocean and received no joy in the Seychelles. The French there were impossible to deal with and funnily enough, even as he sat despondent in a dirty waterfront bar in Mahe he knew deep in the marrow of him that the Indian Ocean was the wrong ocean, that whatever he chose if he were ever fortunate enough to be able to make a choice, had to be close to his heartland.

With a sense of emotional exhaustion he flew back from his latest disappointment and returned to his shack outside Charco where he

pondered the Whitsunday Coast. He had a mouldering pile of bro-
chures plastered with photographs of half-naked youth, blue swimming pools, phoney thatch porticos, happy hour sleaze bars, joy joy
joy. He had an admiralty map in great detail of the coastline from
Rockhampton to the Cape. Dear God, he thought, shuddering into a
half sleep after a night of browsing the glossy pages and striking off
the impossible on the chart, those early beachcombers didn't know the
half of it. His half-sleep took him into a half-dream behind the paint of
the old man's maze where he was the solitary curtained by fabric shot
with blue, green and gold, a curtain so light, so dazzling, it was both
filter and barrier to the world.

He had woken aching for his dream and spent long hours again
plundering the admiralty charts whose secrets had been almost obliterated by monsoon tears. His eyes strained after a magic the stained
and creased maps failed to reveal in his inky voyage past islands in the
Gulf, the Torres Strait down to the inevitable glitter-maw of the
Whitsundays.

And then the man in the bar.

And then the man asking, 'You like this?'

*   *   *

They had pumped their way across bouncing water in a hired launch,
beyond the motel ritz on shore-close islands and had finally steered in
towards a gem whose very smallness had spared it. It lay less than half
a sea-mile of blue dazzle from another larger island whose future, the
man admitted, was uncertain, but which had attracted little interest.
The land on the smaller island rose to a thickly wooded cone from
which foliage flowed like water to at least four small coves with
dazzling margins where the rainforest swept almost to the sea's edge.
Settle here? Here? Here? He delighted in problems, in the elusive QED
of any given assumption and as if the other man had already guessed
his thoughts, 'There's a shack already. Up there behind the trees.'
Mac caught his eye and could barely repress his smile of delight
and acceptance.

He wanted to shout poetry. Green thoughts in green shades.

They took the outboard in as close as possible, dropped anchor and
waded onto the last and smallest of the beaches.

Discovery was enchantment. Later he would find he could walk around the island in thirty minutes and clamber across it in something more. There was a makeshift jetty in one cove. The shack was a one-roomed cabin of timber on a cleared area above the next beach. Behind it ran a small creek rising from a spring near the summit, a spring trickling from a boulder outcrop between the doubled hill folds at the heart of the island. It became a shallow stream, a string of deeper pools then twisted for a quarter of a mile in a last gambol towards the sea. The water was clean and icy under the rainforest and between the fern-thick margins where rocks slowed its progress. In its final laps the gravel bottom signalled blazes of silver across which tiny fish flickered like shadows. He had, perhaps, entered the old man's painting at last.

Mac looked across at his companion for a moment, took in the unbelievable, unthinkable urbanity of him, so juxtaposed on landscape, then lay face down by the water, plunged his face in, raised his head and laughed out loud.

'A libation,' he explained. Then he wept. Inexplicably he wept. He embraced the whole island, its smallness, its roundness, its secrecies and tiny coves. It was the loveliest of women. And he said that aloud. 'Lovely! Lovely lovely lovely!'

*   *   *

He managed to forget the paper maze created by government departments and lawyers' clerks on his first day there.

He had landed with the rudiments of settlement stacked on a half-cabin motor boat he had bought with almost the last of his money and had headed out from Seaforth with the glassy fixed eye of an early explorer.

Yet after the first sumptuous embrace, the months-long sexual plunge, as it were, he found that although he was used to solitariness the final establishment of garden and improvements to the shack left him with too much time. His face trapped in the small shaving mirror above the sink stared back, his only companion. He talked to the face, noted with resignation the deepening furrows between nose and mouth, the whitening of hair, the perplexity, sometimes, in the eyes. A long scholarly face, he had always believed. Now a harrowed face that wanted, he had to admit, to find lineaments in that spotted mirror other than his own. He surprised himself crossing more frequently to the mainland for stores he could have done without. Was it merely to exchange weather documentation with storekeepers, sit over a cup of coffee and watch the town passers-by? He used memories of the last bus trip to the Cape as a warning against human intrusion. That straightest of lines between points A and B. Another axiom refuted! How could such simplicity of direction have created the dizzy con- volutions that sent him fleeing to the shack in Charco resolved never again to involve himself with the whims of others.

Perhaps if the straight line dissolved into circularities and narrower endings, a maze itself would re-define the simplicity of the straight line.

He had always been enchanted by mazes. Once on an early study leave in Europe, his interest had been whetted by a display of Cretan coins dating from the fifth century BC which displayed classical labyrinth patterns. Pursuing his maggot he discovered seven ring labyrinths in Sardinia, others carved onto rock faces in northern Italy. The rock carvings looked like the roughest sketch of a vagina leading to the uterus with two depressions that could well have marked the ovaries. Perhaps, he thought, that was why the penitential mazes of the Christian church were laid out on tiles or stone flagging inside the church itself and penitents performed the journey to the heart of the maze on knees as a crushing, a trampling of the sexual implications.

He would carve himself a maze out of the raw rainforest.

Was he perpetuating the sexual imagery in the fantasies of a dried out old man?

There were the stone labyrinths in Sweden, the ring labyrinths of South India and Egypt.

Is the maze traveller illustrative of sperm entering, penetrating? The emergence of the newborn child?

He would hack out a maze he could penetrate and leave, himself newborn.

Theseus' clue could well be the umbilical cord.

Was the Minotaur the Teeth Mother? Did the Minotaur symbolise the vagina dentata?

He would hack out a maze, give himself to teeth.

There was a stone labyrinth he recalled in the Jungfrau Isles.

Now *his* isle.

The Christian catacombs led, symbolically, to the godhead, the consecration of the wafer in their secret caverns.

There were turf mazes and gravel mazes.

His would be a rainforest maze, a seven-ring puzzle of tracks hacked out of the scrub and culminating in a spy-post at the apex of the island's hill. Mazes had been created out of hawthorn and kaffir apple in this country. His would come from Barringtonia and celerywood.

*   *   *

It took him two months to complete the first circle.

He had drawn a design over a map of the island but his ultimate artistry was defeated by tree and rock. What should have had the inevitability of a curve, a beautifully controlled arc, was angled abruptly by the thickened bole or clawing roots of a parasite fig or was forced back on its course by an outcrop of granite. On paper his plane drawing looked like a flower.

The entrance was placed some distance from the shack and plunged at once into forest shadows. By the time he had completed the first circle and marked in false entrances and barriers and the pathway that would lead to the next, leaves had mulched the scar of the path and the scrub he had been forced to fell was decaying and rotting into the rainforest floor. Working with cane-knife and hatchet was exhausting. On his next trip to the mainland to replenish stocks of flour and kerosene, he yielded to impulse and bought himself a petrol-powered chainsaw.

He knew this to be some kind of blasphemy against the gods of the island. Almost, he imagined some mysterious godhead at the summit, a presence that would reveal itself on completion of the final track.

He thought of little else.

By the time he began the fourth circle and as the circumference diminished, he could see his project ending within a few weeks. He dreaded the ending and longed for it. In at least three places he had been forced to construct rough log bridging over the creek or roll rocks into position to create natural walkways. And all the time the humidity, the sudden rainfalls that preluded the Wet and the build-up of heat kept creating fresh growth that seemed to spring out of the soil with the speed of bean plants, so that by the time he reached the second last circle he had to spend days clearing the tiny trees that insisted on sprouting where he had already cleared. He replanted them within the natural barriers he had left.

Labyrinth.

Over morning coffee between bouts of clearing he thought often of the classical labyrinths of history and laughed aloud, drawing lines of relationship tangency to the three thousand apartment maze near Lake Moeris in Egypt, the thousand-branched conduit of Crete, the tomb labyrinth at Clusium and later, later, the famous Woodstock maze built by Henry II to protect his mistress, Fair Rosamond. Half recollected words of Higden, monk of Chester, came to mind: 'she was the fayre daughter of Walter, concubine of Henry ... a house of wonderful working ... wrought like unto a knot ... but Eleanor came to her by clue of thredde ...'

Who would come to him who had need of no one?

He rediscovered what he had known and what so many millions had discovered before him: working with soil and leaves laid bandages on the hurt places of the heart. Each day returned him to the shack with a foolish sense of achievement. A maze no one else would use. It will be, he told himself aloud, speaking to his inner half as he did more frequently these days, a monument to my last years. He could have seen it as the coiled retractions of a wounded animal that had spent too much of its allotted span traversing the deadly inevitability of A to B. He found himself making excuses. The world had been peppered— a good choice, he said aloud—with solitaries. Seasoned. The South Pacific was a special nurturing ground: Francois Grelet in Fatuhiva, Banfield on Dunk, a madman he had read about, an American named Joe Thompson, who lived and died alone on Vatu Vara in the Fijian group. He wanted to join those elect: *What's your torture?*

His maze was now the coiled snake, ready to strike.

Six barriers were in place on each of the completed six circles.

There were entrancing divergent dead-ends for nosey yachtsmen.

(What's *their* torture?)

During his crazed project he had lost weight and even though he now worked only in the dawn hours, the constant grubbing out of bracken, the cane-knife slashing, all brought him to bed on his camp stretcher exhausted. He had abandoned the chainsaw because its screams ruptured not only the forest about him but that of his mind. The vegetable patch he had laid out behind the shack was neglected, but the banana suckers he had planted were already his own height. The trees would fruit despite his indifference.

Five months almost to the day after he had begun his maze he cleared the last brush at the summit of the island and stood on a knoll from where he could view the blue glare of the passage and the sullen humped backs of other islands. *Star'd at the Pacific*, he murmured. Once Keats had written in a letter to a friend that if he were under water he would scarcely kick to come to the top. *Not here, he wouldn't*, Mac said aloud to sky and trees. *Not bloody here*.

Here he would build his spy post, his beautiful gazebo. Miles out beyond the eastern rim of his island he could see the curtseying of yachts prancing along with the Trades. A little closer a packed launch headed north crammed from stem to stern with reef gawpers on a package run. Over the water came the distorted sounds of the public address system pounding the holidayers' ears with packaged information.

He turned his back on this and looked landward.

Between him and the coast lay another island less than a mile away, a sprawl of a place with long stretches of sandy beach backed by low hills that gazed directly at him. Behind that again, the mainland and the high peaks of the Great Divide in purple and green pleats. The reef waters pearled with high summer. Had Christ, he wondered, been tempted by this instead of all the cities of the world, how would he have responded?

He had expected Minotaur or God presence on this apex.

There was only himself in a Minkowski world.

A fabulous creature now, half man, half bull, he opened his mouth in triumph and bellowed aloud.

FIVE

' "*Luxe, calme et volupté*",' Mac heard Gamble murmur as they drove into Coen.

Below the shallow hills the dying town was still struggling to hold itself together, buildings and townsfolk welded by memory rather than clay, as if the whole fabric—tenons, mortices, nails—were history and portions of history that linked more potently than timber or iron. Forty or fifty houses, like randomly flung dice, dotted the small grid of roads in the parched late afternoon.

Mac turned surprised eyebrows on the young man as he pulled the bus in to the side of the road near the pub. Gamble stared straight ahead, then sprang down lightly and wandered away along the footpath. 'You're a lucky lot,' Mac told the rest of the party. 'It was packhorse up here in the fifties.' His mouth twisted into an uncontrolled grimace. He was prepared to launch into a tour captain's spiel—the Americans seemed to want it—but he was brief as he had been so far on the trip and discovered from the interjections of Estelle

Pellatier and Beryl Dickie that they knew more about the early history of the area than he. They amplified with the zeal of town gossips. The blind leading the sighted, he self-accused, as they all sat later outside the pub drinking beer.

It had been a long day, the bus bucketing like a brumby through parched fever country to the ironic sonorities of Beethoven's 'Pastoral' that Gamble had slipped into the tapedeck as a kind of joke.

At breakfast that morning everyone had inspected Betsy Stager's face lumpy with mosquito bites—or worse. *My Gahd!* she kept saying. *My Gahd!* She had her personal spray, she told everyone. It simply wouldn't work. They were killer mosquitoes. She decided to laugh it off. Mac proffered anti-histamine ointment from the first aid kit and exclamations were stilled. He watched them all munching their breakfast eggs. Something about the names worried him, buzzed like a hornet. Pellatier, Dickie, Gamble. The syllables seemed stitched with their own spangles of last century history, thrown together by no accident to spell out a past in this area.

There had been semi-admissions of sentimental journeying from the women. But Gamble? A real name? Baudelaire amid the scrub turkeys, the compass termite hills!

As the bus had pulled in towards the ghost settlement of Ebagoolah, Beryl Dickie had lurched down the aisle and tapped Mac on the shoulder. 'Could you stop here?' she had asked, just before the last pieces of shackery were left behind. 'Only a moment. Please. I want to walk back down the main street.'

They sat, grimy and sweating as Beryl Dickie walked away from the bus into some lost place in her past and Mac, watching her in the driving mirror, found his own mind filled with the blurred snapshot of an old battler of a prospector, mouldering between the drybones pages of a history book, who had made the first gold finds in the area. He saw him. He saw him. Was she seeing the same man too, pants held up by a cord, gun at belt, stringy hands poised to adjust a shirt button as the photographer caught him with his hat brim rolled back from a face as ragged as the ironbark countryside? She kept walking away.

The others in the bus were craning to discover what she was discovering and 'Let's all go,' Stager suggested. 'Got to stretch these goddam legs!' And so they had piled out after her and placed footprints on the dust of this dead town. When they caught up with Beryl Dickie they saw her eyes were alternately bright and dim with uncovery and regret. 'My great-grandmother,' she said. 'Up here on the diggings. There was an uncle. He worked all through this area.' She was fumbling away in her shoulder bag, digging like her uncle and produced finally a photograph of three people walking away from a settlement of eight houses. The woman held a parasol over her head against the northern sun. Her skirt trailed in the dust. Beside her, a son and daughter paused for that moment to be trapped on glass, their faces under their sailor hats looking hopefully for something.

They all crowded round Beryl Dickie, peering over her shoulder at the yellowed and mottled photograph. 'That's her,' she said. 'Ebagoolah, 1902.'

Even Betsy Stager was silenced by this memento of well-dressed fortitude.

It had been the day of the Coen races—a classic field of three. The jockeys were drinking in the bar as they went through. A radio mazed with static was belting out a Rolling Stones number as they filed past.

'Full house tonight,' the woman behind the bar said. She was a busty fifty-year-old with a warm eye and a hard perm. 'Lucky you booked well ahead. They're camping out by the race-course.'

Mac found he had to double up with young Gamble.

They all made their way back to the bar and the barlady without comment planked six beers on the towelling slop-rag, took a second hard look at Beryl Dickie who had changed and was startling in black, then moved away to the other end of the bar where her husband was yarning with a noisy group of stockmen who had come in for the night from as far away as Wenlock and Violet Vale.

'But what do they *do*?' Betsy Stager sipped her beer in an over-refined way, not quite crooking a finger. 'What do they do up here miles from anywhere? What does anyone do?'

'Don't be stupid, Betsy,' her husband said. 'You know damn well what they do. They work. What do the cowboys out on the ranches in Texas do, eh? God, you ask some stupid goddam questions.'

'Yes but ...'

'They *are*,' Gamble said, flattening his verb deliberately. His ginger bangs were plastered across his forehead with sweat and dust. His myopic eyes blinked seriously behind his hornrims, one wing of which was mended with sticky tape that was beginning to peel. 'They simply *are*.'

'It's a life, I suppose,' Betsy Stager conceded graciously. She pushed a hand through her white hair that from a distance looked like a nimbus. 'No sillier than ours, I guess.'

Professor Stager glared. 'It's a bloody sight better.'

'Now I won't admit that.'

'It's real for a start. They are actually doing something. Something useful. I won't pretend my branch of academe has any use at all. What do we do except take trips and goggle at the natives? God, they must think we're Charlies.'

Gamble said, 'They're anchor lines.'

'Anchor lines?'

'They support each other. That's the beauty of small places like this. They need each other. They interdepend. In Brisbane ...' His voice puttered out.

He was slumped there at one of the rickety tables, skinny body contorted to adjust his weight, what there was of it, on the chair. Mac inspected the earnest face dipping over the beer glass. He understood what Gamble was saying, but it was something now he neither wanted nor needed. Not even this group ... Perhaps his age beckoned him outside the circle, beyond the hearth, the mateship fireside on whose myth the whole country operated. He tried to recall some salient moment in the last decade when he had needed that warmth, held his hands out to it and felt the old glow of companionship and support flush fire down tired fingers.

He could not.

Perhaps it had been the nature of his work; that ivory tower cliché that outsiders flung at academics was true enough for the serious researcher. *Had he ever been that?* Camped down in libraries, haunting the lower stacks, poring over small print and following the snail-trail of footnotes from one tome to the next to the next to the next. And after that, after one decided the goal was reached, further footnotes emerging like atolls rising from the sea within months of that postulated QED of the published article, essay, book. He could realise both the worth and worthlessness, the intelligence and idiocy of the life he had crawled through for years. Students had been the speck in the eye, the irritant that intruded upon the mapped out course of solitary research he sought to pursue. So, too, marriage. *My God*, he admitted, *I never really knew my wife. Never knew the students, my colleagues. There was I and here I am, never once part of that rollicking A's for lays that had so enlivened Laforgue's days, or the marriage-desperate ones of Binnaway; never part of that* bonhomie *that trolled for student groupies and regarded drinking with sottish revolutionaries in libertarian pubs as achieving more than the pedantic nit-picking that debated whether De Quincey really had implied that Coleridge was a big mouth!*

Had he even been scholarly? Words overheard in staff lavatories, through half-closed doors, muttered in asides at staff meetings—*He's Wordsworth's eunuch!*—came back to him now, group eunuch leader for travellers on the cheap, eunuch music masseur for the Genteel Poverty Bus Company.

'Christ!' he said aloud and the others looked at him and he rose and said, 'I think I'll just take a turn round the town' and abandoned his unfinished beer and walked into the stippled dust-heavy air of late afternoon.

He trod every street. Or beginnings of a street. He lingered at corners and took co-ordinates like some maths mutt on the houses and the low ranges behind the town and later on the lights coming out and savoured the dust and being alone and wished suddenly that he had never ventured on this last run knowing he was little advantage to the group, no good for business, for anything really but a hermetic life-style in which he could lick whatever wounds he imagined the years had dished out.

Yet licking over did not heal. Was it healing he wanted?

'I'm content,' he told an empty paddock beyond the race-course. 'Content.'

A straggler on a bicycle rattled by and looked over at him in the twilight. They greeted each other, hands raised in the dusk, and moved apart, Mac down the last crossroad to the pub hearing the cyclist's tyres purring through dust on their way to some white-anted house beyond the town. There came the smallest suggestion of breeze, no more than air-stir and a furring of voices in this last post before the

Cape at the middle of the world. The middle of the world? A pointer
to other islands slouching on the tepid waters of the Strait, islands still
waiting for the computerised *assess and destroy* of first world order.

When he got back to the pub he could hear the sounds of an
untuned piano being played with stunning verve and following the
music through to a tarted up side room that had once been the Ladies
Lounge, he discovered Gamble bent over the keyboard of an ancient
Bluthner. The drunken roar from the bar was obliterated. At each end
of the piano the Stagers posed like bookends, drinks poised between
chest and lip, their faces receding into the silence of smiles. Mac
straddled a chair behind them.

Gamble achieved a crescendo finale, oceans of sonorities. Fish
soared up like Keats.

'Like that?' he asked swinging around and staring into Mac's eyes.

'I know it. Hell, what was it?'

'Sibelius. Black Roses. Accompaniment only. You missed the singer.'
Gamble took a swig from his beer and winked at the Stagers. 'I played
it for Beryl who's in there trying to seduce a couple of ringers.'

They might all have been at a concert the way they clapped.

Liberated rock from the bar radio was again absorbing the air of the
room like a greedy sponge. Mac crossed over to the door between bar
and lounge and closed it. 'Keep going,' he pleaded. What he really
liked about music was the islanding effect, the *mental* atolls that were
evoked and inhabited for the duration of quartet, song, symphony.
Gamble was continuing to amaze. He had said little about himself and
they all assumed he was a drifter, a pleasant one, with just enough
money to see him through from week to week. Curiosity pricked
Mac's tongue with questions the music tossed back for Gamble had
launched into a Scriabin prelude, and yes, the plangent untuned strings
fought him but he surmounted dissonance with emphasis so passionate that the door to the bar was flung back with a crash and the
barlady came through, eyes flashing.

'We can't hear ourselves think in there!' she yelled at Gamble. 'Give
it a rest, will you!'

Gamble ignored her, working his playing to the final tearing chords
before he looked up blinking.

'What was that?' he asked.

He looked almost simple.

'I said we can't hear ourselves think in there.'

'Is that what you were doing?'

Professor Stager cocked his head to one side, an interested bird.

'Excuse me ma'am, but the young man's good. He's very good.'

Gamble ignored him as well. 'Would you like,' he asked, eyeing the barlady, 'something more like this?' And without glancing at the keys began thumping out 'Lay me kangaroo down, sport', watching for a moment to see her face lighten, then turning his back on her.

'You just take no notice,' Betsy Stager said. 'You just play what you want.'

Gamble ignored her as well. He kept rocking the instrument with the vilest of crude rhythms and Professor Stager bent down and shouted into his ear, 'What the hell's that? Jesus!'

'Folk tune,' Gamble shouted back. He began to sing.

Within minutes the bar crowd packed into the room behind him, waving their glasses and singing. Beryl Dickie began dancing with a drunken stockman, Estelle Pellatier scowled and vanished.

'Think I'll stay for a little local colour,' Stager said to Mac, eyeing the dancers.

'Me too,' Betsy Stager said who could not take her eyes off Beryl Dickie's gyrations. Joe Stager had always been a dancing man.

Even an hour later as Mac lay wooing sleep he heard the cheerful thumping through the closed door. He had decided to miss dinner and had bought as anodyne a half bottle of Scotch in the bar. He was pillow-propped up on his bed drinking with the light out, marvelling at Gamble's endurance until eventually all noises—the drunken shouts, the singing, the screech of car engines being savaged, the crash of bottles and glasses—all coalesced into one blare on the edge of dream and he woke to one of those so-called blue-perfect mornings of the Cape without cloud or wind.

* * *

Gamble had become an object of interest. The other travellers were curious about the fuggy landscapes behind those thick spectacle lenses.

Joe Stager was shameless. 'You professional?' he had asked directly.

Gamble had cracked his big-knuckled hands which now everyone was determined to see as having musical genius and shook his head. His pallor on this blue-aired day was appalling. Perhaps it was only the red of his hair that made it appear so. *A student*, he admitted grudgingly. *Still at the conservatorium in Brisbane.* Eyes ate him up as he spoke. Mac, driving doggedly up the stubborn stretch of road towards the Wenlock River through stands of stringybark and blood-wood would hear the unasked questions whizzing through the dusty air of the bus. His pallor? His thinness? How sick was he? Did he have Aids? Take drugs? Was he (hopefully) tubercular? Now *there* was a romantic ring, Mac thought sourly. They could face that better.

Towards mid-morning, unabashed by crow cries ripping the land-scape to shreds, Mac drowned speculation with Bach's Coffee Cantata and nudged the bus in towards the shoulder of the road. Ahead lay the sandspits and shallows of the Archer River. The music was his whimsical signal for a tea break.

'Already?' Beryl Dickie asked brightly of no one.

Mac, observing her tight-lustred face in the driving mirror, decided she was one hundred and twenty. *Oh charity!* he prayed. A hard woman at a loose end. She had been over-attentive to Joe Stager since breakfast. Divorced? Single? Widowed? She was creating pockets of ill-will between the Stagers, between herself and Pellatier. Why didn't the rest of the group turn its probing feelers onto her instead of that one pale silent victim who made no trouble at all?

*   *   *

Beryl Dickie had been everywhere, with her first husband or her second. With or without.

At tea breaks, afternoon coffees, extracting place names was like flicking pips from an orange. But she did not tell everything at once or even willingly. Was she playing at mystery?

'That was in Copenhagen,' she said. 'Or Stockholm. I forget which.'

'Yes?' the others probed, though they were tiring of the game. 'Yes?'

She subsided into a languid remoteness through which their ques-tions could not wade until her face lit up, demanding attention.

They all thought she was lying. Trying to impress.

'A village in La Pampa,' she was explaining one late afternoon. She was feeding small pieces of twig into the campfire. The sun was on its down run into the Gulf, the appalling heat at its peak. 'I was there for a month.'

'Doing what?' Gamble asked.

Mac smiled at his impudence and feared for Beryl Dickie in the telling. She was looking stubborn and the neat structure of her facial bones was making statements through sunburnt skin.

'This and that,' she replied with the carelessness of one who has done nothing. 'This and that.' She was drawing a mudmap with a stick. The company round the fire watched the shape of Argentina appear. They were fascinated by the redness of the fingernail. Then she looked up with the most luminous of expressions, the stick jabbing at an imagined village. 'There. Two years ago. That was the exact spot. Agua Blanca.'

'Remarkable,' Professor Stager said, bending closer to look over her shoulder which he patted. 'Quite remarkable. I was there myself five years ago!'

'And what were you doing?'

'Agrarian economics in third world countries, my dear. It's my field.'

She looked up at him, her light eyes strangely clear, insultingly blue.

'You don't believe me, do you? There was a hostel in town—for the more genteel poverty stricken tourist—I can even give you the name of the street.'

'No no ma'am. Of course I believe you.'

His wife, looking at the hand which had remained on the slender shoulder, was certainly believing something.

'Do you really?'

'Of course.'

If only the wistfulness would leave her voice, Mac thought, watching all of this with irritation. Professor Stager's face appeared lathered with soapy concern. His wife attempted to divert the hand by proffering more coffee. Bach was relentless behind them with his candid notes.

'My lover—at the time,' Beryl Dickie confessed too easily, glancing up at Professor Stager and away, 'Tod—he was an American, too, by the way, *very* deep south—was working for a rancher up in the hills. We saved enough money to get down to there.' And she moved her travelled finger hundreds of miles along the carrot tail of the continent to a place so unlikely, they all had to believe. 'Full of Welsh people, imagine. Well, Welsh once.'

The others were torn between credulity and disbelief. Mac felt she was shattering this present rogue dream. *They do it with such ease. Such appalling ease. Unmoneyed, unskilled, dressed like upmarket gypsies. The bastards move everywhere with such horrible effortlessness.*

They were camping out that night. They all helped raise the tents and by eight Mac had fed the lot of them and was clearing away the last of the debris under a sky slashed white by stars. As they sipped coffee out of mugs, now and again one of the party would move a hundred yards off from the campfire for a call of nature then saunter back to the strange comfort of the fire-circle in this emptied landscape.

'I think,' Beryl Dickie said, erasing her mudmap with a prettily pointed foot, 'I'll hit the sack.' No one asked whose. She rose, stretched elegantly and headed down the track a little towards a convenient clump of acacia.

'Watch out for snakes,' Mac called after her lost presence in the darkness.

'Don't worry,' Professor Stager said, instantly gallant. 'I'll give her a moment or two and then walk her back. Okay?'

They all watched him disappear down the track after her.

SIX

Like Crusoe he found the footprints on the beach facing the other island, where the sand had hardened after an ebb tide. Unlike Crusoe's warner there were several print patterns.

Initial annoyance at intrusion was dismissed. Yachties, he decided. Boat boozers! But he was puzzled that he had heard no one. Farther up the beach he found the pawprints of an accompanying dog. He had heard no barking.

He walked around the island's circumference then tracked its recesses through the maze until he reached the summit. A set of binoculars kept there and wrapped in waterproof dangled from a branch. He took them down and swept the coastline but could see no boat, not even a fisherman on the far shores. Already he had built a shelter at this spot, a rough structure of bush poles and branches closely thatched. Between the double roof he had made was a layer of plastic sheeting to keep out rains in the Wet, for he intended sleeping here occasionally. At times he betrayed himself pondering the gazebo as a guest hut and was startled by his submission to even the idea of visitors. Binnaway or Laforgue playing at castaways and dragging unsuitable girls behind them!

'A pox on visitors,' he said aloud. And added, 'You must stop talking to yourself this way.'

He went back downhill towards the shack, prepared to make vacant his mind and work in the garden. The shack itself was comfortable enough. There was a gas cooker fuelled by a small cylinder he had to take over to the mainland for refills. Ingenious plumbing had hooked up the stream to a kitchen tap over a bench with a sink. Outside the shack was a shower enclosure and earth closet surmounted by a wooden frame seat. Already he had lined one wall of his house with shelves and stacked his books. He surprised himself with his usefulness and had brought timber back from the mainland and fabricated a desk of sorts.

He had begun a journal.

After a few weeks he forgot about the footprints on the beach. The Wet season was drawing closer and fewer boats came up the coast with their crowds of joy-hunters. He had been there seven months and already toyed with the idea of going south to Brisbane over the Christmas period if only to underscore the quality of his isolation on return. There were things he needed: more tapes, a glimpse of current reviews, the live sounds of music.

The Wet was late that year. He travelled south to Brisbane, drank with Binnaway and Laforgue, resisted their flung hints, sated himself with concerts and theatre, made his purchases and returned. He was unprepared for the disaster that threatened.

That night he wrote in his journal: *January 10th. I must put this down. Absolutely must. I have been here ten months now and I find the first indication of treachery on the part of the previous owner. 'Mendax'. Renamed. How could I have been so gullible? Stupid question. All day, from dawnlight practically, there has been the most remarkable activity on the foreshores of Hummock Island, my own island's big brother. All day there have been surveyors moving along the beach and back into the grasslands with tripods and measuring tapes. At times their shouted directions reached me across the water as*

I watched them with my field glasses. I was afraid to show myself in
case it excited their interest. (Whose were those footprints? I ask.)
Workmen were hacking at scrub and in the early part of the afternoon
a barge arrived with a tractor on board that they managed to unload
onto some kind of ramp. All hell broke loose after that. The machine
lumbered up the beach into the scrub and began its cannibal
munching. Trees, scrub—everything fell before it and by the end of
the day the white of marker pegs showed obscenely against the
stripped earth. Something is about to crush my solitude. Resort?
Housing subdivisions serviced by ferry? Hotel stroke casino? God,
I can hardly believe this. Crusoe was lucky. Tomorrow I'll go over to
the mainland and make enquiries round town. 'In solitude what
happiness?' Milton wrote. 'Who can enjoy alone, Or all enjoying,
what contentment find?' Me, buster. Me!

January 11th. Those in the know, the mystic 'they' of shopkeeper
gossips, loose-mouthed real estate agents, a nodding acquaintance
from council, informed me that a multi-million dollar resort is to be
built on Hummock Island. Wonderful project, they all assure my
soured face. Great for the town. Who? I had asked. Overseas interests,
they said. What overseas interests? Well, you know, they said.
Probably Japanese. Doesn't do to sound racist. There's a local bloke
behind it. Has to get the project past the council. It looks as if he's
done that already, I said. You know! They uttered cries of envy at my
prescience. Well he's only a minor shareholder, they said. Just to get
the thing through council. You know how it is!
  Returning I barely felt myself touch the boat, my boat touch water.

Mac brooded over this information for days, enduring wolf-bite
warnings that told him his stomach lining was inflamed with resentment. There was a lull in the activity on Hummock Island for a
fortnight and then the prodigious power of money backed by government produced mind-numbing activity. More bulldozers arrived by
barge, mobile cranes pecked and nagged beyond the sand rim. By the
end of the month workers' quarters were erected and the foundations
of the main building were in place. Load after load after load of
building materials was being dumped along the ransacked grasslands
and in another three weeks a sturdy jetty protruded into the deep

water of the channel. It happened with the speed of nightmare.

His isle was full of noises.

He went to ground on the ocean side of Little Brother and began re-reading mad Banfield's *Confessions.* They were no comfort.

Daily he tracked his labyrinth to the summit to spy from his crow's nest the furious pace of twentieth century greed across the strait.

He could move once more, he supposed, but was so committed to this tiny place with its frail impinging beauty, he was engorged with bitterness every time the notion presented itself. To be realistic, how could he leave? And for where? The world was shrinking before his eyes. A pip. A seed: he could swallow it with the first of the monsoon rains.

*   *   *

Mail arrived at a box number on the mainland.

Mac was always amazed by the amount of mail he received when he had, as he thought, cut off. Binnaway and Laforgue must have talked to their sponging pals.

There were letters from an assortment of strangers all wanting to join him. There were pleas from maniacs, separating couples (sometimes both wrote!), feral freaks and those he suspected of fleeing a criminal life. Most of them he crumpled up and ignored but there were others whose off-beat *curricula vitae* tickled and which he preserved in a folder labelled Screwballs, saving them as a resource raft to which he might cling should this ultimate choice of staying 'put' prove unbearable.

The welcome mats of madmen!

There could have been interviews, he thought, had he been establishing Utopia, doing a Rasselas! He reconstructed them in his mind, setting them informally in southern bars, watching himself tot up the lines of laughter, grief or vileness on applicant faces that had everything and nothing to lose on Little Brother. People with an itch. Women who offered themselves for one thing that had ceased its itch for him. Men who wanted new surfaces to scratch.

He could hear the Socratic dialogue through the stink of malt on a sweating Brisbane day and the pounding of the monsoon rains on his tin roof.

But I'm very practical. I'm quite a cook. I could save you all that work. Really.

I'm quite a cook. Do you read?

Do I what?

Never mind. Do you listen to music? I'm quite cut off up there. No television you know. You'll need books and music. Do you like music?

Of course.

What sort?

Hey, what is this? I thought you ...

What sort? What sort of music do you like?

What do you mean, what sort? Hell, I don't know. What everyone likes. Pop. Heavy metal. Rap. I really dig music. Country and Western. R and B.

What's that?

God! Where have you been? *Oh yes. Sure. Not that long. Rhythm and Blues. Old hat, but I like it. Listen, there've got to be other things to ...*

Next ... letter!

There were approaches from a qualified psychiatric nurse, a politician who had lost a recent by-election and several teachers who were failing to find job-enrichment.

*   *   *

Mac had a sudden filmic flash of Binnaway's wife cornering him petulantly at a farewell party only a month ago. *There I was*, she had complained, *with a handful of accountancy tickets, a degree in business administration and a husband who wanted me waiting each evening with a martini shaker and a well-tempered oven.* He had murmured something placatory about her finding a job. *But the rows!* she had cried so loudly half the room had turned to listen eagerly. She was watching her husband's intransigent back across the room. *The endless endless rows! My dear*—and her hand had found Mac's knee as if by accident—*I did get a job once. After a month James took my boss to lunch and had me sacked. Redundant was the word. Last on, first off. Of course, I sulked for months.* Mac was aware of Binnaway's head strained backwards to catch every word. *So I went on spending binges. Then I gave up and took a course in dramatic art. You hardly need that, James told me. You've refined your vulgar domestic dramas into an art form! Well, I ask you, Mac. I ask you.*

Binnaway had given up listening furtively. Why be furtive? The rest of the party was agog. He crossed the room to tower over them both. *She wants a screw. A great long undistinguished screw! She is testing the waters, Mac. Be warned.*

Warned.

He placed James Binnaway's letter alongside that of his wife and compared them under lamplight. They deserved each other. Then he tossed out Marie's marital plaint along with the other outpourings of opportunists and lotus eaters and re-read Binnaway's. *I have left Marie finally and utterly*, he wrote. *I shall visit.* No plea there. More a threat. He wondered how he could postpone the conviviality, the drunken evenings of marital remorse. How allow any of his southern friends always ready with the I-told-you-so to observe what was happening across the water? He had mentioned nothing of the resort. He was afraid of looking foolish, of reaping fake commiseration, bogus compassion for misjudgement. Laforgue, that professional guest, named actual dates! When the rains eased he crossed over to the mainland and sent scribbled messages to each of them: *Hopeless at the moment. Shack blown down in high winds. Will be in touch.*

Across the water the racket of electric drills, cement mixers and graders were the sonic metaphor for what was now becoming three unattractive storeys of glass and concrete that raised its shell back from the beach. Ten-foot palms were shipped across by the score, poised above holes scooped out by bobcats and firmed into place. He wished he didn't wish they would wither. An enormous swimming pool had been gouged out above the waterline to be fed by reef water. Lawn appeared overnight. All day the workmen's transistor radios blared across the sea and drove him from spy-post to fox-hole. Even there, a blurred cacophony assailed. Now toadstool villas were sprouting, bars, boutiques, a landing strip. He went down to Mackay and sought comfort from lawyers, lobbied local politicians skilled in evasion and wrote letters of complaint to the local paper. He received little sympathy. 'Didn't you make inquiries first?' they all asked him. 'You slipped up there, eh! Listen, mate, it's doing great things for the town. Why don't you put up or shut up?'

He bought a generator.

That night back on his island he wrote in his journal: *The first weapon!*

Inevitably there will be a constant flow of nirvana seekers jetted from economic springs in foreign lands. There will be constant bliss and electronic frenzy ripping the sumptuous darkness. I shall respond.

He bought a powerful amplifier and two sets of speakers, one set of which he rigged high in a tree at the focal point of his maze. The solution! The monster in the cavern, a twinned pair of spheres, art decorator green, housed under fibreglass and protected from forest animals by a tough mesh screen. The power line from the generator raced directly up hill from his player, cutting across maze paths in a more or less straight line suspended from branches. The speakers were positioned so that they faced the resort across the water.

He felt like a general preparing for battle.

He even disgusted himself when he realised he could hardly wait for the first confrontation.

Late at night, he decided. Wagner. The launching of his first stealth missile.

SEVEN

On a sandspit by the river he quickly got a small fire going to boil the billy. Gamble came up to help. Beside them the Coffee Cantata flowed on, transferred to Stager's battery player. The others had wandered down to the shallow freshwater pools of the river and presently there filtered back a chorus of giggles and splashings.

Gamble stared dreamily into the billy, waiting for it to come to the boil, stirring with a gum tree twig and inhaling the eucalyptus fragrance as it rose with the steam. Stager was wallowing in a waterhole downstream from the women. Mac set out the tea mugs beside the fire. He looked at Gamble stirring and humming along with the music.

'Don't you feel like a swim?'

'Oh I feel like it.'

'Then why not? I can handle this.'

'Don't think,' Gamble said slowly, still watching the twig, 'that I haven't noticed the curious looks. No. I don't have Aids. Shall I bellow it out over the PA system and put their minds at rest?'

'If you like. If you really want to.' Mac grinned and threw a handful of tea into the billy. 'Be a good lad,' he asked, 'and fetch the milk from the bus. I'm not functioning properly this morning. Oh, and sugar.'

Gamble propped the twig carefully against a rock and went back to the road. The bus stood on the grass marge like an alien slug. The whole trip was a laugh. But he was enjoying it, enjoying the gradual breaking down of those staged personalities who had begun the journey. Wankers! All of them wankers! He dug out the powdered milk and the sugar tin from the supply box and went back.

'I've been pretty sick.' He resumed his squatting position and flicked the twig away watching it loiter along the gentle river current. 'I lost a kidney last year. God, you don't want to hear about it, but I'm still pottering round, you know, feeling dickey. Probably shouldn't have inflicted myself on this trip.'

'Why not?'

'Could be a handicap. For you. For the others.'

'I'm glad you're here,' Mac said, meaning it. He hesitated. 'What about your career? Your playing?'

Gamble inspected Mac's pleasant worried face as he began pouring the tea. The others had left the water and were wandering back to the campsite towelling their heads dry. 'Oh I've given that away. Haven't the strength to do the practice needed. You know, you have to be pretty fit to be a musician. Good wind. Stamina. I've got brass player pals who work out regularly. It's not all Chopin spewing blood on the keyboards.'

You have to be even fitter to do nothing at all, Mac wanted to reply. The mind goes first, without rituals. But he had learned to turn each day into ordered patterns: that first cup of coffee, the preparation of notes for classes, the time set aside for grading assignments, for visiting libraries, for lunch, dinner, bed. Days carved out into masses of tiny practicalities. He had become what Coleridge contemptuously called a 'goody'. But it worked. He had even set a time for simply staring into space.

He said aloud, 'You've got to be really fit to do absolutely nothing.'

Gamble looked at him thoughtfully.

'I like the sound of that. I like it very much. It makes me wonder why you're doing this.'

'It makes me wonder too,' Mac said.

The party camped out that night off the road somewhere near Wenlock station. As Mac prepared to insert himself into the narrow opening of his pup tent he was stopped by Gamble's white face, another moon, peering down at him.

'Do you have time for a yarn?'

Mac crawled back out of the tent and suggested they go back to the bus so as not to disturb the others. His bony flanks ached from the driving, his heart ached for what he could see was a mistaken venture. How much time was there left to talk or not to talk, for him anyway? He had long passed beyond impetuous moments, those bursting hours of youth when ideas had to gush out or choke. The world had enough ideas to sink it. And was sinking. The world never learnt from its errors, except in the technological sense. He envisaged a planet where notions of morals and justice were replaced entirely by computered decisions. The little time left was perhaps too much.

He said all this to Gamble who blinked and sat forward on the edge of the bus seat, shuddering in unexpected cold.

'I'd planned,' he said, 'on not coming on. One of the boundary riders told me there was a mail plane back to the coast in the morning. But now.'

'If you're finding it tough,' Mac said, 'I'll understand.'

'It's not that. My body's still coping. It's the whole sodding ambience those others are creating.'

The afternoon had passed with compressed lips. Everyone carried that lightning exposure of Beryl Dickie emerging naked from the river to wander ostentatiously past the campfire in search of clothes she claimed she had misplaced. Her white body had glowed with the shock of a *fête champêtre* against red earth and sombre scrub and they were forced to accept the outrageousness of her insisting she drink her tea before clothing herself. 'It's so *hot*,' she had whispered, the force of her emphasis challenging them all. 'It's so *hot*. Aren't *you* hot, Joe?' She sidled up to Professor Stager to borrow his spoon. 'Or you, Mac?'

'Skin cancer!' Estelle Pellatier had warned flatly, and had flung her a shirt, knocking the tea from her hand. There had been a lot of querulous squealing and the shirt flung back.

'Nothing too genteel about this company,' Professor Stager commented, giggling maliciously.

His eyes were riveted.

All of them sat it through until they reached Weipa. 'Here's your *luxe* and *calme*,' Mac said softly to Gamble as they checked into the town motel made available by bauxite courtesy. Perhaps it was the air-conditioning that unhinged the Stagers, the hot water, the insect screens. Over breakfast they announced their intention of flying out on the company plane to Cairns. 'Blame the little lady,' Joe Stager kept saying. 'Once she gets to taste those fleshpots!' He winked at Beryl Dickie. His wife kept staring stubbornly ahead. 'Maybe we're getting a little old for this kind of thing, huh? Well, maybe Betsy is!' He laughed appreciatively at himself. 'Feel like we're deserting. But what the little woman wants goes!'

Everyone maintained a threatening silence. The disappointment on Beryl Dickie's face was palpable. She had spent the previous evening edging Stager away from this wife, displaying late-girlish awe at his travellers' tales. He was a man who had to touch when he talked. He touched a lot.

*   *   *

The town squats on the rim of Albatross Bay, a boringly geometric assemblage of almost identical houses, a company town twelve degrees below the equator, hot and sticky in the Dry, intolerable in the Build-up, barely livable in the Wet. The large-leaved tropical plants in the gardens remain alien, hostile. The old mission on the Embley River has been gobbled up by the mining town. The government has taken over the mission and salved its conscience for past crimes against the original owners by easy handouts.

The diminished group wandered the streets as far as Duyfken Point, stared lack-lustrely at dozers, screeners, crushers, open-cut mines and a giant freighter moored at the town wharf then fell back into the air-conditioned bar at the motel with cries of relief.

They barely noted the Stagers depart.

'Do you still want to go to the Tip?' Mac asked, more out of politeness than anxiety. They hardly seemed a group at all.

Estelle Pellatier suggested a vote on it. Her blighted handsomeness was swollen with confidence now the Stagers were a forgotten pair of dots waiting on a dusty tarmac. Mac warned them it would be camping for the rest of the way. Privately he hoped they would vote for a return.

'Right to the Tip,' Estelle Pellatier insisted.

Beryl Dickie nodded sullenly while Gamble raised eyebrows and shoulders in a wry 'whatever' fashion.

So they had packed their belongings, checked out and back-tracked to the Peninsula Road, the tapedeck unsuitably playing Delius, Gamble paler than death but hanging in out of some peculiar loyalty to Mac's theories, if not Mac, squeezing out weak jokes about finding the perfect Baldwin piano abandoned near Somerset by a passing tourist liner. Beryl Dickie sulked.

Hour after hour after hour.

The road ran in an almost straight line north, always north; and after a while even the empty landscape demanded that the tapedeck be silenced with the intruders as they bucketed along a road a little better than a track to come late in a star-hung dark to the ruins of Somerset, emptied of all but the coconut palms that had been planted years before. Offshore the islands prowled like whales.

A place teeming with ghosts.

After the tents had been erected and a meal of sorts eaten, the quality of those lost settlers and the memory of dispersed tribes blunted need for conversation. The two women spoke quietly beyond the fire, civil at last; Gamble rolled himself in his sleeping bag and fell instantly asleep. They could have been the last humans on earth.

Like the two women, Mac trod old ground.

It was forty years since he had camped only a few miles from this spot. He sat on now, feeding the fire, feeding memory where he strode, the youngest patriot in a light ack-ack unit positioned at the Tip. Although he had enlisted for overseas service, he had seen no action beyond this outpost during the Pacific war and the closest he had come to terms with disaster was hosing down the bomb turrets of returned planes, trying not to vomit at the jelly of blood and flesh that had been spattered by enemy fire. He had hated the war, the boredom of it all, the reported brutality, the death stews he cleaned up, the sheer pointlessness of everything that was happening.

But there had been lighter moments in the monotony of heat, flies, bad meals. The genteel company of soldiers!

His unit had been composed largely of men from the university regiment. When Japanese pressure mounted on the eastern seaboard he enlisted. Reluctantly. But enlisted. Most of them were originals, better educated than the fuzz-chinned lieutenants who were handing out orders in futility, and sharply aware of the comic idiocies of protocol.

Trembath. How well he recalled Trembath.

He sat grinning in darkness at the memory of Trembath on sentry duty outside Tobaccotown headquarters presenting arms to the family goat in the yard of the house the army had taken over. Trembath had done it deadpan, po-faced with satiric militarism. He had taken sentry duty lightly too. On night-watch in the Cape he would prop his rifle to act as deputy while he wandered off into the scrub to sleep. Despite these quirks, Trembath had magically received one pip. Even then he failed to take his duties seriously. When the unit was harangued by a visiting colonel, Trembath took up position behind his senior officer and a little to one side so that the lined up ranks could see him. Mac laughed at the memory. 'And I tell you men,' the colonel had roared, 'that if there is the slightest repetition ...' and all the time Trembath had nodded exaggerated agreement, made mock horror faces and silently mouthed large parodies of the colonel's words, 'the most severe punishment ... all leave cancelled ...', while behind him Trembath nodded yes's and shook no's and waggled his head in mock horror at the unit's misbehaviour as the unit stood to attention, straining not to burst out laughing.

'God!' Mac said aloud. 'Oh my God!' Those were the years of gregariousness, the lust for talk, for company. Trembath had vanished suddenly a month or so after he had been made a lieutenant and hauled south to join the diplomatic corps as a cadet and had survived over the decades to become a bongo playing ambassador marooned in South-East Asia with the same disregard for *gravitas*.

He stubbed out his cigarette in the dirt. The moon had risen, a burning orange paper lantern that faded as he watched. Sandflies bit his arms and legs. Mosquitoes droned in from the lank grasses. *God*, he said again, and heaved himself up dusting off the sand still powdering his shorts to trudge up over the crest towards the sea. Looking back, he saw the fire watching him like a red eye. He shivered for no reason and set off down to the beach and walked its length.

When he returned the fire was nearly out; he stirred up the embers, fed in a few more twigs and boiled up the billy again, dropping fresh leaves on the old, creating a brown stew. From the pup tents came no sound, not even the snorting noises Estelle Pellatier seemed to make all night, snuffling through dreams he had eavesdropped on through canvas and wall.

A vagrant line from a story of Chesterton's kept coming into his mind. *I want nothing*, the man in the story said. *I want nothing I want nothing*. Variants created by different emphasis each time. I want *nothing*, he had stated. Ah, that was the tricky one. He thought of that other old man in the gun emplacement stuck out there some miles to the south who had told him and Binnaway that he, too, had wanted nothing. Was it nihilism they craved, a melting into the void?

Despite himself and the steaming brew of tea that he sipped as delicately as if it were some rare wine, he shuddered.

Nothingness could fall from the air. He feared they were on a journey from nowhere to nowhere.

EIGHT

Over-priced ecstasy and tourists converged within another month. The vine blanket that screened much of the canopy on the hill created a baffle but nothing could muffle the raucous screech of the newly opened disco that pounded the nights until one in the morning. Evenings were shredded into vile ragged lengths.

Sometimes tourists on their hired windsurfers or canoes attempted to land on Little Brother. They did land. At first Mac requested politely that they leave, then ordered, then took to pacing the accessible strands with a shot-gun, blasting away at an unruffled blue sky. A mainland police officer came over by launch and cautioned him. He posted large notices that said 'Private', a word that seemed to excite the curiosity of intruders and fire their interest. He began wandering naked around the sea marge and received another caution.

Mac smiled a secret smile and in the heavy peace of three o'clock dark started his generator and gave the sleeping resort two hours of *Die Götterdammerung*. He went up through the maze to watch the lights come on across the water.

Behind the speakers in their eyrie, he had built a kind of sound board with side wings that formed a funnel. With the amplifier turned up full, music channelled itself across the strait to blast an entry even through the plate glass and air-conditioning. With delight he observed the terrace by the pool wash with sudden light and saw figures moving rapidly backwards and forwards across its glow. In the main building half the rooms were lit up. He felt godlike, powerful, watching illuminated agitation.

All the next morning inquisitive boats nosed about his shores but stayed a hundred yards off. People peered through field glasses. A number of them played radios challengingly. But Mac was to be found, a picture of inoffensive meekness, dangling a line from the end of his jetty. Later he went back to his shack and read for an hour before catching up on sleep to ready himself for the night. Yet his dreams were bashed apart by the thud wham of electronic revenge, so devastatingly resonant even the tourists must have been pleading for mercy. In his eastern facing shelter tucked as it was beneath covers of leaf, the thwack and blast of reciprocatory rock made the cups on his table rattle. He made himself a meal to the pain-screams of male singers and sorted through his tapes and records for something equally devastating. The waiting was tedious. In his journal he prepared concert programmes to delight Hummock Island. *Little Brother is listening to you,* he wrote facetiously, and then found himself cursing them aloud. To have done this to him! To have reduced him to a throbbing vengeful pulse! He hated them most for that.

At two in the morning he gave them the whole of the *Carmina Burana* and rounded off the evening with acts one and two of *Parsifal.* 'Too good for them,' he was muttering, red-eyed from lack of sleep in his hut. 'Too bloody good.' His shaving mirror scowled back.

Five nights of this.

Berlioz. Stockhausen. Webern. Bartok.

He felt no guilt. He felt guilt.

He was reviling his own gods.

He had read recently that America made no bones about using heavy rock music as a weapon to terrorise an embassy. They understood the viciousness of the culture they had created, whole generations of kids brain-drained by the noise-cult, their jerked-up nervous systems craving hubbub as a drug. *Here's to you, Uncle Sam! Up yours!*

On the morning of the sixth day as Mac lounged on his jetty trailing a line in high tide, a meanly powered speed boat describing the curls of a flash watery signature rocked to an insolent pause, motor still throbbing at his jetty's end. He watched two men clamber up onto the footway. They stared long and hard at him then began to walk across. A third man remained in the boat, allowing the engine to roar for a whole minute before cutting it.

A squat powerful man, Mac wrote in his journal later that day, *leather-tanned, balding. His companion was over six feet, built like a house. The minder, doubtless. He sported reflective sunglasses in a menacing blue that dazzled as they threatened. I had a deckchair with me on the jetty and a plate of breakfast cereal. As soon as they came towards me I took to my chair, and began spooning Weeties as if those bastards of intruders weren't there. It gave me an advantage.*

Mac neither greeted nor smiled. He wedged his rod into the leg of the chair and steadily shovelled up mush. They watched him for a moment and then the shorter man said, 'I think we have a few things to talk over.'

The journal commented: *I assess this oaf to be a man unaccustomed to thwarts and baffles. I must have looked disingenuous enough slopping up my breakfast. He has, I hear, powerful political friends in the south of this state who take their bribes in brown paper bags. The packed lunch! They believe strongly in the fluidity of used and crumpled currency.*

Mac looked at them briefly, decided on silence and scraped up the last of his breakfast. It was almost pleasant to sense the rage in the man standing over him, more pleasant still to have his sense proven correct when the minder swooped unexpectedly and snatched the plate away.

'Why thank you.' Mac smiled. He took a handkerchief from his shorts pocket and fastidiously wiped his mouth, brushed off both hands and replaced the handkerchief. Nothing must ferment his calm. He gave them wide-eyed interest.

'Who are you?'

'You know bloody well who I am.' The short man was contemptuous. He spat his own name. 'Truscott. Clifford Truscott.'

'Spell it.' Mac was interested to see the man's hands clench.

'Listen!' Truscott shoved his porky face horribly close. 'I am the owner, developer, whatever, of the resort across the water, built, I might add, with government approval. And I'm not going to have any shitty little two-piece beachcomber putting me out of business. You are driving me mad with your night-time bloody racket. The guests are complaining. I'm complaining. If you don't stop I'll have your lease rescinded quick smart and you'll be off here for good.'

'I play only the best music,' Mac said. He smiled again. Oh they couldn't stand variety, these baboons, they couldn't bear intricate melody lines, rhythmic innovations. It hurt! They craved the repetitive thump thump thump thump as mindless as the copulation of rutting animals. That was it! He'd stumbled on it! The source of popularity was the drum wallop of the sex act backed by the orgastic cries of over-stimulated young. 'Would you care for something lighter? The Romantics, say? I've a great Schubert collection. Or Chopin? Everyone likes Chopin.'

'In twenty-four hours!'

Mac picked at a dried fleck of mush on the edge of his shorts and licked a thoughtful finger.

'I don't think that's possible.'

'You'd better believe it,' Truscott said straddling the timber decking of the jetty, bulging in his beach shirt. 'You can do a lot in a day.'

'Oh nonsense,' Mac said. 'Absolute nonsense.'

Gossip on the mainland had informed him Truscott was a man to be careful with. The acronym FBO stood for first boat off and was applied without even a moment for argument to employees who overstepped the mark. There was a piratical coarseness about this stocky bugger whose rage now had the incandescence of cartoon animation.

'I've given you fair warning.'

He swung about, head-jerking his bully-boy to follow. Mac waited until the boat vanished around the little headland.

That afternoon, note against note, a collision mid-strait, he gave Hummock Island the rest of *Parsifal*. Wind-sailers trapped mid-dissonance should have chosen obliteration, a salty plunge. At three that morning he played Beethoven's last quartets.

Truscott sent a letter through his lawyers making an offer for the lease, an offer of such magnitude that Mac could only laugh. That, plus an alternative island, to be chosen with his approval.

'What power!' Mac breathed admiringly. 'What authority!'

He did not reply.

*   *   *

A few days after this a small dinghy with outboard puttered into the landing stage and a plump city type uncoiled himself from the stern, tossed a rope over the mooring post and stood for a minute gazing at the blank face of the island, shuttered in trees. He raised his hand to his mouth and cupped a shout that brought Mac from his shack, shuddering at the recognised singsong of Binnaway's voice. Nevertheless Mac parted the tree screen and walked down towards the beach, his mind rattling with opposites: he hated intrusion; he needed reinforcements. He forced his face into smiles, made dubious syllables of welcome while Binnaway explained what a job he'd had tracking him down.

'I don't want to be tracked down,' Mac complained, half-sourly. 'I don't need to be rediscovered. I have enough problems right here at the moment.'

'Problems?' Binnaway's face lit up. 'Well, that's cheering. I'd always thought you were the self-sufficient man! More righteously adequate than the rest of us. My God!' He cocked a listening head. 'What's that frightful noise?'

On Hummock Island morning joy had begun.

'Come up to the shack,' Mac suggested, wincing, 'and I'll tell you all about it.'

Not only had he left Marie for the last time, utterly the *last*, Binnaway explained over drinks, but he had left the job as well. 'Left' was hardly the word. They had, he protested, forced his resignation for refusing to accept the directions of head of school. 'Jesus,' Binnaway said between sips and self-absolutionary giggles, 'the only direction Bronco ever gave he gave when he went on his last sabbatical. Typed up, pinned on the notice board.' He gave a fair rendition of Bronco's high-pitched chant. '"One: Chairs must be replaced in the exact indentations already made in the common room carpet. Two: Water the mother-in-law's tongue from *both* sides."

I read that and at his little farewell morning tea—dried cheese and three packets of old crackers—I shifted all the chairs and dropped the mother-in-law's tongue five floors into the car park. Chaos. Chaos.' His bright spiteful eyes became doggy. 'Just a week or two, Mac. I've got some grog in the boat, a bit of food. I just want to sort out priorities.'

'Not the remnants of the crackers, James, I hope.' Mac leant back against the wall. Binnaway had taken his only chair. 'You know I don't need anyone, don't you? The whole point of this exercise is *not* to need anyone.'

'I know,' Binnaway said humbly. His eyes were bloodshot. His creased unfit body was the essence of gloom. Any moment, thought Mac, there will be tears and was granted an immediate trail of moisture on Binnaway's puckered baby cheeks. Mac eased himself round on the stretcher. The bony framework was biting into his thin flanks.

'I could buy in, you know. Shares or something,' Binnaway suggested. 'Severance pay and all that.'

'I don't want anyone to buy in. We weren't exactly a great business partnership in Charco, were we?'

'Look, that was a long way back. I never claimed to be a business type.'

'You're not a recluse either. Look, James, a month. And that's generous. I'll give you a month to regrow your social skin or whatever, and that's it. How about that? And I do mean a month. You can knock up another shack if you want. Or camp. But well away from this spot. Sorry if that sounds unwelcoming, but that's the way it is. And maybe when you're desperate, say in a year's time, you can come up for another month. That's if I manage to stay put. Those bastards across the water are trying to edge me out.'

'You mean Truscott's place? But that's how I found you. I was there for three nights on one of those package deals. Don't ask me how or why. I won it in a raffle, for God's sake! Knew it was a mistake the moment I arrived. They're all talking about you over there. You kept me awake for three nights, mate. God, have you fired a boil-up!'

'And you came across from there?' Mac was suddenly infuriated. 'Do they know you're here?'

Binnaway shook his head. 'No,' he lied. 'I checked out. Rented a dinghy back at Seaforth, stocked up and found my own way across.'

'And are you to be followed by reinforcements?' Mac asked. 'Have you prepared another little surprise for me rather like the one you organised with Laforgue?'

'Oh come on, now,' Binnaway said. 'You never could take a joke, Mac.' He was knuckling at his reddened eyes like a small boy.

'Could I not?' Mac looked at him and wondered if Binnaway were simply another barrier to the spiritual maze he was constructing. 'You're on your own, then,' he warned him ungraciously. 'Shelter, food, whatever. I'm good for the occasional coffee. Very occasional. Can you take it?'

Binnaway sat up, surprisingly recovered, on Mac's one chair. He stopped rubbing his eyes. He forced a grin. 'Sanctuary. It's like the mediaeval church, Mac. Sanctuary for a month.'

NINE

'*P*ellatier,' Gamble murmured over breakfast.

They had all bathed briefly in the sea shallows, aware all the time of the possibility of crocodiles. Beryl Dickie had insisted on nakedness for herself, splashing closely to Mac and Gamble who had said absent-mindedly, 'Did you know your back is a mass of bites? I'll get Estelle to slap some ointment on.'

'I prefer,' Beryl Dickie said, her nipples affronted by his indifference, 'the intimacy of sandflies.'

And now Gamble repeated the name that had been jogging Mac's memory. 'Wasn't there,' Gamble asked, messing baked beans round on his cardboard plate, 'some Frenchman? Some ship-jumping sailor?'

That triggered it.

Of course. Of course. Nearly a hundred and fifty years ago, up here, on the Tip, Narcisse Pellatier had been marooned near Cape Direction by sailors escaping from the wreck of the barque, *Ste Paul*. He had been only a boy. Aborigines had found him and he had lived as one of

their tribe for years. Seventeen. Anco, they called him. Anco. Then he
had been rescued—Mac forgot the facts—but he had returned to
France and been so unhappy he ached for the solitudes of the Cape
and returned to live with the tribe whom he regarded as his family.

And how many children had he sired?

Estelle Pellatier's face was a mixture of distances.

'You know as much as I do.' She looked away from the others
across the terrible blaze of morning water and her words floated out to
it. 'Go back ten generations. More. I've tried to discover. It's almost
impossible now. It's all guess work, more or less. But what I believe.
One of his half-castes, one of Jardine's by-blows at Somerset to mate
with. Then the Aboriginal protector moving their offspring to white
townships to act as domestic or farm slave labour. That's how it went,
wasn't it?'

Yes, Mac agreed silently, *that was how it went.*

She was still befuddled by distance and by time. 'It breeds out fast,
the colour. After five generations of marrying white who would know?'
she asked almost anybody.

'Only Joe Stager,' Gamble said with a giggle. 'Yanks have a nose
for it.'

'Pellatier,' Estelle said half to herself and half to the sea, ignoring
Gamble's joke. 'Yes. I tell everyone my great-great-great et cetera was
French. It's not a lie. And my other great-great-great et cetera whom I
am artistically vague about came from Somerset, thinking I mean
England and not that feudal outpost set up by Frank Jardine. I held it
as shame for years. But not now. Not any more.'

Mac understood why she had come back, come on this luckless trip.
There is spiritual life to be extracted from treading the places of long-
gone footprints. It was as if Estelle Pellatier were absorbing the soul of
the Cape, her ancestry, through her feet. 'I almost want to stay on,' she
said. 'Never move again.'

Surprisingly Beryl Dickie moved across to her to offer comfort.
She put an arm around the other woman's shoulders. 'You could,' she
said. 'But don't. This place is made for hermits. It's hungry for them,
like nourishment. It feeds on them. I felt that even down in Charco and
there are planes in and out there, other people, a hospital, shops. But
there's nothing here. Nothing, Estelle. You need all those other things.

You've been too softened by our century. I couldn't have stayed in Ebagoolah despite what it meant to see it. We need connections.'

Again Mac was tempted to tell them about the old-timer squatting on the eastern seaboard no more than twenty miles from where they were. He opened his mouth to speak but something held him back. If he took them there on the return trip he knew it would be an intrusion, a rupturing of that membrane the old man had created around himself, a caul protecting from the failing years of the twentieth century.

'I could leave you all behind,' he joked instead, 'one by one in your selected spots, and come back in a year to see how and what, how and why. Gamble, where would you choose?' But Gamble only smiled.

More and more he found himself wanting the trip to end so that he too could investigate the uses of solitariness like that old man. Two more days. Two. He had made up his mind. This was it, the last trip, the penultimate venture before he found his own funk-hole. The genteel poverty bus company would carry one passenger only.

* * *

Mozart took them back down the Peninsula Road and soothed them. They would be camping that night near Yarraden but on impulse Mac swung the bus towards the coast north of the Archer River and took them up the track past Iron Range to Portland Roads. There was a small commune living in a vestigial shack on the rim of the Coral Sea.

'A diversion,' he explained over the PA system. 'A divagation. Apologies to Wolfgang. A group who survived flower power and moved beyond.'

They were delighted by the unexpected and more delighted when the commune greeted them with cries of pleasure. They were the first friends Mac had made in the north. They respected his need for separation. They loved it when he showed need of them. Within moments his little party was supplied with drinks and food. 'Herbal,' their hippy hostess warned, producing a flagon of sallow liquid.

'It looks like pee,' Gamble whispered.

'Of course it's pee,' the woman said. 'We waste nothing!' And laughed. 'No. Sorry to disappoint you. It's all vegetable. Mac's an old hand. He'll reassure you.'

Names were exchanged and instantly forgotton. 'Names,' their hostess warned, drifting round in her caftan, 'are a bourgeois hindrance.' Her accent was impeccable.

Mac watched his troupe's eyes glisten with envy at this carefree lifestyle. 'I could stay *here*,' Estelle Pellatier said jealously. 'Oh I could really stay *here*.'

'You haven't much time,' one of the men said, 'before the high rise, the Cape launching station, the resorts. These are the last of the good years.'

By now they were all picking at reef fish and damper. Beyond the airy shelter the landscape offered its perfection like a whore.

'It only looks like perfection,' their hostess warned. Her hair was plaited back into a braid that touched her hips. She picked up the end of the plait and fiddled with it. 'I measure time by this,' she said. 'It started here.' She touched her shoulder briefly. 'We've been here five years now. Developers have tried to move us on but we own the land and no one's on the dole.' She smiled engagingly. 'They hate that. They'd really like to be able to boot us off. You see we have our hard times.'

'Like what?' Estelle Pellatier wondered. 'Like what, for heaven's sake?'

'We get cut off, you know, during the Wet. That road you came in by is impassable. We're not entirely self-supporting. The sea gets too rough to take the tinny down to Charco. Oh we have our problems.'

'I wish they were mine.' Sea breezes blew unimpeded through the shelter. Banana trees rattled messages. 'This was once all my country.'

The other woman turned on her eyes suddenly, amazingly aware. The two of them looked at each other for a long while. 'Yes, I know. It was. I know exactly how you feel.'

'I don't think anyone could know that,' Estelle Pellatier said.

They were silent back in the bus. Each was furnishing a private dream. Mac played 'On Wenlock Edge' on the tapedeck as they bumped back to the highway and thought of Billy Lakeland, an early settler who had blazed the track from Laura to Coen and later built himself and his family a house in dense rainforest teetering two thousand feet above sea-level just south of Vaughan Williams' tone-poem and had created his own. Earlier hippies! A battery powered by water-wheel. Supplies lugged in from a boat landing on the coast. The good life. He winced at the parallels. Lakeland had returned to Charco and established a brewery to sate the miners. What was *he* tapping with his smell-of-an-oil-rag bus tours? The bush had reclaimed Billy, dying alone in some scrub fox-hole. Tears for that. Tears for himself. Tears for all of them.

And tears, too, for that visit in two o'clock camp darkness that night by Estelle Pellatier pushing in through the opening of his tent and lying beside him in the snuffling dark. There was no sound from the other tents. Through the fly-opening he could see the ashes of the evening fire still glinting. She had lain beside him without speaking but he knew she had sensed his recoil into rigid wakefulness.

'Hold me,' she had whispered.

He had propped himself on one elbow, leaning towards her so that he could make out the outlines of her face. Outside the landscape was ragged with moonlight.

He began, 'You can't ...' and saw, heard rather, that she was shaking with unshed tears.

'What is it?' he asked gently. 'Tell me, what is it?'

She was silent so long he thought she would never answer.

He repeated his question softly.

'I have nothing,' she whispered. 'Nothing.'

'Neither have I,' he replied. 'Nothing I can give.'

'But you want nothing. That's the way you want it.'

'Then why me?' he asked. 'What could I possibly offer?'

He heard her sigh. It seemed to well up from the very pit of her.

'Just hold me,' she pleaded. 'Please. Nothing else.'

His arms had long since become unaccustomed to gestures of warmth, to the shielding of another. He reached over awkwardly and eased her to him with one arm.

'Now the other,' she said. 'Please.'

They lay there uncomfortably together in the dark. The last of the glinting ashes in the campfire died. He felt the woman's body move in more closely, stretch and press its length along his side. He felt his shoulder grow wet with the tears she had been fighting. His heart gave way at that. He reached up one hand and stroked the portwine birthmark over and over.

'You'll have to learn to like it,' he whispered into her smoky hair. 'You'll just have to learn. I did.'

TEN

*B*innaway was not a practical man. The crude sapling shelter he finally put up collapsed on the second day. He persuaded his unwilling host to help him return his hired boat and take him to the mainland to buy a tent. 'You're a hard man,' he accused Mac, standing hopefully in the doorway of the shack on the fourth morning. The scent of Mac's breakfast had drawn him round half a mile of foreshore.

'There's always a solution,' Mac said.

The nightly playing of records went on. Binnaway resented this too but held his tongue. More police called at Little Brother to give warning on malicious noise pollution. Mac walked them round to the landward side of the island to make his point. The amplified joyland screech left the police unmoved. They were young. They didn't even hear. 'No one objects to *music*,' one of the young coppers said, giving his last word italics. 'It's that stuff you play that's got them objecting. Can't you see that?'

'No,' Mac said. 'I can't.'

He was careful to keep the police ignorant of the monster at the heart of the maze. They had no search warrant but he politely showed them the small tapedeck in his cabin and let the police wonder how the sound could track uphill and over. Eventually, he knew, they would search.

After they left he went over to his player, replugged for hill speakers and gave the revellers the Sibelius violin concerto at full volume. Neveu playing her guts out! And his. The strings built plateaux of sound that bridged the narrow strait and would pack the *al fresco* dining area of the resort with almost tangible vibrations that would tear the heart. They would also prevent conversation.

Binnaway, sullen and thoughtful on the far side of the island, lay stretched out on the beach under the arc of music, the ocean breeze urging the pages of his book, hearing those passionate assemblies of instruments building cathedrals of heartbreak. Or would have had the sounds not met like some tidal wave the speaker-crash from the opposition. There was a pause at one stage while a record was being changed and then a nameless counter-tenor sang high and effortless above the rainforest canopy.

'Fuck,' Binnaway said quietly. 'Fuck.'

'It's not,' he said later to Mac, 'that I don't like your sort of music. I think you're crazy, that's all. How long can you keep this up?'

'I didn't think you'd last out. Never were a great backstop, were you?'

'You're hardly the gracious host, mate!'

'You're hardly a guest.'

'Right. Right. So that's it. You win. I'll be off the moment you want me to go.'

'But how will you leave?' Mac asked slyly. Consternation made hollows on Binnaway's baby face. Even in a fortnight he had lost weight. His food supplies had run out a day ago. 'Think you'd make it to Hummock?'

'Let's be civilised,' Binnaway said. 'Let's not get unpleasant. If you want to run me across now, I'll be happy to oblige. At least I can warn Laforgue. He's been threatening to invade. You'd hate that, wouldn't you, a professional guest like him.'

They made a bundle of Binnaway's belongings ('You can keep the tent,' he said generously), put them in the launch and set off down the tides towards Seaforth. They were a mile or so south of the island when a powerboat cut close across their bows, missing them by a few feet. In the turbulence following, Binnaway was flung backwards and opened the flesh above his ear. The powerboat described a wide circle and returned to rake in again across their stern. Their own launch pitched wildly for moments, water washing into the cabin, drenching them both. Someone on the powerboat waved insolently as it sped away.

'That was no accident,' Binnaway squawked. 'That was deliberate.' He kept prodding at his bloody temple. 'If I were you, Mac, I'd take that as a distinct warning.'

'You're not me.' He was inclined to snap.

He dropped Binnaway off at the little town's wharf.

'There's a bus of sorts,' Mac said, smiling gently. Binnaway pulled a reminiscent face.

'I won't say I'll be back and you don't have to say any time. Look,' he urged, 'take it easy, old chap. Despite everything, buddies, eh? You won't win.'

When Mac got back later that afternoon, an anonymous foot had scored a message for him along the hard sand beyond his jetty: *Next time we won't miss.*

He went up to his shack, expecting the worst. He found it.

His player was smashed, its dismembered pieces littering the floor. The records had been hurled into the rainforest. His tapes were in a tangled drapery from window ledge to doorway, a macabre form of streamer. He thanked God he had removed the hill speaker plug and tucked it out of sight in a tree branch as he usually did when he left the island.

He hardly knew what to do next. Going to the police was an exercise in futility. Royal commissions had proved that—public charges of corruption were substantiated but made little difference to offenders. In this state the wealthy and the corrupt had rights of passage.

He gazed at the mess all round him. Everything was replaceable, more or less, but the collection of tapes and records he had built up over the years would be expensive and difficult to restore. He could make an attempt to fill the gaps. He could go to town, buy another player, order records. That was easy enough. But how long could he hole up on the island? Two months? Three? His fruit trees were bearing, his vegetable garden producing stringy silver-beet, tomatoes. There were fish to be caught. But the basic comfort assured by his generator required gluttonous amounts of diesel fuel. The gas cylinders for his refrigerator and stove lasted only a couple of months, used sparingly.

He accused himself of softness, the decadent centre of civilised man that yearned to make it the easy way. Remember Grelet. Remember Banfield. They lived before the efficiency of generators and refrigeration. He had done it himself for the first couple of months. He could do it again.

Candles. Lamps. A brick-lined cooking pit.

He was afraid to leave his love, his island.

He was beginning to be afraid to stay.

He organised a primitive winch and hauled his launch up onto runners on the beach. His dinghy runabout he concealed in the shelter of the treeline, and padlocked the outboard to a stake.

Ritual.

Establish a ritual.

At the end of another week he crossed over to the mainland in the launch, with the outboard trailing behind. He asked the boatshed owner to store both for a week, then he picked up his van from the garage where he stored it and drove down the coast to Mackay.

He reported the break in. The desk sergeant was uninterested.

'You can't prove it was the people on Hummock,' he kept insisting.

'You could come up and have a look,' Mac argued. 'I'm reporting vandalism.'

'You want to make an official statement?'

'Yes. If you can bear the bother.'

'Don't use that tone on me,' the desk sergeant said.

'Then I won't use any tone at all,' Mac replied, and stalked out into the burning streets.

Blind, driven, fanatic, he had intended going down to Brisbane for replacements but the thought of the long drive, the time away from

Little Brother caused him a change of heart as he sat in a side street restaurant and munched sandwiches. The electrical goods shops were full of reasonably priced equipment. He decided it would be better to buy two players now, the ploy of a zealot, keeping one hidden in reserve. Madness, he told himself, as he watched the salesman box up both sets. The word vindictive crossed his mind. He erased it. Justifiable rage were the words substituted. 'And these.' He had selected an armful of discs and tapes. Perhaps when he got back they would have attacked the generator. He went to a hardware store and bought drums of fuel, maintenance tools, batteries, and box after box of candles. He purchased several kerosene lamps to supplement the two he already had.

Food? He could hardly move through the humid streets of the town drowning in the stink of sugar beside its river. He begged spare cartons from the supermarket and stacked carton upon carton of tinned food into the back of his van then he stood back and examined the crammed interior. There was enough there, he hoped, for a few months. Eked out by what he caught or grew, longer, perhaps.

* * *

He noticed the hitchhiker when he was half a mile away, a young man limping along the shoulder of the road, one hopeful hand raised but the head not turning as the cars whizzed by.

As Mac drew near he saw fully the poverty of movement, the effort with which the young man put one foot ahead of another. He pulled up on the side of the road a few hundred yards ahead and watched him approach in the driving mirror. The young man's face was half-concealed by a wide-brimmed hat under which a draggle of ginger fringe showed. He came round by the passenger door and stood politely waiting for the signal to hop in, one hand tentative on the handle.

Mac reached over and flicked up the lock to find himself looking into Gamble's stunned face. Recognisably Gamble. Undoubtedly Gamble. Thinner, paler, minimally five years older, but Gamble. His shirt flapped like a flag on bones. The grin he gave Mac dragged the taut skin of his face back into a rictus of pain more than mirth. He wore only one sandal. The other dangled from his hand by a broken strap. His shoulder-pack was pathetically limp. 'My God!' Mac said softly. 'What on earth! I thought you'd gone back south.'

Gamble fell, almost, into the seat. With an effort he lowered his small pack between his feet and leaned back with his eyes closed. His face was carved like a stone saint's.

'Just give me a minute,' he breathed. 'Just a minute.'

His eyes remained closed. The lashes fluttered on his ashen cheeks. His breath came irregularly, with a rasp to it.

'You're sick,' Mac said. 'You poor coot.'

'Sicker,' Gamble agreed. His eyes blinked half open. Mac recognised the glint, the blue. 'I only went back south for a while. Couldn't handle it.'

'What have you been doing these last years for God's sake? You look as if you've been punishing yourself.'

Gamble opened his eyes wide this time then shut them again.

'Oh God, I do feel sick. Oh God. Doing? Playing palm court music in various places. Nightclubs. Cafés. You name it. It was fun for a while and then it got terrible. Couldn't live on what they paid. So I pulled out.'

'And where the hell do you think you're heading for in this state?' Mac asked.

'I've been looking for you,' Gamble said.

ELEVEN

*T*he last day.

His eyes met those of Estelle Pellatier's squarely across the breakfast mugs of tea.

There had been nothing but the huddling of bodies. There had been no exchange of pasts.

Yet there was a limpness to all their feelings on this final morning, he could sense, a regret for the ending of something. He drove steadily south, forgoing the temptation to take sidetracks, to extend in a last burst of geographic emotionalism, their experience of the Cape and its loneliness. Enough was enough was enough. Beryl Dickie had produced her old photograph again and had sat mooning over it while she drank her tea. He realised why she could never have enough of it. As he drove he kept seeing, as if his mind were a screen that permitted only this one image to emerge, that dusty road, the bleak houses of settlers corrugating the skyline while down that main track, alone in her awful dignity posed against the desolation of the outback despite the presence of children, the woman with sunshade strolled and strolled through dust and scrub, her skirts trailing, removing her footprints, challenging her impertinent gesture to surroundings. *Forever wilt thou tread.* His mind was puddled with Keats. And the woman walking forever through a dusty street in a lost town. He was teased out of thought by her gallant poise and her face shifted on the screen to become that of Dickie, Pellatier, his wife and an urgent Marie Binnaway. He understood everything and nothing, even the need for the little houses to cling for comfort as one body sought the other warm one in the bed, the touching of feet, the exchange of smiles over a breakfast cup.

Now?

He had had the huddling once, the warm body, the touching of feet. He had had the over-proximity of all other people and things that crowded the space he had designed for himself, selfishly, yes, but crowded. From the marrow of him, the very marrow, he longed for the untouched space, the silence. A Simeon Stylites perched on his saintly pole, peeing into space, defecating? He had spent thirty years on his pillar. No. Not that way of eremitic discomfort. More of a desert father, say. He understood well that craving for arid lunar landscapes picked clean as bones by wind and the abrading teeth of sand.

Gamble was fiddling with the tapedeck. In a moment the bus was swollen with lament: *Fremd bin ich eingezogen, fremd zieh' ich wieder aus, der Mai war mir gewogen mit manchen Blumenstrauss.* Oh the deadly accuracy of the choice! *A stranger here I journeyed, A stranger here I go.* He found himself singing softly with the tape. He caught Gamble's eye and nodded. Glancing in the driving mirror he saw Beryl Dickie dozing, her head propped by a cushion against the window. Why had she come? She didn't like music, had no interest in it that he could discover. It was the hunt. The lusting flesh refusing to give her peace. The chance of encounter. He felt almost sorry for the relentless nagging of that body, for the wasted pilgrimages on which it pushed her. Estelle Pellatier trapped his eye and smiled. She was braced rigidly against the onslaught of the road but her inner eye was fixed glassily on the Cape country she had left. But she smiled. She smiled. Even the blotch across her eye and cheek smiled.

The music unrolled and the road unrolled and they took a lunch break by a creek that fed into the waters of the Endeavour. The air was dense with leaf and sound, unending water-music, the metallic clicks of insects in the branches above them. They were bound at last by simplicity before Charco.

To Charco.

In the worst part of the afternoon.

*   *   *

Estelle Pellatier discovered in these last hours as she lay on the river sand of her almost personal beach, that she had developed astonishing fluidity in her left hand. She could draw like Picasso. There it came in one swift movement, the overnosed profile sporting two huge almond eyes. *It looks like Beryl*, she decided; erased the profile and drew a meltingly lopsided left-hander of her long-gone husband. He, too, despite glasses and a spiv moustache, looked like Beryl Dickie. She looked at the drawing. She had tried to obliterate those years of failure. Her past was a bland sequence of years spent as a librarian in the lower recesses of a mining corporation. She filed nothing but facts. She catalogued nothing but details related to the process of disembowellment. She thought of it that way. She would emerge blinking from fluorescent light and air-conditioning to the lemon bite of a late Brisbane afternoon aware there was only the bed-sit, the television, the meal she scrambled together without appetite and ate, plate perched on knee.

'Oh God!' she said aloud to the mutter sounds of the river, the crash of the falls upstream. Behind her the scrub creaked with the movement of lizards, ticked like a watch with insects. Two falcons swept over the bluespace and rasping birds in the thicket made notes of torn wire.

The others had hiked upstream on this last day to come to the lip of the falls. She felt content on her own. She had no wish to return to Brisbane, the library basement, the lonely meals, the evenings spent clamped to the television set. For a moment she contemplated walking off, simply walking off down-stream to become lost in this particular place with a music that froze to deadness all the music that bus had spilled out in the last week. She smoothed out the sand once more, changed to a squatting position and in half a dozen swift and graceful left-handed movements, reproduced the whirls and serifs of the wonga vine she had seen clambering about trees at almost every campsite. Sitting back on her haunches she smiled at the drying arabesques and was startled into a shriek by a sudden soft hand on her shoulder.

She looked up into Beryl Dickie's unsated face. The hand remained.

'My God,' Estelle Pellatier said, 'you frightened me.'

'Silly!' Beryl had been unexpectedly kind in the last day or so. The truculence had yielded to an inner planning. She was absorbed by future programmes, had ceased expressing impatience with the trip, the members of the party. She could afford this generosity of spirit. It was almost over. She would wipe it from her memory as if it were an unsuccessful party. Wipe everything except Joe Stager and a moment in Ebagoolah that would insist on living with her. She had so wanted to be like that woman walking her children to nowhere. She knew she could never be. *And without a man*, she always marvelled. *Not for me*.

She sat down in the sand beside Estelle and regarded her with bright curious eyes.

'Now what?' Estelle Pellatier asked.

'Tell me,' Beryl Dickie said.

'Tell you what?'

'For a . . . well, ugly bitch,' Beryl Dickie whispered watching the hurt and shock flush up on the other woman's face flaring the birthmark into a horrible plummy crimson, 'you're quite successful.' She looked down at the drawing of the wonga vine and rubbed it vigorously with her sandalled foot.

'What do you mean?' Estelle Pellatier asked, knowing.

'My God! All innocence, aren't we? I mean last night. Getting off with the tour captain, if you can call that any kind of victory.' She was determined to debase. 'What a pedantic old woman of a man, with his tapes and his puling bits of travel talk. I never, not ever, want to hear Mozart again.'

Estelle Pellatier pressed her mouth tight and stared straight ahead. *Did you ever?* she thought bitterly.

'Not talking, eh? Was it too exquisite to describe? What a sly puss you are, Estelle. You've been doing the perfect schoolmarm job for a week now. Come on, tell me, what was it like?'

How could the other woman reply? How answer 'nothing'? 'Nothing and much.' Automatically her hand flew up to her cheek and began to stroke the disfigurement that had been touched with such kindness during the night. Only that. A hand stroking tortured skin. And briefly. Despite the containment of his arms into which she had fallen asleep, she had been aware of those arms' distance, their uninvolvement. The stroking, the containing had been acts of kindliness that forgot all reference to flesh. In the dark of his tent he had asked nothing. He had not wanted to pursue the pain of her personal history. She had blubbed out this and that, isolated incidents he might string together later to form some kind of whole, but she knew he would find the pieces of her existence an intolerable burden.

She had slept, but briefly, and on waking sensed him lying cramped and watchful in the dark. Without speaking she had eased her body away and crept back across the clearing to her own tent, sliding quietly into her sleeping bag, imagining Beryl's deep breathing spelled unconsciousness.

Her face dragged down into a curve of misery.

She wanted to screech obscenities, to shout *Slut slut* against the gabble of the falls but her tongue was trapped on the syllable.

It was when Beryl Dickie put her hand out again, this time on the other woman's lap and said, 'If you won't tell me, then show me' that she fully understood the horror of the force behind the question and hand. She recoiled in disgusted pity realising, at that moment, the torture of driven flesh, when the two men came climbing down the bank above the water-hole and one of them, she was too confused, too opened up with realisations of another kind to distinguish which, said, 'Time to be off.'

*   *   *

The office stank from being closed for over a week. The louvres jammed when he tried to open them. A vase of croton leaves he had put in water and left on his desk had withered and dropped leaves across the top, their stems still stuck in a disgusting broth of green.

And there was awkwardness, too, over parting. It had not happened before. People had rolled off his bus and away without a backward glance. This time there were hesitancies, unfilled conversational blanks. He agreed to run the two women to the airport to catch the evening plane. Gamble declined help. He intended hitching a ride to

Reeftown, his pack already on his shoulders.

All the hands had been shaken, Beryl Dickie's clinging moistly longest. All the thanks, regrets, false assurances of remeeting gone formally through. At one point Estelle Pellatier had attempted a ladylike speech of gratitude that fluttered into embarrassed gaps swooped on by Beryl Dickie who had regained brassiness as they neared terminus point. 'Again,' Estelle was assuring the room, faking an over-bright smile, her birthmark painful to see against the sallow quality of her skin, 'we will come again. Take some other route, perhaps, some ... We ...'

'Oh do shut up!' Beryl Dickie said boredly. That was the cruncher. That she uttered the words so languidly and with such indifference. 'You make it seem like one of your dreary public service staff farewells. Mac ...' and she gave him the coyest of smiles 'could you let me have the Stagers' address? I want to keep in touch.'

I bet you do, he thought. He smiled at them, suffering these last moments as a necessary punishment. 'You might all want to keep in touch.' He hunted through a drawer and pulled out copies of the original list which he handed around. 'There's even an extra name on it you might find useful.' He could have bitten his tongue off for that last thrust. But Beryl Dickie took it like an old pro. 'You never know,' she said. Now it was over she could forgive everyone. She glanced quickly down the list, folded it and packed it away in her shoulder bag like a trophy.

On the way back from the airport Mac spotted Gamble still waiting hopefully at a service station for a lift to other places. He pulled over feeling a peculiar wrench at this second parting.

'Sure you're okay?'

Gamble nodded. He looked like a grubby waif. 'I'm fine.' He nodded the words into place. 'Look, I did want to say thanks, well, personally. I enjoyed it, because of you, mainly. I know you must have lost on the deal but it taught me something.'

'It taught all of us something.'

Momentarily Mac feared for the Stagers.

'I'll keep in touch,' Gamble said, half-watching Mac and half-watching a long-distance haulier that had pulled in by the bowsers. 'This year. Next year. Sometime. But I'll be in touch. Really.'

'No promises,' Mac said. He drove on down Charlotte Street.

It was time to assess.

He could not assess.

He went back to his rented office. It had the feel of a raided tomb. He emptied his desk, shoved aside the memories of Binnaway tacking posters to the wall and pulled down the route maps, the planned itineraries. Then he locked the door hearing only the smallest sound as it sighed, delivered the key to the local real estate agent and drove the bus out of town towards Helenvale where he pitched, at last, at last, personal camp in a rainforest glade he had used before.

His bus company days were over.

TWELVE

Mac took him back to the island. He borrowed a fold-
away camp bed from the boatshed owner, unloaded all his gear into
the launch and puttered into the late afternoon wondering if he should
have taken the young man straight to a hospital instead of lumbering
himself with nursing duties in the middle of a war. For it was war.
As tragi-comic in its way as his other war, nearly fifty years away.

Hummock Island was pounding out its quick-kicks message as he
cut past it and round to the jetty. Gamble could barely manage to
stagger along the beach and up through the track to the shack. Mac let
him topple onto his own bed where the young man mumbled, *sorry
about this sorry about the trouble* before he dropped into slumber like
a stone and slept for the next twelve hours.

It was true. Gamble had been looking for him. In the way news
travelled in the north, tales had filtered through to the places he
worked at of this madman on his island, its approximate location,
exaggerated blow-ups of inter-island warfare. 'Some stubborn old

crackpot,' he had been told. Gamble brought out this information in withered phrases between sleep and invalid meals over the next three days. On the fourth morning Mac, clearing the maze tracks, was surprised by Gamble panting up to the fifth circle. His eyes were clear, the once-flaming rims of his eyelids faded, his skinny body peeled clean by sleep.

Under the shadows of the forest they confronted each other, sinking in soft-leaf mould. Mac knew what was coming. He anticipated the young man's request. 'Yes,' he said. 'Yes.'

Gamble grinned, the old familiar grin lost five years back near Charco Harbour. 'I haven't asked yet, but yes, I would like to stay for a while. If you can stand it.'

The other looked beyond him to the curve of the track, the track itself racing into obliteration in a wall of stinging plant. Offshore came the whine of revved up motors, the faint and faded shrieks of joy-festers ploughing the sea. He was conceding, submitting. So much of his solitude now was raped, nothing much more could affect it. For the last week, out of care for Gamble, he had desisted from playing his new equipment. Should he cede his lease to the larger island and start the search all over again? In his heart he knew that to be useless, that he was running out of time. The two-faced monster called progress would slide in wherever he went, one head smiling, the other munching. *I'm too old*, he thought, *for moves, for change. Yet how can I tolerate this?*

He hated the thought of running away from battle. Even though in the last one he had never seen front-line action, and he had nearly died of boredom for his country, he had stuck it out. He would stick it out now.

He looked back at Gamble, his ginger skull catching fire from one penetrating sunspear.

'Man Friday,' he said. 'You're stuck.'

Gamble, he discovered during the next few days, balanced words and silence nicely. He did not flog him with the story of his life. He knew when to disappear. He took to sleeping on the boat to give Mac back his privacy but also managed within that week to knock up a bush shelter two coves away from the cabin, a charming lopsided structure laced with air and lawyer vine. Mac wondered where he had learnt such a skill. Gamble blinked. His freckles loomed enormous against the pallor of his skin. 'Mallicolo,' he said. 'I like islands too. My father was an engineer up in Santo. I was there, oh, six, seven years.'

'But it's all breeze-block and cliplock now.'

'Not everywhere. Only round the towns. Go out from there into the hills. It's different.'

He was carefully plaiting and weaving more leathery straps of lawyer vine leaf, lashing the half-finished mat he was forming to a slender bush-pole with lengths of the vine itself. 'Screens.' He grinned again. 'It's what you need up on the summit. The perfect camouflage.'

Sprung! Sussed out! Mac blinked in his turn. He had neither discussed his form of musical revenge nor shown Gamble the monster at the heart of the maze.

'Oh I don't blame you,' Gamble said, eyes busy on his plaiting. 'I know you've been holding off for my sake. Go ahead. Sock it to them!'

In a strange way Mac was beginning to find his flitting presence a comfort. He had his uses. Returned from fishing, Mac would find the vegetable patch forked over and hilled. He had begun another garden section behind his own airy lodge. The night they tested the player for the first time, Mac made a ceremony of it, opening a bottle of wine to launch the music bomb. Above them through the night sky, Rhine maidens rioted for an hour.

'You know,' Gamble suggested in the three a.m. silence afterwards, 'they could get to like it. How would you deal with that?'

'I doubt it,' Mac said.

In the morning he discovered he was right. The launch was listed to one side at its mooring, its hull flooded from a hole drilled below the waterline.

His first impulse was to call for Gamble. Consolation requires another. He regretted his carelessness in not winching the boat up onto its chocks. He wished either he or the boy had continued sleeping aboard. How he wished.

'Tell me,' Gamble said after they had spent a morning taking turns on the pump at ebb tide to the chiacks of passing wind-sailers, 'do you ever think that solitude is a selfish pleasure?'

Mac was so stunned he strode back to the winch and began the painful haul. The boat jerked on the rollers they had placed under the hull and moved up the beach a foot. 'No look!' Gamble began to gabble. 'I was asking a serious question. It wasn't aimed at you. Well, not really.'

Mac eyed him suspiciously. 'I've often thought,' he replied, 'about the utter selfishness of saints, of the deeply religious who let others minister. Yes. But I'm not trying to be a saint. I'm not a rainforest father, if that's what you're getting at. I've done my share of serving. More than my share. Now all I want is to be left in peace by the world out there and get on with it.'

'Get on with what?'

'I thought you understood. I really thought you understood.'

'I thought I did. Until last night. I thought all you wanted was to be and let be. Then I saw you animated—no really—*animated* by contact. And you were making contact. You were energised, kind of, by animus.'

'That's a good word. Oh that's a very good word.'

Gamble flopped onto the sand and stared hurt across the water.

'I didn't want to quarrel.' He looked as if he might weep. Mac detected a furtive rub at the eyes. 'It's just that you haven't really cut off, have you? You can't.'

'You're ignoring the fact that I had. That I was. I didn't ask for that goddam resort to plague me. Everything was fine until then.'

'No,' Gamble said. 'No. It's simply not possible, I can see that. The world resents loners. Do what you like, the world will still nose you out and make you pay.'

*   *   *

A Malvolio of the Tropics. That's how he saw himself.

Puttering back the next day from the mainland, happy in the knowledge of Gamble as watchdog, crammed with advice and repair gear lent by the boatshed owner at Seaforth, Mac retravelled Gamble's comments of the day before. He was right. There was no doubt. He was right. Even the hermit of the Cape made contact with towns once in a while. And he was more fruitful. He painted a journal of his last days. Mac couldn't even claim to do such a positive thing.

Forgiveness had never been his style. Colleagues apologising to *him* had been pulverised by another verbal blast. Could he forgive himself for that? 'You'll become a soured and totally loathed old man,' his wife had warned as they flew back from their disastrous last trip to Europe. 'But maybe that's your idea of achievement, universal loathing.'

The words had haunted him again on this day and he was bringing a gift as apology, an acoustic guitar and a dozen sets of nylon strings. He was resigning himself to a long hosting. It wasn't until he was pulling the dinghy up onto the beach that he realised he hadn't asked if Gamble could play such an instrument. Today, of all days, he found in himself an inexplicable yearning to talk, to confess need. Down the years his wife's summation floated its rancour. He had always imagined himself a stolid chap, not one easily moved by transitory emotions; never one for a quick response to a pretty mouth, a moist eye; insensible to the fanfares of male buddy-dom. Yet here he was trapped in a welter of gratitude to a stray washed up on his beach.

'I have my toys,' he said more abruptly than he intended. 'Here's one for you.' He watched Gamble's delighted face reflected and distorted in the honey-coloured surfaces of the guitar. Almost immediately he had stroked chords of wistful energy from the instrument. And yes, of course he could play. Everyone, Gamble assured him, of his age had flirted with the guitar. 'It was like a disease,' he said, looking up grinning. 'The big guitar scare! It was just that I had to make up my mind between one instrument and another.' He did some bravura flamenco phrases, tapped the wood, and laid the guitar carefully on the table beside him. 'Or just,' he added, 'I looked bloody awful in tight jeans.'

Mac laughed. The unaccustomed sound left his throat as more of a croak. But it was a laugh. He felt it heal some small bitter place.

'I'm glad you're here,' he said. He could not stop himself from adding, 'although it may not be for long.'

Gamble's eyes lifted towards him in question and Mac allowed the question to hang in the air.

*   *   *

Gamble carried his thatch mats through the maze and mounted them on saplings above the speakers, teasing down the overlap. His hands were deft. His mechanics precise. From fifteen paces it would have been impossible to assess concealment let alone imagine the objects concealed.

They stood around and admired.

The day was slipping into the quick tropic dark. Lights pocked the shoreline on Hummock. Music was already blaring from the dining terrace.

'God,' Mac said, 'let's get down from here.'

He had given Hummock silence for five days. 'The beauty of unexpected assault,' he explained to Gamble. 'What an old unforgiving bastard you are!' Gamble said, softening the words with a smile. 'My wife's words exactly,' Mac replied.

They ate together that evening, a reef fish Gamble had caught in the morning. The flesh was thick, white, sweet and tasted of the sea. Gamble cleaned up and stacked dishes away, took his guitar and went off to his own cabin. 'Thanks,' Mac had said looking at the shining plates, the wiped down table. 'Not even Crusoe had it this good.'

All the patterns of history he knew repeated themselves in recognisable curves. He lay back in his deckchair in the sea-noisy dark under the pisonias outside his hut. Caterwaulings from the other island clawed at him across the water but on the summit his own warheads thundered out a choral Mass. The notes collided mid-stream and annihilated each other. He, too, was waiting for a curve in history, the unambiguous curve that would run, roughly parallel, concentric more or less to that other curve more than a century before when natives from Bentinck Island in the Gulf paddled their canoes across the glittering water to Sweers Island and made an abrupt and hellish attack. The previous owner's name now obsessed him and his mind was unable to release that sad history. His own brain glittered with travellers' tales of settlers among savages. Yet he was not the intruder. The savages had come second.

Would come closer.

In a way he longed for it.

Weaponless except for his music missile.

The martyrdoms of history ran like an overfast length of film through the gleaming rotten spaces of his skull where he was the projectionist controlling the light fully and powerfully, a doomsday glare.

He would make the enemy a gift.

He would give them their own sounds back.

* * *

Gamble had become useful. He took the dinghy to the mainland and bought half a dozen tapes of heavy metal rock. 'Have you been converted?' he asked ironically when the request was made. Mac didn't bother with a reply. The blaze of intention was searing all other thought.

That evening he inspected the purchases with insulting forefinger and proceeded to persecute himself with earphones. Reeling! Reeling! It was all so cacophonous, so one-celled in structure, choice became unimportant and a high-pitched ecstasy carried him through to launching time. During dinner the muffled hammerings of bass guitars, the persistent deadly thud of them sounded like thunder on the left.

'On the left indeed!' Mac dragged up a Roman superstition to fortify, took a sleeping pill and set his alarm for three thirty. At five minutes exactly after that time he was bellowing with joy as other bellows rocked out from the summit. He would not be able to endure that for long himself, so he made his way round the island to watch the lights flash on. The cracking sound of slammed doors and the raised voices of complaint all came to him like fuel. Lights blazed out around the swimming pool and a string of flares leading to the marina. Within seconds there was the sound of a motor launch.

Invasion at last?

He wanted that.

Gamble was waiting for him back at the shack. 'Funny,' he said. 'That really sprang them. Not one of your classical bullets but that, the tape they've been playing all day. I think that says something, don't you?'

They worked crazily for a few minutes lugging the player to a waterproof box concealed in the undergrowth. They moved carefully. The tape played on. At the last moment when the noise of the motor boat sounded close to his beach, he switched off the tapedeck, disconnected the leads and rehung the speaker terminals in the trees, turned off the generator and, half trembling, stretched out on his cot and pulled the sheet up over his head. Gamble raced away to the launch and feigned sleep on its deck.

It was like a police raid.

Flashlights created a clotted geometry of black and white in the brush outside the shack, flinging tree-shadows through his door and up the walls of the room. There were feet rocking the veranda and in moments hands clawing away at the mosquito net and his own face pinned like a waning moon in the glare of a flashlight. Behind the glare was the glint of metal and behind that the velvet of the cabin crammed with threat, a velvet that seemed to billow and wilt with heavy movement.

'Out!' someone ordered as hands dragged him from his bunk and filled him with a perverse joy. He tried to back away from the lumpish shapes in front of him, grabbing at the rough wood dresser. The skin of his neck jumped with nerves that spelled anticipation rather than fear. The adrenalin rush. His nose began to run.

Voiced like a prophet he shouted at the faceless currents of the dark, fulminating from his pillar like Saint Simeon. A hand whacked blackness into the back of his head and he noddled forward, tripping over the leg end of the stretcher to fall into the bear-clutch of another lump of darkness that held him crushingly and hissed in his face. Light bounced across the ceiling thatch and he could only smell the bear, the spirits, the rage.

He could barely breathe. His mouth was plastered against hair and flesh. His prophetic voice had become a mumble. He kept struggling with words. 'Why don't you shoot me?' Challenging them. Saliva dominated.

The voice in his ear hissed with contempt. 'You want that, don't you? It's what you want. Well, you'll have to beg for such a mercy, mate,' and there was another thud as something thick and metallic took him across the ear and his head rang with the wildest music of all. He sagged downward in a stupor of discordant ringing and was barely conscious as they lugged him outside and down to the beach. By the time the cold sand revived him, the tide was pecking at his feet and he crawled up into the tree fringe and watched as the cabin burst into stunning flowers of scarlet.

THIRTEEN

*I*n this unambiguous light, the crack in Nirvana.

'We can patch up, I suppose.' Mac was kicking about charred fragments of bookcase, poking testily at blackened tomes. He stood uselessly before the burnt-out shell of the shack. Gamble had managed to douse the fire with bucket after bucket of water that at first seemed to pitch uselessly onto flames that hissed greedily for more. The structure leant its bones towards the sea. Only the floor, a mess of sodden planking, retained a memory of its shape. He could no longer savour the parallels of last century in Gulf waters. Pettishly he picked up, examined and then dropped *Recollections of the Lake Poets*, biography glued by disaster.

'This makes me angry. Really angry.'

'The books?' Gamble asked.

'What else? Books, records. I can stand losing the shack. I don't need houses. I've grown beyond houses. The barest of shelters. But these other things!'

'You still don't have to give in.' Gamble appeared to be testing his lower lip with a flickering tongue crowded with questions and dubious answers. They beat, too, across his eyes like birds.

'I'm not an aggressive man,' Mac insisted. 'It's been forced upon me. But not this way.' He wanted to howl long and lewdly, a dousing cry that would blanket his small world. He watched Gamble shoving the debris aside, sifting the mess. The young man picked up an unbroken cup with a rose of ash at its heart, a doubly fired earthenware plate and two scorched saucepans. He placed them carefully on what was left of the sink bench.

'Passivity,' Gamble volunteered slowly as if he had spent a lifetime thinking it out, 'drives people crazy. Not the passive ones. The viewers. That turning the other cheek! Best advice ever given.' He grinned at Mac. 'For a stubborn fighter, that is. As I think you are.' He nodded his words into place. 'They don't know about me. They don't know I'm here. Another plus. They don't know about my shack. They haven't found the Minotaur. I've checked. Even your player's safe. And by the way, Mac,'—he put one skinny hand onto the older man's shoulder for the briefest of moments—'I saved most of the tapes and records, believe it or not. I stacked them at my place. You could be back in business tonight.'

He added, 'But I think you should wait.'

Gamble seemed to be growing stronger as circumstances flayed them. He had been on the island a mere three weeks and already his body was losing that excessive thinness. He moved with speed and confidence along the beach and the tracks of the maze.

'I'm not a strategist,' Mac confessed sadly. 'I think I'm cut out to be the perfect passive resister. I'm in your hands.'

Gamble held them out, long, thin, dirtied with ash. He waggled his fingers comically and coaxed Mac down to his own hut to absolve him from the spectacle of ruin. He made tea on a primus and in his turn watched while Mac drank. Mac dribbled tears but was relieved to find they were of rage.

Self, he accused. *The old* mea culpa. *Self self self.*

* * *

There's a lot to be said for remaining perfectly still. The static state disturbs others. The two men moved quietly about Little Brother, concealing their presence as far as possible. The launch still crouched on its chocks waiting for the final patching. The dinghy skulked in undergrowth. For three days the generator remained silent and they cooked on a fire-pit deep in the maze.

Heat bright, Mac said to himself. He was trying out words, filling in journal time, combinations that he chewed like spearmint. Heat bite. Green fright. Green heat. Wet bright. Bright fright.

That last made him quiver, quiver all back through his ancestry, from that great-grandfather who had lived and written hermit style on a tiny south Pacific island called Mauke, coming rarely to Sydney on trading ships puffing against the trade winds. Mac's past was patched with missionaries and sailors, a hotch-potch that was slapped into a genetic framework that included eighteenth-century Scottish adventurers. There were glimpses of Quiros and Spanish deckhands three centuries before that.

No wonder he loved islands.

He said to Gamble as they fished that night from a beach out of sight of Hummock 'You're free to go, you know.'

Gamble ignored that.

Mac pulled in his line and walked back to his own beach and up to the shack.

He bent to pick up a clear triangle of glass that had escaped his notice when they swept the fire-tailings off the veranda. He held it so that the stars burned cold and hard through it and said aloud, 'Stay' and dropped the tiny fragment to shatter on a forest rock below.

In the morning he walked up through the narrow tree-crowded circles of the maze, savouring freshness, the prismatic glitter of water dropping from the canopy, the chatter of the creek. He unslung the field-glasses from the tree and moving to a clearer section of the plateau focused on the enemy across the water.

Things appeared unruffled. Couples were out on the wide deck beside the pool drinking. Waiters moved to and fro. Water-scooters and wind-sailers dotted the sea. Oh tropadise! Music came in a morning-clarified wave across the strait. After this, he imagined, he might write a new version of Crusoe, his ferocious pages vinegary with resentment. He caught a glimpse of Truscott swanning along the poolside untroubled by guilt, stopping every now and then to speak to guests. '*Rot you,*' Mac whispered.

Should Gamble leave? Should he be made to go for his own sake? Was lotus-eating for solitaries or pairs? The dedicated communism of shared living simply did not exist. Not in the real world. They would eventually argue, fight. One of them would assume leadership status, the other that of servant. He dreaded being a Crichton.

He rehung the binoculars and trotted back down the twisting paths then worked his way round to Gamble's hut and sat outside on the narrow ledge in the mottling leaflight of early day. Gamble's dreams were pierced by his presence. The young man rolled over on his narrow stretcher, opened his eyes and stared blankly for a moment. Mac observed an ant threshing through the ragged plantation of Gamble's emerging beard. He let it thresh. On his own ankle a leech was attaching itself, undulating disgustingly before it gorged. He wondered why he did nothing about it. The leech settled into a loathsome draining and again he was amazed at his own passivity. Soon, engorged, it would drop off his elderly flesh in a splatter of blood.

'Are you still bent on staying?' he asked Gamble's now focused eyes.

'They'll crucify you,' Gamble said, 'if I don't. They can savage one easily enough, toss him aside. Two makes it harder.' He frowned. 'By the way, there's a leech on your ankle.'

'I know,' Mac said. He smiled. It was a metaphor for Truscott.

*   *   *

Mac was counting out cans of food in what was left of their larder. Six of baked beans. Four assorted vegetables. Five bully beef. 'This is, after all,' he admitted, 'pretty boring. Boring if it weren't desperate.' Had he always been a time-waster? He had felt separated from work colleagues who, he imagined, were nursing hyper-tension and shimmering tracts of time. Like himself. *Time in which to write*, he had always explained to his unbelieving wife. But did he? And write what? He remembered his cabinets stuffed with quarto, the peckings of his typewriter on summer evenings, peckings so desultory his struggles for *le mot juste* might expand the moment into whole quarter hours. The peckings formed a natural equation to those unmemorable occasions on which he and his wife slept together, effacing them later with teeth-cleanings and gargles or some other bathroom mundanity.

Pricked, he gave meticulous attention to his shopping list. He added the words 'kerosene', 'cooker', 'batteries' to the dreary catalogue of essentials.

Four nights after the fire, just before dawn streaked the bay, they rowed across to the mainland taking raw-palmed turns at the oars, afraid to use the outboard in case Hummock Island nosed them out. The sea-miles bit endless. By the time they had picked up the van and driven down the coast highway the sun was well up and Mackay already starting the daily swelter. In a back street they found a café open for breakfast.

Mac mopped at his plate with a wedge of cold toast.

'Forgive me. I've forgotten how to eat. The little niceties. I think I've just gone native too long.' He looked hard at Gamble. 'You're here now. This is your last chance. Go or stay.'

Gamble pulled a face. 'Go to what?'

'Back south. To your family.'

'I've written. They won't worry.' He had dropped a soiled envelope in the post office the moment they reached town. He was lying. They would worry. But he had done his best to reassure. There were still a few hundred dollars in his savings account. He could get by for another month or so before penury drove him back to the piano bars and the out-of-town gigs. He could see his mother biting her lip as she read between the lines, despite his offered tentative return date. *Don't worry,* he had scrawled. *I should be back by the end of the month. I'm staying with a friend on an island just off the coast from here. There's no phone, no nothing really. But I'm getting plenty of rest. I know you like to hear that. And when I get back maybe I'll give up the music bit and go in with Dad in the business like he's always wanted. Okay?*

The okay hung now in the heavy wet air, cocking an ear for reply above the dirtied breakfast plates, the drained teapot, waiting for an answer. *Warum? Wohin?* He found himself whistling the latter melody between his teeth, but softly, so that the dark-eyed Greek behind the cash register wouldn't be upset and start reporting a madman.

'I'd like to see this out, if that's all right with you.'

'But it could go on and on. On till I weaken. I don't think this is the sort of fight that can be settled in days. Months, probably. I don't know whether I could face years! Anyway, anyway, they'll wear me down ultimately and I'll yield, I know that, sicken into some soft amorphous splodge of submission.'

Gamble picked up the last of the cold toast and dragged on it.

'God,' he said, 'God this is awful. Look, I know you're right. I know that will probably happen. But you don't have the right, not the moral right, to give in so early, so easily. Maybe there'll be compromise. I mean it's really cultural war with you, isn't it? Would you feel the same if they were bashing out Beethoven or Brahms day and night, day and night? You might. Think of that. It's noise, I know. And it's that *kind* of noise. But any noise, really . . .' His argument trailed away. He gave up on the toast. 'Own up, Mac. Now you're just after the aggro, right?'

Mac bit his lip. 'Man Friday attacks Crusoe, points out the thinning of moral fibre.'

His Eden! And the serpent arrived amplified!

'I've told you. You don't have to stay. I could order you not to stay.'

'Don't do that,' Gamble pleaded. 'It's going to take both of us to wage even the tiniest war. There are just two sides to the problem. That's about it. I'm trying to make you see both.'

'I can only hear one.'

Gamble giggled. Mac was pushing his protest along. 'I don't even believe complaints to authorities would make the slightest bit of difference. It will be complaint against complaint. Look, we've got a country run by people who aren't all that much older than you, a rock generation. They won't have the slightest sympathy for me. The whole country has grown up with racket, shops to racket, works to racket, relaxes to racket. I'm a passive racketeer, for God's sake, and I've got to make a gesture. A gesture for silence.'

Behind them, on cue, the café proprietor switched on his radio and there was a sudden screech of male hysteric advertising in the nudge-wink voice of the breakfast jockey.

Jesus! Mac's face contorted. Humans had changed along with technology. It was cultural aggression being foisted on the masses. After all, he was convinced the Berlin Wall, the whole communist set-up in Eastern Europe had been brought down by the Big Mac and the video clip. No one seemed to be able to function any more without background noise. There was *horreur du silence*! That was it. The horror of being left alone and knowing there wasn't one bloody thought going on in those ringingly empty skulls. *They have to fill them*, he thought bitterly, *with anything*.

'I'm a horse and cart man fundamentally,' Mac groaned as they steered the van through traffic. 'Born too late!' They drove up to a garage for a gas cylinder as the owner was opening up. 'Half a mo,' the man said, wrestling with padlocks. He flung back the double doors on his workshop, switched on the fluorescent lights and went instantly to click the wall radio to the programme they had abandoned in the café.

'If you'll turn that bloody thing off,' Mac said, smiling as nicely as he could, 'you'll have a sale.'

The garage man turned, hands on hip, jaw out-thrust. 'What's the matter with you, mate?' he asked. 'You some kind of wacker?'

＊　　＊　　＊

The Minotaur was reconnected. A new ice-box was put to suckle its gas udder, the patching of the launch more or less complete.

Already work had begun on a new cabin despite protests of non-need. They built this beyond the second barrier of the second circle of the maze in a blanket of scrub at a point where the hill stream detoured on its way to the sea. Cued by Gamble, Mac parodied his raised platform mounted on poles. Gamble spent days plaiting vine screens and making a roof thatch from layers of wait-a-while frond. The work took them both nearly a fortnight and they waited until evening on the day of completion to test its vulnerability. Mac lit a kerosene lamp and surveyed this leafy cave with its bucket sink, slab table and rough shelving warming in lamp glow. It seemed composed of delicate shivering blocks of leaf doubles that moved as he moved the lamp, that swelled and shrank with every flicker. Somewhere on the fringes of the beach below Gamble prowled to detect light.

He came up panting in ten minutes. 'Not a sign. Not even a glimmer from either end of the cove. You've picked a good spot.'

Mac rubbed his hands in a satisfied way. 'Organisation,' he gloated. 'That's all it takes.'

During the day a helicopter had flown low over Little Brother, circled it several times and hovered above the plateau at a dangerously low level. Two days before Gamble had spent a morning trailing wonga vine between trees to camouflage the small clearing. Around the makeshift gazebo he lashed the lower branches of the parasite fig and then he climbed up to the speakers and tied more branches into place across his thatching which had dried to a shiny giveaway brown.

All the while Hummock Island raged.

They warmed the new cabin that night, getting mildly drunk, and out of winey exhilaration started the generator now rehoused even farther up the hill and sat back to a rousing session with *Till Eulenspiegel.*

'Truscott wouldn't mind Johann,' Gamble said.

'I know that. Don't want to please him, do we? Have to stick to Richard.'

In the morning the helicopter prowled their airspace again.

'The *deus ex machina*,' Mac began mock ponderously, 'or the god from the machine, was a classical device for intervention in time of trouble. I think our friends above are some inverse kind of intervention.'

A week went by with no further action than the daily inspection from the skies. The men were beginning to feel confined, only moving about the beach after dark. Each felt the need to swim in the worst heat of the day. They had to content themselves with the shallow pools of the spring. Because they had decided no light should be shown, there was no way they could read. Once Mac was warned by the gentlest of splashings beyond the deck. He raced out with a flash but could see nothing. There were unexplained crashings in the under-growth, muffled cries of pain as wait-a-while scored a point. Gamble, using Mac's cabin that night, and reading by furtive candlelight, huddled braced for whatever might come out of the darkness and heard tentative paddling along the path below that could have been any night creature on the prowl.

They were impatient with each other, the impatience disguised as humour—and missing.

'Trip wires?' Gamble asked, grinning ferociously.

'I don't think so.'

'Barb wire snares? Tiger pits? Electrified fences?'

Mac walked away. Gamble went back to his hut and played his guitar. Mac could hear the sounds only when he was close—the music was like the clearest fall of water. If I could do that, he envied. He wrote in his water-damaged journal, he read, he spaded the garden, tended the fruit trees and felt beleaguered. The speed boats of the tourists were circling the island even more closely. Water skiers sliced the days to ribbons of sound and flung confetti'd blue. The end of endurance. To fill in his day, Gamble had begun building a raft, a clumsy affair of logs from old fallen trees which the young man dragged painfully down the path towards the beach. He was busy plaiting lashings of treevine when he became aware of Mac hunkered down watching, his face critical and alien.

'I'll be able to take myself off,' Gamble said. 'You won't have to lift a finger.'

It didn't look as if it would buck water.

'I don't even know Archimedes' principle,' Mac said, squatting beside the clumsy structure. 'Maybe it won't float.'

'I weigh so little,' Gamble said, thrusting out one skinny arm. 'I carry no luggage. Less than I had on the bus.'

It was the first time either of them had mentioned the bus.

'A year ago ...' Mac began. Then he stopped, wondering if he should speak of Laforgue's little gathering.

'A year ago what?'

He told him. 'In a way, that's what made me look for an island. Oh the excuses can roll in, but there was something about that forced unwanted reunion. Only you were missing. And the unfortunate Betsy Stager.'

Was he a man who had to keep running or was he being pushed?

For a moment he regretted his house on the beach outside Charco. Yet it had had its days with him. It had been time to move on. *Goodbye*, people had been saying to him as long as he could remember. *Goodbye*. Or was it he who said the word?

Have I been angry all my life? he asked himself, remembering academic years destroyed by an inner savagery at the phoniness of the system, the brutish laziness of some of his colleagues and most of the students; the hey-nonny acceptance of ignorance and semi-literacy on the part of the staff; the faked-up exam results aimed at keeping politicians happy and staff in jobs.

Squatting there in that blazing sun that ate through the shell of his panama, whittled by the throb of bass amplification to landward, the shrieks of motor boat engines and the hovering spider shadow of the chopper as it racketed above them, he grew suddenly dizzy, all his resentment packing into his head in a blood rush that found him swaying and the sand rushing up to abrade.

*   *   *

'I'll be off in another few days,' Gamble announced unexpectedly.

He had helped Mac haul his body up through the trees to the shack and dosed him with coffee laced with brandy.

His words stank of desertion. Mac didn't care.

'All right,' he mumbled. He didn't want discussion. He wanted sleep. His body was relaxing in an unaccustomed and delicious way, not having to fake slumber. It was as if a vast dispensation of charity had taken over his whole being; as if he were at last about to understand the sheer bloody humanness of people.

A necklace of rafts, Gamble had said at some time during the hot morning. *A flat immovable plane on an undulating mobile surface. A moral paradox of physics and aesthetics.* Had Gamble said that? It described .. him? Macintosh Hope?

Picture Mac. Picture him working his way through the mazes of sleep towards three in the morning, his kerosene lamp still burning. The lamplight attracts moths in their scores. Bodies zing and plummet, singe and flop, fluttering to the ground beside his cot, whacking the walls of the shack with a rubbery thwock. In his dreams he is worrying at it, bone-like, the next step in his re-lived history, the ultimate invasion with boats pulling in across the early dawn and the flitter shadows of attackers as they move from boat to beach, beach to tree-line, scrambling over rocks into the protective shadows of the forest to enter, finally to solve the maze that was himself.

He snapped awake and contemplated the maze, more an idea of a maze than the neatly executed one such as that where he had lost his wife one long-gone summer in a garden in Suffolk opened to spring visitors. Briefly again, he heard her wistful bleat then a series of angry cries as he headed for the exit in the high cropped hedges, heard her anger change to panic and tears, fading, while he pondered heading back to the car and driving away for ever, her whitened bones to be discovered in later decades by clipper-wielding gardeners. He was actually in the parking lot planning a speedy removal of her bags when she burst—irrupted, he decided—from the hedge, dishevelled and panting to capture him with a well-cast screech. 'Dear God,' he murmured, remembering. 'Dear God.' No amount of protest that it was unplanned, fortuitous, could convince. Why should it? It was not long after that that they separated. A day after their plane deposited them at Brisbane airport they were living separately and he was filled with a peace he had not known for years.

The maze was in the mind.

The Minotaur was two dangling sound pods on a gangling creeper.

FOURTEEN

*H*e made a final gesture. He played Mozart until dawn. Who could fault Mozart?

Carcasses of moths littered the table, the floor, his papers, his bed. Everything was powdered with the grey dust of their wings.

He went outside and leant into the dawn, a small wind off the sea sustaining him as he strained through the grainy air. He trudged up through the maze to the summit and watched Hummock Island wake to morning. Two small moving hyphens, paddles dipping gently, were slipping across the water towards him, recapitulating his dream, the long-read history. Hidden by trees, he waited and searched out the boats with his field-glasses. There were three men in each canoe. When the boats were a hundred yards or so from the island they separated and swung in opposite directions. Now he could make out the tight co-ordinated movements of the rowers. He lowered the glasses, confused.

He hadn't expected an army.

He had expected an army.

He began to race down the tracks of the maze to the launch, cursing momentarily the divagations so carefully planned that now worked against time. Vines whipped and cut. Necklaces of blood appeared on his chest and arms. His breath could barely sustain his pounding body as he broke through the beach scrub and stumbled along the jetty to the launch.

Gamble was thick with sleep and dreams that Mac pummelled out of him.

'Quick!' he gasped, half-choking for air. 'There's six of them. Two boats.'

Gamble struggled naked from his blanket and dragged on his shorts. He shook his head to clear it.

But Mac was sick with history and its repetition.

'Take a bag,' he ordered, 'and get up to your shack and mine and pack whatever you can. There isn't much after all, and get it down here. No, wait a minute, I'll do that. You get up the hill and watch those speakers. See if you can get them higher up the fig. I'll get the dinghy down and take both the boats out. At least that way we'll be safe.' *Safe?* Why did his mind harp on hurt to the flesh? He looked at Gamble. Already his own feet were tapping impatiently longing to be gone. 'I'll keep circling the island and find out where they've beached. Stay up top till you see me come round by the western side again. I think we've lost, mate. I'll be waiting to take you off.'

Minutes wasted while he gabbed.

Gamble was ahead of him in seconds. 'Forget my shack,' he shouted over his shoulder. 'All my gear's on the boat.'

Too old, too old for history, Mac confessed as he thumped his elderly legs back to the maze entrance they had camouflaged a few days before with branches and vines already withering into a dying flag of disclosure. He had created his own nightmare, thrust it on himself from a fevered reading, a wistful longing to repeat that which would inevitably repeat itself. Man had learnt nothing from history except technology. In the matter of morals man was still as primitive as the first dragging animal that heaved itself out of sea-slime to land. 'Oh Christ!' he whispered. 'Oh Christ.' Already they could have landed on any pair of his enticing inlets.

By the time he reached his shack he was trembling. The absurdity of it! A greying ex-academic forced into the lurid possibilities of an airport paperback. It should be funny, life mimicking history, but life and history in the late twentieth century were merging and played out their scenarios in grotesqueries that far outreached the most horren-dous scripts of film makers.

He shoved tapes, records, books, groceries, cooking utensils in one untidy load into a travelling bag. The player he rammed into a smaller one and struggling with the weight of them set off on teetering ancient legs towards the sea again. *Time*, he kept gasping. *Time*. He barely had the nervous strength to stagger back to the place where they had concealed the dinghy. His chest lashed with its tremendous pain. Spasms contracted the muscles in his gimcrack legs.

By now the sun had played scarlet over the eastern rim. The sea ran red.

As he dragged the dinghy down to the water he found he was counting aloud, counting as he heaved on its mooring rope, counting as he tied it to the launch in waters now leaching to an eye-searing silver that almost blinded him. It was too late for caution. He slipped the boat's moorings, clambered in and started the engine. There was a convulsive roar as the motor caught and then he was sweeping out from the little bay in a wide arc to the north of the island. Behind the stern silver was chewed into a wild pattern of white that caught brief fire from the risen sun. If only, Mac thought, to be able to sail on directly into the heat of those fading rosy dyes, drowning in russet. But he forced his attention to the shoreline and in another quarter of a mile spied the first of the boats beached into the elbow of the tiniest cove and wedged under the shadow of the west-facing boulders.

He cut the motor, dropped an anchor over the side and watched.

There was no movement from the shore. He waited another mo-ment then slipped over the side, swam and then waded up to the elbow of the beach to where the boat snuggled in shadow. The paddles were nearby, shoved against a log and camouflaged with carelessly heaped sand. He felt a surge of rage and dragging out the paddles one by one he wedged the blades in turn beneath a boulder exerting all his strength until he heard the wood crack. Panting, he dragged the canoe down to the water, smacked it lightly and sent it off on the outgoing tide. He heaved the useless paddle shafts after it.

'One,' he said aloud. 'To sail beyond the sunset and the something something.' Good, his memory was going as well! He knew himself to be the complete monomaniac. By now Gamble should have hoisted the Minotaur and its umbilicus into the topmost caverns of the canopy to dangle amid birds and leaves.

He swam after the bobbing canoe, nudging it farther out, climbed back into the launch, hauled anchor and restarted the motor. Without a qualm he clipped the canoe and was pleased to see it founder and fill with water. On the resort side of the island he saw nothing, not even an early morning guest on Hummock. He completed the circle of Little Brother, then swung the tiller and backtracked close to the shore, his eyes barely leaving the rocky fringes. He must have missed the second canoe somewhere. He circled again, a maze in water, his eyes sore from scanning. The sun was almost fully up. The water was running blue. He slowed down nearing his own jetty and then he saw the second boat. Impudently it had been hitched to one of the shore-end piles and was slapping easily against them in the shadow of the planking.

Jetty and beach appeared lifeless as Mac moored the launch but kept the motor idling. Quickly he ran down the jetty and waded out under its shadow to the canoe, unhitching and relashing it to the stern of his dinghy. Then he took the launch out again, his own necklace of rafts.

Turning his boat into the heart of the risen sun he travelled for nearly a sea-mile before he unslipped the canoe and sent it on its way.

* * *

Above Gamble the trees held that pre-sunlight stillness. Together, Gamble and trees, they stood holding their breath, straining after dawn sounds and noises that did not belong. Above him, rope-hauled from sight, the Minotaur dangled in the top contortions of the strangler fig, the end of the rope secured and tucked in a fork of the tree just below. The yards and yards of leads he had hauled from branch supports on his way up were coiled into a thick bundle of loops hidden behind the speakers.

As he stood and listened from somewhere farther down the hill came the sound of furtive movement, the cracking of twigs and the subdued oaths of men tangled in a mess of tracks and becoming angry.

The maze was easy enough. Gamble had learnt its secrets in a day. But the sounds were too close, he decided. Too close. Swinging himself up into the lower branches of the fig he began climbing until he reached the wide fork where speakers rested on a makeshift platform. Edging around speakers and leads he climbed even higher, thirty feet up now, the branches becoming thinner, more brittle and less capable of bearing his weight. Carefully he edged along one limb until he reached a point where the leathery leaves formed the densest cover and waiting, his skinny rump carved by the branch on which he perched, he stayed motionless, hearing a muffled cough below him and to his right. Downhill. Whoever it was, was in one of the dead ends. The entrance to the final circle was another hundred yards away and uphill.

Not only was Gamble well-hidden. The sea was also blotted out. He had no way of seeing Mac's launch swinging its guardian ellipse around the island. He had carried the field glasses up with him, dangling around his neck by their strap. Useless. Mentally he cursed. There was nothing for it but to dodge his way down to the beach, avoiding the tracks and forcing his way through the thinner parts of the rainforest. He was torn between waiting and attempting an immediate run for it. Already he had one impulsive foot placed on a lower branch and was preparing himself for the swing down when without warning two men burst into the clearing. He parted the leaves and looked down. They were big men and despite the still low temperature of the morning, appeared flushed and sweaty as if they had been wrestling with landscape. In a moment a third man joined them, a fleshy red fellow who broke the rules by shouting. He was mopping at scratched arms and legs; a thorn had torn his cheek from eyebrow to lip. They were gazing perplexed at the emptiness of the clearing until one of them moved across to the sapling gazebo and began shaking with such force the whole flimsy structure swayed, tottered, cracked and fell apart.

From the debris of dead fronds, dead leaves and split timber, one of the men picked something up and held it out to the others. Gamble caught the glint of light on its surface and then he could see as it was passed from hand to hand that it was one of the clips Mac had used to anchor the leads.

He held his breath. The men spaced out and began inspecting the glade more closely. What else would they turn up? He craned forward, trying to gauge their movements. The slight shift of weight undid him. In seconds he was crashing forward, slamming into one branch after another before he managed to grip one and break his fall. The three swung round and stared up but Gamble was still fighting the giddiness of his downward rush, too shaken, to speak.

'Okay,' the fleshy one ordered. 'Down.'

He stared at them with what, he reminded himself, recalling his schooldays, would have been dumb insolence. He was barely ten feet above them at this point. Something had torn his shoulder as he fell, and there was blood running freely down his right arm and dripping onto the grass below.

'Move!' the fleshy one roared. 'Or we'll pull you down.'

Gamble bit back reply and began climbing cautiously to the lower branches. The next minute they had moved in so fast he knew only that his legs were hooked from under him and he found himself face down spitting out a mouthful of dirt and twig. One man straddled the small of his back, pressing his left arm into an agonising angle. Another had bent his legs back and was squatting across them. He knew that if he moved even a fraction the wrong way, a bone would snap.

The fleshy man squatted on the ground beside him and swung Gamble's head about so that he was forced to look up into oily skin and light unblinking blue eyes.

'And who the hell are you?'

'I'm a dropout,' Gamble said. 'I'm nothing.'

His face was slapped smartly.

'No sass, matey. Who are you and where's the boss?'

'Not me,' Gamble managed cheekily. 'You've got the wrong bloke. I'm a visitor.'

He spat out more soil.

Fleshy smacked him again on the side of his head.

'Where is he?'

'Who?'

'You know bloody well who. The man who owns this place.'

'He's gone. Gone away. He runs a bus company. The Genteel Poverty Bus Company. He's the tour captain.'

'The genteel what?'

'Tours up the Cape. I'm the caretaker.'

'You're bloody lying,' Fleshy said. 'Our boss wants to talk with him right away. You'd better find him quick smart.'

Gamble raised his head with an effort, smearing dirt away from his mouth. His tongue tasted the island and he understood momentarily Mac's sensual attachment but the slaps had made him giddy and he felt more like burrowing his head into the soil, closing his eyes and sinking into oblivion. He forced words out.

'You don't listen, do you? He's gone. I can't find him. Now, can I just get up? Your bloody bully-boys are breaking my back.' He tried to pull himself up against the pressure of bodies but weight forced him back. The sun had begun to light the tops of the rainforest and was inching into the clearing.

He let his head rest on the warming earth, his ears still ringing from the flat comment of hands, allowing his body to become as limp as possible until the pain eased. He wondered where Mac was at this moment, thinking he could hear muffled shouts from the southern end of the island, shouts broken into pieces by rock and tree. Was this happening? Really happening? He thought of triads and mafia and tongs and comprehended finally the reasons for Mac's puny fight against the power of money and corrupt political preference. He understood why Mac raged against the bland stares and shrugged shoulders of front men who were salting away the profits of this most specious of industries. Perhaps the whole country should be taking to rafts looking for sanctuary in other lands. As one lot came in the back door they would be leaving by the front.

He giggled. It wasn't funny.

Oh but it was! And he heard himself laugh and was rewarded with another clout.

He lifted his head again. 'My grandfather died in Changi,' he said, not irrelevantly. 'He was beaten to death. For smiling.'

Sounds of anger were invading the clearing. They came like clarinet snarls. He thought rapidly. The men pinioning him were in a kind of hatchback dead-end. To cross the island or even get down to the jetty one had, against better judgement, to double back at the second turning from the exit to the summit. In his mind the map of the maze was laid out precisely, the barriers in position, the false entries, the hazard of stinging tree and rock. The clear sounds of running were now coming from the sixth circle. Somehow he must encourage his captors to let him up and lead them downhill, lose them along one of the tracks if he could, and reach the beach.

'Okay,' he said. 'Okay. I'll help you find him. If you'll just let me up.'

He sensed the weight on his body ease.

Fleshy shoved his mug down alongside his own. 'No bloody tricks, mate.' His face loomed out of focus with its own maze of broken capillaries.

'Right,' Gamble said. 'Just let me up. I won't be much damn use if I'm bent like a pothook. Just let me up and we can talk sensibly. If you understand sensibly,' he added.

Bodies moved off. He rolled over and began massaging his thighs, his arms. The cramp spasms subsided as blood flowed back. Groggily he got to his feet. The sounds from the sixth circle died away as muddled men headed off into the false leads of the track. If I can just dodge them, he thought. A chance?

They frog-marched him out of the clearing into the first opening they saw. It was the wrong one. They were baffled by scrub whichever way they turned.

'You'll have to go back,' Gamble said. Movement was returning to his limbs, the throb in his skull fading. 'You'll have to start again.'

'Jesus,' one of the other men said. 'What kind of nutter is this bloke?'

They trudged back to the clearing. The sun was fully up now, the trees glistening with overnight rain that dribbled in a continuing spatter from the branches. Gamble glanced all round with a kind of love. He knew it would be the last time he saw it. 'This way,' he said, a kindly guide. 'Over here.'

He led them round the sixth circle but deliberately took a wrong turning at the fifth. The sounds of the other group were fading downhill as the men gave up trying to solve this riddle of trees. He could confuse them well before they reached the third circle where a stand of Gympie bush formed one of the barriers near the exit to the second track. '*Dendrocnide moroides*,' he could hear Mac pontifically pronounce. 'Don't touch! They have all the qualities of the human heart. Deceptive shape and capable of inflicting vicious pain.' He had pointed to an enormous tree at the rear of the barrier. '*Laportea gigas*, if you're interested. The daddy of them all. Don't be deceived by those bleeding-heart leaves. The pain will last for weeks.' He had poked one of the leaves down so Gamble could see the dense covering of stinging hairs.

Matters of the heart, Gamble thought, stolidly leading the three bruisers towards their doom. *Theirs.*

As they drew near, he made up his mind quickly, stumbled deliberately and pretended faintness, swaying despite their manacles of hands, and sagging at the knees.

'Just a minute,' he pleaded, infusing weakness into his voice. 'I need a breather.'

The men's faces were dogged with uninterest.

He tapped his chest. His pallor should be enough for them. 'Heart,' he said. 'I've got a dickey heart.' His nose had begun to bleed and the blood trickled unstaunched over his lips down onto his chin and began dripping onto his chest.

Fleshy regarded him stolidly.

'Please,' Gamble said. He closed his eyes and swayed again. The track lay each side with no visible break in the high walls of green. 'You want me to help, don't you? If you keep pushing me at this rate I won't be any help at all, you stupid sods.'

Fleshy grinned unpleasantly. 'So you've got a dickey heart, mate? Who gives a stuff!'

'The others,' Gamble gasped, lying quickly. He feigned cramp and bent forward, trying to grip his side.

'What others?'

'The others. The others here.'

'How many? You're lying. There isn't anyone else except that nutter you're with.'

'Four,' Gamble began to gabble. 'The Stagers, Dickie, Pellatier. Just four. The whole busload.'

'We don't want their fucking names,' Fleshy said.

As they came opposite the stinging trees, Gamble let his knees buckle dramatically, letting out a yelp of pain, trying to grab for his heart. They hauled him up roughly and he let his groans increase, knowing without looking that they half-believed him for he felt the grip on his arms slacken.

At this point on the track there was a narrow screen of celerywood. He began to gurgle and choke, the horrible sounds bursting out

between a mouth rosy with blood. *Genuine method theatre!* He felt
the restraining hands shift and with a jerk he was away from them,
speeding off down the track into the celerywood, hurtling past the
poison trees, swerving and dodging until at the last moment he placed
himself in tantalising stillness on the other side of the grove where he
knew they could still glimpse him, casual, static, behind the great
heart-shaped leaves. He smiled. He waved one impudent hand and in
response, reflexive, his pursuers thrust directly into the Gympie bush
to be struck and stroked on face arms chest legs by the murderous
hairs as they dragged the foliage back to get at him. Gamble turned
and began trotting away from the barrier into the thickets of the
rainforest hearing their howls and yawps as they floundered between
the branches that, thrust incautiously back by their scalding hands,
returned to whip them across their faces and the upper parts of their
bodies. The noise of their cursing faded as Gamble pushed deeper into
the trees, only an isolated shriek reaching him as he came to the first
track, cut across it and scrambled down towards the beach.

* * *

Gamble was some kind of grinning pup as he recounted.

He had crouched hidden behind a rock outcrop until the launch
circled the island for the fourth time. His waving arms attracted Mac
who brought the boat in closer and Gamble raced into the water and
began to swim, wallowing mock-comic until he found himself surfac-
ing at the stern of the dinghy. The other three invaders (*Was that the
word?* Gamble asked Mac) had come pounding along the sand-strip as
he reached the launch and watched him being lugged aboard. Blood
still trailed from his torn shoulder.

The island was infested.

'A cruel word,' Mac deliberated. 'But there's no other.'

He remembered solitude, uttered the word, tasting its solid round
reassuring syllables and what they connoted. The memory was dim-
ming the outline of a long-lost atoll toy. He allowed Gamble to gabble
on, not listening, wondering about the next step, if there were a next
step, and turned the boat in the direction of the mainland, hardly
conscious of what he was doing.

* * *

'It's time you left,' Mac said as they sat on the veranda of the little pub outside Seaforth. 'Time, I think.'

Gamble became voluble. He didn't want to leave now, he said. Despite what he'd said the day before. He had nowhere to go.

Go, Mac wanted to order. *It was easier with my wife.* They couldn't wait to separate by the luggage carousel. Not even a backward glance. Not even the deadliness of follow-through phone calls: my dear are you all right is there anything have you enough do let me know if. None of that. Why did this have to be so difficult?

Then 'I'm sorry,' Gamble said humbly. He pushed his drink aside in a submissive way. 'I didn't mean to be a handicap.'

Mac was silent a long time. Finally he said, 'You've been cracking the edges of my dream. Didn't you realise? Cracking them.'

'I'm sorry,' Gamble said again.

'I've decided, anyway.' He hated to admit it. 'They win, the bastards. They win. I'm leaving too. I can't wait for the ultimate.'

'And what's that?'

Mac lit a cigarette. The ritual. Everything a ritual. 'Greed,' he said in *non sequitur*, 'is probably the most appalling sin of all.' He was silent so long, Gamble had to prod further words out of him.

He was greedy himself, he admitted, greedy for isolation, for being alone with himself. He thought again of the desert fathers, the buddhist monks, the whole lot of trappist-like human prayer wheels who ultimately became dependent on others as they indulged themselves in ejaculatory cries to their god, expecting their begging bowls to be filled without stirring a hand to produce a thing. Those who had no time for prayer worked. A balance there. A terrible balance.

His eyes distant, busy with historic ironies, he was stuck with his own memories. 'Work is prayer, boys,' Brother Anselm used to say to a cynical class of sprawlers and loafers. 'Make no mistake about that. Work done for the right reason is prayer, whether it's pasting labels in a jam factory or mending boots. Whether it's digging drains or spading the garden. Whatever. It's all *ad maiorem dei gloriam* and don't you forget it. Learn to have respect for work well done.' 'Yes, brother,' they had all chorused mockingly. And then one of the kids had raised a hand. 'What about Trappists, brother? They don't work. They only pray.' Brother Anselm had looked at the kid for a long time,

a strange flicker passing over his face. 'You want me to say they're
prayer bludgers, don't you? That's what you want to hear, isn't it?
Well, prayer is hard work too. Believe that. You'll never know how
hard. Especially when you don't seem to get any answers.' And at that
point he had swung out of the room, gown flapping, his face set lean
and hard, heading for the chapel. Mac had followed him. He had
stood at the doorway of the wax-scented flower-drowsy little room
haunted by the presence of the Sacred Heart and the Virgin staring
down with compassionate plaster faces and had seen Brother Anselm
close up by the communion rail, head burrowing into his arms and
could hear the muttered muffled sorry sorry sorry.

'I'll be gone in the morning,' Mac was saying. 'I'm going back for
one last look.'

'Let me come,' Gamble said. He seemed perilously young, lost.

'No,' Mac answered. 'I want to be on my own.' He felt as if he had
been running for a month. A loser. A born loser. He saw himself
running out the last years of his life breathless, gasping towards a
finishing tape forever moving beyond reach.

'You know,' Gamble said reflectively, 'I feel I've never been off the
bus. Not even in the five years in between then and now. Wherever I
worked, wherever I went, there were Stager clones and Dickie clones
and replicas of sad old Pellatier. I kept remembering you and your
assault on pop culture. And we were still all alone and you more than
the rest of us.'

Gamble had begun to see the Genteel Poverty Bus Company as a
symbol for something larger than those five travellers bucketing to the
Tip. He rose and came round the table to Mac and held out both
skinny hands.

'I'll push off now, then, if you don't mind. No ceremony, eh?'

Mac took the offered hands and squeezed them.

'It's best,' he said. 'I think it's best.'

'There's a truck pulling out in half an hour. I don't want to miss the
chance of a hitch.'

'Where's it heading?' Mac asked.

'I don't know,' Gamble said. 'That's the beauty of it.'

Mac understood. He stood up and walked with the other to the
head of the pub stairs. For a moment as he watched the young man

grab his pack and head off to the roadway he felt as if he had given birth to the young man he once was, as if that body had been torn from this.

'Take care,' he called. 'Take great care.'

Gamble raised one arm without turning his head. Then he was gone.

*　　*　　*

Mac took one last walk through the damp trackways of his maze and found the summit clearing purged of all presence. From the base of the strangler fig he could just make out where Gamble had hidden the speakers. It was too high for him to climb, too dangerous. Anyway, he didn't care. It was as if a nerve had been severed, withdrawn. His kindly Minotaur was dead. The bellows the bullhead gave were no more than the music of long dead men stretching the white elastic of their souls tuned to a gut-point high in search of an ultimate perfection. As he. As he. Across the water rocked the din of the Minotaur's natural enemy, alive and kicking and he turned away and walked slowly back down the seven circles of his maze, taking one last drink from the spring as a sort of communion. Down. Down to the jetty to stand for what he knew was the last time looking out across the water, listening to its repeated message as it hit the piles.

What was the message?

He should have been weeping that an answer was lost to him. But he wept instead that he had not the generosity to give without bile. He lit one cigarette after another and the morning swelled into its great heat bubble exploded by the engine of the resort runabout as it swaggered round the point and cut a vast loop in to the end of his jetty.

Truscott clambered up onto the boardwalk and the two men stood staring at each other for what seemed hours before either could find words.

Truscott asked, 'Why won't you know when you're beaten? It's a losing battle.'

Mac still baulked at admitting, admitting he was leaving, admitting defeat. He bit his tongue and waited. Behind him was the glistening beach, the high hill that had nourished the dream, the forest with its maze. He watched Truscott lean back against the jetty rail, heard and did not hear his suggestions for compromise, offers of monetary soothing, resettlement. He heard and he didn't hear. He was absorbed by the face confronting his, that of a middle-aged beach bum, the flesh fattened by good living, the eyes hard as rock. He heard and he didn't hear until finally Truscott burst out, 'Christ, you're an amateur. You're just a bloody amateur.'

At that Mac said in a kindly way, 'Piss off will you. Piss off and don't come back.'

He turned on his heel and went back down the jetty and made his way to the northern end of the beach where Gamble had been building his raft. Behind him the runabout's engine hacked into life and he heard the sound of its motor receding round the point. He refused to look at the victor's wake. *Like this?* he was questioning himself. *I have to leave like this?*

He looked instead at Gamble's makeshift raft asleep beneath the scrub. Maybe the boy had had a point. *Haul out, drift.* It was a question of historic irony, a reversal of the process; the new boat people heading off from what was called progress and looking for a primitive welcoming shore. *And what shore might that be?* he had asked Gamble whose eyes had been set beyond the black line of the horizon. *East,* the other had replied. *East east east.*

Mac dragged the raft inch after grating inch across the narrow beach to the water, waded in behind it and shoved it farther out. It sank immediately. The weight of ill-planned dream, preposterous invention.

Life was a never-ending accretion of follies. It was nothing without them. Energised, he strode back quickly to the jetty and his boat while the decision still fuelled him. He stood on the deck's rocking skin before he started the motor and took one last look at his island with the eyes of a lover.

It gave nothing back. Nothing. It remained floating above the sea, tiny, perfect and unknowable, indifferent to the tearing he felt in the heart of him.

'I love you,' he said to the island. Its perfection remained unmoved. East east east.

He didn't look back. He took the boat straight out as he had once taken the bus to the Cape. The bickerers of that journey crowded his little deck, jostled for room and ripped the edges of his dream.

The genteel poverty boat company stood along the rails like figure-heads, each distanced from the others, connected only by roll-call. *Gamble*, he said. *Dickie. Pellatier. Stagers.*

Humming to himself he headed straight into day, straight for the outer reef and the ocean beyond.

Void.

Inventing the Weather

*I*t is seven years now since I came to this town, this sluggish hot-smelling sprawl of a place, immodestly supine like a woman with her skirts hitched up, along the banks of the river. I've never warmed to the place and that part of it I inhabit has never really warmed to me.

I don't know why. I feel I am a lot more warmable to than Clifford. Clifford is my husband. Well, that's a misuse of a term as well. There's nothing husbanding about Clifford, even though we are legally tied. (That word should be spelt with an 'r'). I keep remembering that devastatingly vicious quatrain Byron (why is it *women* they call bitches?) penned on his sixth wedding anniversary: *This day of all our days*—I'm sure you know it!—*has done the worst for me and you*—interested?—'*Tis just six years since we were one*—what an epigrammatist, hey?—*and five since we were two.* If I had access to my gadabout corporate husband's laptop I could give you in a minute the days to the hour since we were two, the precise number of suckophantic managerial dinners attended or cooked and proffered, the infinite private school (the firm helps with the fees) canteen attendances with choral accompaniments from one-upping graziers' cane-growers' dentists' doctors' lawyers' politicians' and other corporate directors' wives. I could list that unlisted grind of morning coffees and afternoon teas taken beside tennis courts, pools and mandevillea-swagged patios with the girls, as the girls coyly describe themselves, endured to promote the efflorescence of our bank and credit card accounts. Theirs as well. Look, I'll tell you something. Lend me your tropically mildewed ear: most of us are skint, as they say. It's not only culinary makedo of cane-toad-in-the-hole. It's the full gamut—the sneaky shopping for clothes at cut-price supermarkets and charity recycling barns.

I'm getting tired of all this.

Only last week Flora (the most tolerable of the lot of them and a former school friend) admitted she had to choose between buying herself a new dressing-gown for the winter or paying Chubbsie's second-term music fees. The music fees won. Musicians come cheap in this country—the serious ones anyway—so she couldn't have got much of a dressing-gown.

In any case Chubbsie has no talent.

Not only is Flora struggling to educate Chubbsie, a large girl in the mode of Mrs Worthington's daughter, but she also has older twins at the acne stage called Hengist and Horsa. I can never recall their given names and to me they have been that since they first started punting balls through other people's windows. They are attractive boys, almost identical with their surfer-blond hair and impudent mouths. Hengist is distinguishable by a scar across his left cheek that he acquired when trying to terrorise a neighbour's dog. Apart from that there is nothing to separate them, not even mentally.

'Must you always talk like that?' Clifford demands of my light aside. 'Must you always put down?'

As I write that I can see Clifford sounds the more lovable. Men can afford to be more lovable. They have it made. Sometimes watching television I suspect there is only one sex in the world. All the news is about men making money, cheating each other, killing each other and playing football. Who's getting on with it? I ask myself. Who's doing the boring stuff? Don't answer that. So I ignored his remark as I tend to ignore most of his remarks these days. He spends an inordinate amount of time away from home locked, or so he says, in conference and policy discussions. Want to bet on it? I am busy making twelve dozen madeleines (God! That trendy mothers' committee!) to be sold at a fund-raising fête for Sweetgrass Grammar and the flour has entered my soul.

Clifford is not really a self-made man. He has failed at a lot of things but an inheritance from his father set him off on a career of real estate buying, a pursuit that is so lacking in humanity and moral purpose it is on a par with playing the stock exchange. Perhaps stock exchange activities are worse. After all share buying and selling is nothing more than gambling and adds zilch to the total of human achievement. It is a sterile, almost moribund activity, structured for people who are too selfish to give anything to the world. Takers! Two-legged wallets! Clifford's real estate ventures were like that. He began modestly. He had perfect pitch. A block of land here, an old dump of a slum house there (a coat of paint, slap wallpaper over sagging ceilings). Then he waited twelve itching months and doubled his money.

I must confess to a brief monetary symbiosis and amusement on the first few outrageous occasions—it was so pleasant to see him successful at something instead of choking with sun and allamanda—but when it became obsessive and he was waving his athletic tentacles over tracts of woodland and pasture hundreds of miles away, buying and selling without sighting (oracular ocular!), I was sickened by his cynicism.

'Why don't you hang out a tile?' I asked. 'Make it a full-time operation? Buy yourself a gold chain? Wear Harry Belafonte shirts?'

He did that.

He became a developer sliding into the morass of subdivision without missing a beat. Cane farms along the coast north of this town were transmogrified to suburban sprawl. Clifford became precariously wealthy. On paper. There never seemed to be any cash around. But there were lots of credit cards, the monthly payments of which we barely kept up.

Me?

What about me?

I was once a cadet reporter on a regional newspaper in Rockhampton. Now I am a bored housewife and mother of three.

How did this happen I ask myself often and can attach cause only to a chain of coincidences, the prime mover being an assignment to report an end-of-year high-school play evening (we're very parochial here). Clifford, then employed as a lack-lustre English teacher, was attempting a pretentious production of *The Master Builder* (you might have guessed!). I noted this in my review but the sub-editor blue-pencilled every negative remark, every tiniest criticism. Clifford wrote me a small note of thanks which I placed on the sub's desk.

The heat up here makes everyone short on irony.

We met again, unplanned, on the *Spirit of Capricorn en route* to Brisbane, both on annual leave, travelling sleeperless and locked into a sandwich line on a midnight station in Gympie. Our faces fell as we recognised one another but the sheer *longueur* of the journey forced us into conversation and, one thing leading to another, three candlelit dinners and a planned weekend on the Gold Coast aborted by my boss telephoning and requiring my immediate return.

Perhaps the frustration of strategy prompted Clifford to propose marriage when he came back. Perhaps the security of my job prompted him to give up his. Certainly he remained teaching for only a year after we married and I must admit it was a relief to have an end to his moanings as he ploughed through a weekly load of illiterate student assignments. I think Clifford must have been one of the few remaining teachers in the country who actually marked anything and even he wasn't so punctilious. Once I looked through some of those appalling essays (preparations for university entrance) and found dozens of errors he had failed to correct. Sometimes the assignments appeared to be written in another language altogether.

Clifford shrieked at me when I pointed out his omissions.

'You think I don't know?' he screamed. 'You want me to wreck their self-esteem by having corrections all over? Do you? Is that what you think teaching's about, just stuffing in non-creative facts? My God!'

Words failed him.

They failed me. You couldn't deny the stuff was creative!

I wanted to ask if teaching were all about letting uncorrected misconceptions linger on like mouldy packing. I'm glad I didn't because a month later he handed in his resignation and we tried living on one salary while he negotiated the possibilities of being a travel agent, a seller of insurance, a barman. Fortunately his little inheritance arrived at this time. I was pregnant with Daniel and it was at this point that he made his move into real estate. Between bouts of buying and selling Clifford made me pregnant twice more: Etta, Timothy. There is a six-year gap between Etta and Timothy which brings me to now. Add seven years. Daniel and Etta are fourteen and twelve and are five-day boarders at Sweetgrass Grammar. Timothy attends the government primary school where he is about fifty years older than his classmates. All three children are surprisingly well-adjusted despite seeing father only two days a week. (Clifford's path is strewn with libidinal disasters I have so far ignored.) Or perhaps that *is* why. I used to think *I* was suprisingly well-adjusted. One of these days, I tell myself, I might even get back to newspaper work.

I mention this ambition to Flora. (Christ, Flora, I have said on several occasions, you have the most godawful name! I know, she always replied. I know. It's so awful I've come to like it.) She is aided in this by superb looks. It gives a kind of quirkiness to the whole persona. Who's that gorgeous woman? people ask at parties. Oh, that's Flora, we say. Flora! they cry. God!

And why not? Flora responds to my tentative ambition. She encourages me, that old me dragging my limp ego over the cobblestones of my subconscious. She also is testing her wings now Hengist and Horsa and the formidable Chubbsie are fully potty-trained, vocal and in the school first eleven (the boys) and dramatic club (Chubbsie. Mrs Worthington hasn't taught Flora a thing!). Flora used to be a weather girl on Sugarville's one commercial television station but there were complaints during the cyclone season that viewers were so busy looking at her they missed the vital announcements. And despite the passage of years she is still photogenic enough to give news of year-long droughts, drug hauls and police harassment. But her goals are set higher. She would like to be a political commentator. She carries a master's degree in political economy that she tossed off when the twins started primary school and believes she is destined for something more cerebral than warning southerners of approaching lows and unspeakable temperatures. (I don't mean to sound grudging when I use the phrase 'destined for more'. I feel it too.) But we do tend to spend—read 'waste'—our days when she is not spilling out degrees in Celsius drinking endless coffees, offering our bodies to the gods of carcinoma beside swimming pools and planning or recovering from dinner parties.

Flora is kind. She actually likes her husband.

'I can't understand this,' she says wistfully, twiddling her toes in our pool and making tiny tidal waves. 'Maybe it's his ears. Maybe it's because he makes me laugh.'

She makes him laugh quite often and is totally unaffected by her dazzling appearance. She acts as if it isn't even there. We all like Flora.

Things came to a pretty pass a month ago. Clifford's infidelities long suspected emerged as fact substantiated by a gossip-monger husband in our circle who assumed the passing on of such information might give him an advantage with me. Forty love! Bored housewives were open game.

'What makes you so certain?' I refilled his glass. Timothy, just home from school, made car-accident noises round the back of my guest's chair. 'Ker-vroom ker-rash,' he kept crying excitedly and describing deadly parabolas with two clutched matchbox cars he swung within inches of Foster's head.

'There's a good kid,' Foster soothed whipping his skull out of range and trying hard to maintain sweetness. 'Take the cars over there, Timothy. Yes. Of course. It was the Brisbane realtors' AGM. I'm sorry, darls, but Clifford had this ... well, he had this woman ... you know like they were kind of stuck together. Like clones the whole weekend. God, Timothy, mate, not so close, old chap.'

My initial spasm of jealous rage engorged and subsided. I was enjoying Timothy's assaults on this po-faced Cassandra.

'Does she have a name?'

'Laramie.'

'Laramie! My God!' I couldn't help laughing.

'I wouldn't put up with it if I were you,' Foster said helping himself to more Scotch.

'But you're not me.'

'No. I'm not.' He eyed me cloudily over his glass. 'Thank God.'

'What do you mean, thank God?'

'Just that.' He smiled smugly at some inner proposition that was only beginning to be formulated. 'I'm a man. You're a woman.' His loathsomely confident smile widened. 'If you take my point.'

'I'm afraid I don't,' I said infusing coldness into my voice. Foster was so basic. Timothy miscalculated and two matchbox cars crashed together grinding the rim of Foster's ear. He screamed with pain and the pretty pass entered another dimension entirely as I staunched blood and applied iodine.

So I was not surprised when Clifford returned from what he calls a familiarisation trip to a beach area ripe for rape a few hundred miles north of here.

'There is something I must tell you,' he said having waited discreetly for me to prepare dinner, serve it, clear away and bed down the children (the older two are home for the weekend). 'I have decided to move out.'

I think here that the crunch with Clifford had come a month back on the day he insisted I park the kids with Flora because we were going boating. As part of the jewellery required by white shoe developers he had recently bought a launch called *Allegro*. He had, too, a secretary of alienating charm whose relationship with Clifford I suspected was not entirely secretarial. 'I've promised Mimsie a run on the boat,' he announced that Saturday at breakfast. 'She's really earned it.'

'How?' asked innocent Timothy.

Clifford ignored him. 'I'd like the kids to get stuck into their assignments,' he said. 'But Julie, a run would do you good. There's some property I'm interested in inspecting. This could be the big one. Think you can whip up some lunch on board?'

There we were, the three of us, heading north towards the Whitsundays, me slaving in the minuscule galley, tossing lettuce and tomato salad, slicing the boiled eggs and arranging them prettily round a glutinous pile of potato salad while Clifford and Mimsie, topless, disported on the deck above, my spouse giving elaborate hands-on tutorials in tiller-handling. Gales, but gales of laughter! Occasionally there came bellows from my husband demanding to know whether lunch was ready as the tired crouched lions of the islands came up on the starboard side.

It was, as Clifford explained with a mouth full of impressionist egg and lettuce and busily swilled Riesling, a business trip. The *Allegro* was anchored and rocking in a small cove of a snoozing islet that he ogled with the greedy orb of a producer interviewing a potential star. Mims, as he called her and who had not bothered to dress for lunch, sprawled back, her nipples appearing rather bored by the whole business but her injected comments supporting Clifford's claims to being on the edge of the biggest resort development along the coast. I let them witter on, my eyes scaling the peak of the tiny gem that lay across the strait from our anchorage a bare few hundred yards. I suggested diffidently that that would be a more idyllic choice. Clifford and Mims did a two-part invention of patronising laughter. Too small! they said. Oh God! Too small! We're not in this for the idyll. It's the money. The money. This was going to be the biggest, the most elaborate, seductive ...

I hid from their superlatives under another layer of sunblock and began to stack plates.

'While you're doing that,' Clifford announced *ex cathedra*, rising to his feet and displaying the thickening torso that had not then reached full term, 'Mims and I will take the outboard and check out the sites. The possible sites.'

Check ... out ... the ... sites!

He even produced a survey map.

Before I could make the merest annotation to his suggestion, indicating a wish to accompany them, they were off, racketing away from the *Allegro, allegro molto*, Mimsie with a T-shirt knotted carelessly about her shoulders, Clifford doing a Viking stance in the bows. 'So long, buddy,' I whispered, piling unwashed dishes into the galley sink, fighting the temptation to take *Allegro* home, leaving them stranded even though I knew nothing about boats. Clifford had seen to that. When, two hours later, they had still failed to return, I chucked the unwashed dishes into the tide. Yep! Right into the tide. Then I made an ill-founded spontaneous decision to run *Allegro* back, willy-nilly, but discovered that Clifford, the clever devil, had removed the ignition key.

Bless you, Clifford.

At four they returned with a sated look. Did I imagine that? An ammoniac stench like a nimbus? The fishy stink of sperm? Of course I imagined all that, too, but their faces were oiled with some kind of temporary release and I barely glanced up from my sulking bunk when they poked noses round the cabin doorway, gluing my eyes to a page I hadn't read once in the hours it had challenged me.

'Some marvellous sites!' Clifford gloated. I'll bet! 'Did I tell you we tied up the lease last week? Absolutely superb! Should be able to get things under way in the new year. How about a coffee, love? We're tuckered out from crawling around those beaches.'

'Ask Mimsie,' I suggested without looking up.

He glared at me. I could feel the glare.

'She's a guest.'

'She's your girl Friday, *n'est-ce-pas?*' I said nastily. 'She does it every day, doesn't she?'

Clifford backed out of the cabin and hitched himself up the companionway. I could hear him conferring with Mimsie and later, cries of fury on discovering I'd heaved out the crockery. 'I think you're mad, Julie,' Clifford said when he had calmed down sufficiently to address me. 'Bloody impenetrably mad.'

Oh Clifford, I do agree.

We puttered back through a miasma of sulks.

I can only plead provocation of the most extreme kind.

So I was not surprised, etc etc, when Clifford announced his intention of leaving.

I think Clifford wants drama at this point but I find I am unable to say anything except, 'You have metaphorically done that already.'

'There you go,' he accuses. 'My God! There you go! Always the quick crack. Don't you realise that's half the reason I'm going? You've brought it on yourself.'

'What's the other half?'

He is furious. Where are my tears? Where is my hysteria? Where is the pleading, the wild accusation, the old Canossan knees-to-the-carpet humbling? His inner man demands medicant grief to his indifferent cool, the wringing of hands and uncontrolled sobbing far into the night that will ultimately give him the excuse to fling out with the final words 'There's no talking with you.' (That's how it's done!)

I deny him this pleasure.

I deny him this excuse.

'Well if you must go, darling,' I say.

He ignores this.

'Of course you have!' he rants. 'Of course you've brought this on yourself.' (He'll take the other direction now. He'll call me frigid.) 'You're a frigid bitch, Julie.' He has decided to give cool for cool and that unimpassioned utterance is intended to be all the more offensive with its lack of emphasis because it is so dispassionate, so reasoned. For one chillingly mean moment I am tempted to switch courses and open the floodgates for him just for the pleasure of seeing him shift modes again. But I can't be bothered.

'You can have the house,' he says to an unbearable prolonging of silence.

'I don't think I want it.'

'Of course you want it. The kids have to live somewhere.'

'I don't want the kids either.'

He goes red, then white.

'God Almighty! What? What was that? What did you bloody say?'

I pour myself another coffee. It is freshly ground, a South American brand an airline pilot pal smuggled in for us. The flavour is sharp and full-bodied at the same time. Like the present situation. I gesture with the pot towards Clifford's cup. He shakes his head and says, 'I can't believe what you just said.'

'What was that?'

'That you don't want the kids. I can't believe I'm hearing this.'

I take my time, adding sugar and cream. Stirring.

'Oh that,' I say. Clifford is a mottled colour.

'It's not,' I add, not looking at Clifford's big blue bloodshot eyes but through and beyond them, 'that I don't love the children. It's just that I think they'd be better off with two people who love each other than with one bitter resentful one. I am thinking of them.'

'My God,' Clifford cries, 'you're a selfish bitch! A selfish unnatural bitch into the bargain. Timothy's only seven, for God's sake.'

I agree he is only seven.

'Well?' Clifford demands. 'Well?'

'Timothy is a well-adjusted child. He'll have you, his daddy, and ... um ... Laramie.'

At the mention of her name Clifford's face contorts.

'How do you know her name?' he asks.

'I know everything,' I tell him. 'Look, do have more coffee. It will calm you down.'

I am thinking fast. Should Clifford decide to walk out now, the high prance of outrage, I will be the one lumbered. Somehow or other he must be persuaded to remain, for this night at least, so that I can make my escape first.

You think me heartless?

Wait. Wait.

'Or a whisky.'

He glares at me but moves automatically to the decanter. Clifford has a small drink problem, a social inability to say no. When he came in he had his first Scotch of the evening. Several others had followed in the last hour. He now stands at the side table pouring and comes back with his glass refilled, his tongue flickering around his lips lizard fashion.

'Listen,' he says, 'let's be reasonable about this. I can't ask Laramie to give up her career and stay home to mind kids. It's not on. You know it's not on. They're not *her* kids, after all.'

'Agreed. But they're your kids. Yours. I know how much you love them, Clifford. I can't deny you having them. It wouldn't be right, now would it?'

'I can't believe this,' he is muttering. 'I can't bloody believe it. A mother walking out on her own kids. Jesus!'

'But you're walking out. On your own kids. A father.'

'That's different.'

'Why?'

'You know bloody why.' He is becoming furious again. 'Mothers are supposed ...' He can't find the words, shovelling through his basic English vocabulary, and throws back the Scotch in one ferocious gulp then goes and pours himself another without prompting.

'But if you and Laramie love each other ...' I let the implication of their sacrifices drift.

He says, spacing each word and enunciating with pure vowels, 'You ... are ... the ... most ... selfish ... woman ... I ... know.' His eyes are glassy with rage.

'I'm rather tired,' I say. 'Could we talk about this tomorrow? You promised to take Timothy and his friend to football early in the morning.'

He had forgotten. A scowl interprets his amnesia.

'Christ! Why can't you take them?'

'He wants you. His daddy. Man stuff.'

'What time?'

'I think it's an eight o'clock kickoff.'

'You think? You think? Can't you be sure of anything?'

'Okay. It *is* an eight o'clock kickoff.'

'Oh Jesus,' he says. 'Jesus.'

I rise and take my coffee tray into the kitchen, picking up his car keys which he had discarded on the phone table as I go. He will never notice until it is too late. Clifford has, for sixteen years, been in the habit of divesting on the move: jackets ties shirts wallets, even trousers, have landed where they fell across the living-rooms of years. In the kitchen I make washing-up sounds and drop his keys quietly out the window onto the grease trap lid. He'll wonder later how they got there. By the time I look back into the living-room, Clifford has passed out on the cane lounger and is snoring vigorously and rhythmically.

Coolly I go to our bedroom, stuff a softpack with clothing, scribble a note for Clifford that he cannot fail to see in the morning and in a moment of compunction rescue his car keys from the grease trap and place them in his shirt drawer. Then I tiptoe into Timothy's room torn, I confess, I confess, between going and staying, and sniff in his beautiful small boy scent and kiss him lightly on the cheek.

He stirs briefly and I whisper, 'Soon, Timmie. See you soon. Very soon.'

Wifely to the last I check the older children, put a light rug across my sleeping spouse, dim the lights in the sitting-room and tiptoe through the back lanai and out to my own car that I reverse, engine off, down our hillside drive. I manage to get it a hundred yards away under its own volition before I have to turn on the ignition.

Where to go?

Where in God's name to go?

*   *   *

I offer prayers, of course, hissed aspirations, as I drive to the outskirts of this steaming sugar-scented town, to Saint Sparebed, fourteenth-century English patron of unreturned hospitality.

I am owed plenty.

Yet though names flash to mind, the thought of explanation is so tedious. It might be better to drive into the night, plunge into that highway river, thresh north and locate some down-market motel eager for custom. You see I have this monetary problem. My small savings account might support me for a few weeks at the most; and if, as I plan, I send for the children in a month or so after having frightened the amorous life out of Clifford (Yes, I am weakening already. Biology certainly is destiny!), I will need a reasonably paid job and suitable accommodation.

I intend taking nothing from my dreary spouse.

I am not sure why I married Clifford.

I'm sure he isn't sure either.

Somewhere along the highway, swamped by cane and drizzle, I stop the car and smoke thoughtful one, two and three cigarettes. I am near the turnoff to Flora's avocado farm. Though I know Flora could be trusted to keep secret my whereabouts, I hate to burden her with the guilt she would feel at the notion of Daniel, Etta and Timothy abandoned to the capricious care of Clifford and/or the resentful ministrations of Laramie. The chances are she would scoop them up at once and play earth mother. I can't have this.

Clifford must discover what it is to be a parent.

Clifford, to give him his due, is not a thumper. Of flesh.

Over the years in fits of drunken and guilty irritation he has flung pots, plates, books. The smart crack he could never handle. Unable to respond with barbed word or pointed phrase, he would, like most men, resort to the physical. Fist force has always been the prerogative of the moron. We've always been short on crockery.

He developed, as well, a clutch of dubious friends, out-of-towners who visited the house late, talked long and excluded me from their presence. I began to suspect all manner of things when gouts of money dropped unexpectedly into our lives, when Clifford departed after late-night phone calls and was gone for hours. He destroyed a dinner set after one of those calls. Perhaps I had subjected him to some kind of Socratic interrogation.

Drugs, I would wonder.

Calabria, I would wonder.

Clifford has an anglicised form of an Italian surname.

Terrascati became Truscott, an alteration made by his grandfather shortly before the outbreak of the Second World War.

Does Clifford go back to the days of black-hand gang warfare in these parts when ears were sliced off and people shot in main street sugartowns in broad daylight, when cane farms were burned to the ground?

I asked him this.

He killed a *cloisonné* vase given me by my mother.

No, Clifford. No. It is really all too much.

Above me in the darkness is the black bulk of the treehouse Hengist and Horsa built in the mango tree on the fence-line. The treehouse and I have familial links: Flora's twins would barricade themselves in its rickety fastness while Daniel, three years younger, screamed for an elevation the twins denied him. I spent a night there one year ago crawling up the rotting handholds nailed to the trunk to sob my eyes out over Clifford's latest infidelity in a night drilled by mosquitoes.

I stub out the last of my cigarettes and drive over Clifford's engorged face, crushing one plate-flinging hand as I go. North, my mind instructs me. North.

*   *   *

Townsville is far enough to pitch tent for a while. It is, unfortunately, the orbit of Clifford's development company which is attempting to turn the coastline in these parts into one uninterrupted line of joy stalags. Tenement joy stalags. Terraces of joy stalags like upmarket Sydney slum housing. Locals living half a mile from the beach-front will never glimpse the sea again as the resorts link arms and close ranks. I decide to pull rank and throw myself on the mercies of a one-time journalist boyfriend who has now risen from the swamps of produce shows and petty crime reporting to become managing editor of one of the town's dailies.

I pull in to the shoulder of the highway and count my money. I have less than five hundred dollars and it is apparent that the most practical ploy would be to go to a caravan park, clean up and then plead for work.

I have been driving all night. The sun is bleeding along the eastern sky, hesitant in its rising, skulking behind Magnetic, as unwilling to face the day as I am. But a trailer park on the southern perimeter of town accepts me when I pay upfront for a week.

My caravan is eighteen feet by nine. It smells as if it hasn't been opened in years. Inside the temperature is ten degrees higher than that of the flattened parkscape outside. I dump my bag on the bunk and head for the shower block where the lack of hot water is a matter of indifference to park management. All the walls of the female amenities building are scrawled with the diary graffiti of loss and despair, of hope and perilous consummations. Amanda 4 Trev, a primitive algebra solved instantly as A = 0. There are hearts with diagonal *verboten* lines drawn through them. There are longer scribbles telling me Trevor is a fink, a suck, an asshole. I learn that a multitude of men have no balls. Over and over again comes the real message, the subliminal A hates B.

Shall I add my own grief to this wailing wall?

I shower, change into bag-crumpled clothes and feel better.

I never travel without a Texta pen in my handbag.

Now I write up, best cursive, a parody of Lord Byron's remembrancer, changing the word 'worst' to 'best' and the numerals to suit my own situation. Yet as I comb out my dripping hair and stare at my exhausted double in the blotched mirror above the greyish basins, I deplore my unoriginality. I can do better than that. From behind me comes the sound of someone being sick in a lavatory cubicle. I write:

The wilder shores of love
Spell doom for you and me.
Don't tread the quicksands of his beach.
Swim safely out to sea.

           *   *   *

It is seven years since I last saw Baxter. He is just returned from an alcoholic lunch and I catch him between the stages of *bonhomie* and irascibility. Each of our faces is registering embarrassed unbelief at what time has done. Baxter's private school soft good looks have long melted into a blue jawline, thinning hair (where are the locks of yesteryear, bud, those thick golden bangs?), the beginning of jowls and unassessable extra kilograms of flesh.

And what does Baxter see?

He sees an over-anxious set of unspectacular features playing at sophisticated adventurousness, a thickening not-so-youngish woman in a skirt and blouse that display all the crease marks of runaway packing.

Baxter exclaims, *My God, Julie!*

Julie exclaims, *Baxter!*

Baxter queries Julie.

Julie queries Baxter.

The queries are composed of *non sequiturs* and polite inconsequentialities.

We draw *verboten* lines through coupled initials.

I am brief to the point of obscurity.

'I have left Clifford,' I announce.

Over the last few dollar-filled years Baxter has encountered Clifford on public platforms and has written coruscating editorials attacking Clifford's development company and its urbanisation of the coastline. They are natural ecological enemies.

'And I am looking for a job.' I add those words before he has time to draw breath. 'Something. Social notes. Births. Weddings. School fêtes. Anything.'

His face relaxes. Perhaps for one horrible moment he had feared I was hurling myself at him for emotional recovery.

'Julie!' he says. 'Julie! After all these years.'

That spurious throb! Now he feels safe he can afford a little sentiment coupled with that wagging of his head unbelievingly from side to side as if this impromptu encounter was the one thing that had been missing from his life. Perhaps I have been too precipitant in my request emotionally/chemically speaking, so I allow him to meander through groves of nostalgia while the indissoluble elements settle and I smile, look wistful (I am wistful) and brave in turn.

Eventually he recovers from a paragraph of do-you-remembers and admits I have caught him and the paper at a bad time.

'We're cutting back,' he tells me. 'We're putting people off.' Freelancing, he suggests, admitting he had noted my occasional byline over the years. I explain, less forcefully but slowly and rationally, that that would not be enough to keep me, let alone support three children as I intend and want.

'Let Clifford support them,' he says callously. 'The bastard's loaded.'

'It's a question of pride.'

'Pride! Pride!' He is impatient. 'You're not in a position to have pride. That's a luxury, dear.'

I remark that he needn't twist the knife so thoroughly and with a grin he asks, 'And who's the girl?'

'Who's the what?'

'The girl. The new lady. Clifford's paramour.'

I tell him and he laughs silently, shaking all the way down to his swivel chair, a ghastly lewd choked-up mirth that unsettles. To my offended interrogative face he gabbles explanations. 'I know her. In fact I once threw her out of the office. You know she works for another pirate realtor, don't you? My God, it's our convict past coming back to haunt us.'

While I am satisfied Baxter's sympathies tend my way, I am still desperate for security. Behind Baxter's head two palms in the main street hang listless in the muggy weather, swooning with humidity. Castle Hill raises its scraped orange cheeks to sun assault. There's graffiti there as well. I flick my eyes back to Baxter's blotched pink face which is beaming at me in a kindly way through gold-rim spectacles. I offer to do anything at all—tea-making, proof-reading, copy-running, first-year cadet wages.

At this Baxter eyes me interestedly. He always had a nose for a bargain in flesh or brain.

'You're serious? You'd do anything?'

I nod, wordless now, frightened of misplaying a syllable.

'This will have to be a gentleman's agreement, Julie, strictly between you and me. The AJA would come down like a ton of bricks. If I sign you on. At least for the moment, you understand. Things will look different in the new year but now ...' He does finger tappings and cheek suckings and takes his glasses off, polishes the lenses and replaces them, looking at me all the while as if assessing whether I am worth the trouble. Finally, 'General dogsbody, eh? You could pop your age back, dear. That way I could avoid flak. And maybe the odd feature article. A different byline, till things settle. You know, something sexless and indigenous like Flinders Moll or Magnetic Eye. You know the sort of bullshit, love. But it will be junior rates at least until Christmas.' I fail, during his breath-pause to point out the sexism of either byline. 'Can't let an old mate down,' he is saying. 'Can I?'

Is he leering?

Oh God, Baxter, I say. Oh God.

Outside this knockabout town is still a mess of palms thongs singlets work shorts beer guts skin rot and glaucoma.

The air walls of my now town require no added graffiti.

I start work that afternoon.

*   *   *

During my second devoted-parent phone-call check-up, Flora tells me that Clifford has deferred his move to Laramie's house (check!) and is bad-mouthing me all over town. He has installed a part-time house-keeper and takes the kids to Laramie's for the weekend. Timothy believes I am on an extended holiday, a fable concocted and dissemi-nated by Flora, and that he has almost forgotten me in the joys of acquiring a two-wheeler which Clifford (who has hitherto been un-believably mean) has given him to demonstrate what a great guy Daddy is. Daniel and Etta are less pleased with my absence, missing that weekend ministering, and have asked if they can become full-time boarders. Clifford will be only too happy to oblige.

How does Flora know all these things?

Her husband is a member of Rotary to which Clifford also belongs, not because he is a community do-gooder but because he might make useful contacts. One of Clifford's most traumatic periods was five years ago when he was torn between becoming a Mason or joining the Holy Name Society. Rotary provided a happy middle way.

I write to each child separately explaining that Daddy and I have separated but that as soon as I have suitable accommodation they are to come and live with me. Daniel and Etta write verbally grudging notes after a fortnight. They don't actually tell me to drop dead but they indicate strongly that the thought of visiting me now or in the future let alone moving here full-time would be unutterably dreary. Timothy asks for a crash helmet.

I sob quite diligently for half a morning and then harden my heart.

Baxter is working me to death. I go to cattle shows, dog shows, garden displays, school swimming carnivals and play nights, suburban musicals and the Magnetic Players' (there's a misnomer!) unbelievably bad performance of *Private Lives*. I spend whole mornings in the magistrate's court, whole days in horse salesyards. I have taken over the agony column and am tempted to do a Miss Lonelyhearts. I write questions and answer them and publish both without a qualm. I write the daily horoscope.

For the first few weeks Baxter had been avuncularly subbing my copy but relieved by my literacy finally gave me a free hand permitting me to introduce material into Susie's Advice Column and Your Week by the Stars that gave me, at least, quirky pleasure. I eschewed such clichés as 'You will travel and meet lots of interesting people this month. Your stars are in the ascendant for money matters.' Little throwaway lines like 'The man of your dreams is lying', 'The stars indicate the possibility of an embarrassing illness. See your doctor', 'Avoid all property deals. Real estate agents have the finesse of fast-food servers. Keep their thumbs out of your financial soup' lasted only four days.

Baxter called me into his office.

'Julie,' he said, all heart, 'I understand this. I understand what you're doing. But you mustn't let personal grief colour your journalism. There've been a lot of complaints. Got it?'

He took me off my more creative work, handing over the agony and the stars to a junior typist. I devoted myself to the magistrate's court.

My life is spent on the run between the metal capsule where I try to sleep in temperatures like those of a nuclear reactor, the upstairs office of *Magnetic Sun* and the assignments laid out for me. With my first month's pay I buy a table fan and manage to sleep for seven hours straight for the first time since I walked out of Clifford's back door. You note I say 'his', making no claims to the family estate. At night so that I won't stay awake worrying about the children I take a sleeping tablet with a brandy chaser. This is not proper behaviour. I fight the impulse to ring or write to the children every few days but I check in with Flora long distance.

'You're not made for this.'

'Made for what?'

'Abandoning the family. If you're going to walk out on your husband, at least do it thoroughly. Cut free. Totally.'

'But the kids?'

There is an expensive silence. 'Flora? Flora? I said ...'

'I know. I know. Look, Julie, I don't know how I'd behave in the same situation, but if you cut off from Clifford then you cut off. What a sleaze!' she adds comforting me. 'And if you're not prepared to take the kids or you can't, then I think you've just got to wear that, as they say. I can tell you from what I hear that Clifford is not very happy. He did try installing Laramie. I wasn't going to tell you. That was before the housekeeper. But she refused to give up her job, Timothy ignored her and after two nights she walked out.'

'What spies you have!'

'Not really. It's largely Daniel and Etta. They worm it out of Tim and then they tell Chubbsie and the twins who tell me. I think Clifford is thinking of boarding school for Timothy.'

'But he's too young. God!'

'He'll be eight soon, won't he, going on fifty-five. Might be the best thing. Then you can visit for all you're worth. Meet Clifford at Parents' Nights.'

This isn't what I want. I don't want Clifford to escape so lightly from parental demands. I want him to suffer. There he is, an adulterer of bravura style—Laramie must be his tenth affair in as many years— poor sod, intense about it all probably because his hair is thinning and his paunch showing and it looks as if he has not only achieved his grand passion but achieved it without the nagging of tiny voices and feet. By now I realise that my name has become a byword for unnatural behaviour, the lacking of maternal instinct. I have become the partner at fault, the abandoner of children. Had Clifford waltzed off and left me with them, eyes would have blinked sympathetically for a day or two and then the situation would have become acceptable. *Men do that sort of thing. Well, yes, but he's a man!*

That old double standard has me gritting my teeth. I am now the heartless one, selfish beyond credence, and at this very moment Clifford will be floundering under the weight of soup tureens, roast chickens, beef casseroles, assorted cakes and puddings rushed to him by the moist-eyed wives of colleagues who already suspect—no, *know*—their own husbands are capable of the same behaviour I endured for over a decade.

O wondrous world!

Time passes.

Clifford does not approach me demanding I ease the burden of child care. My phone calls to Flora have become more widely spaced. A coolness has entered her voice and I find unspoken criticism harder to endure than the fling of words. I try to put the children out of my mind. I recall fright-tales told me by a friend working in the local welfare office: 'Would you mind looking after Brucie?' one bedraggled young mother had asked, flicking Indian junk beadery about. 'I'll only be a minute. I have to go to the washroom.' The minute had expanded to an hour, to two hours. Darkness fell from the air. At closing time the welfare office found itself the proxy owner of a screaming year-old baby. My friend was vague about the aftermath. 'A grandmother, I think. It's always a grandmother, isn't it? Someone in their seventies. Just when they thought they were going to get a break. Anyway, they had to fly from Adelaide to collect. God! Can you believe it?'

There is probably something wrong with me. My feelings go out to the grandmother. 'What about the father?'

'Who knows!' The girl had vanished farther north.

'Where?'

'Portland Roads. That's where the dole cheques went,' my friend explained.

'And what about the grandmother?'

'Who knows? Who cares? That's what they're for, isn't it?'

'And the baby?'

'Oh, the baby would be all right. Babies are great survivors. They're stronger than grandmothers. Brand new motors.'

I tell myself that sneaking back to check on Timothy would not improve matters. Indulgently I inform myself such a visit would only make him fret for me. In more rational moments, I know, rationally I know, that Timothy thought I was a bit of a fool. He always was a frightening child with an over-large head and boiled egg eyes that would apprehend the wavering perimeters of any situation almost immediately and evolve a domestic geometry that inevitably worked in his favour. The spoils of marital battle had filled his room with large and expensive toys and one particular Borodino had given him a personal computer. Clifford thought we had bred a genius. He was fond of telling people this. 'It's all in the genes,' Clifford would say modestly, meaning his. Perhaps Clifford's apogee of fatherhood came when the local TAB rang to tell us our son was placing bets he gauged from a carefully worked out computer programme.

Forget it, I kept telling a chewed sleepless pillow. Timothy is all right.

By the end of three months Baxter's conscience impels him to give me a salary rise and I am able to afford a beach apartment twenty minutes from town and three minutes from a school.

✳   ✳   ✳

But I *like* Laramie!

Timing my arrival for late Friday evening, an hour when all children should be back in residence, I had driven south on my next long weekend. The boringly familiar street buzzed with sprinklers. Cars snoozed in driveways and there was that lingering smell of Aussie sacrifice, smoke from the barbecue pits of hundreds of houses.

I parked the car neatly and unobtrusively in the shelter of our hibiscus hedge, closed the door with no vulgar thump and walked quickly across the lawn under the jacarandas, up the steps and onto the veranda.

The house appeared to be in darkness.

I rang the bell and waited. There's irony for you!

No one answered.

I went down the steps and along the side of the house beneath a shower of television commercials from next door. The back of the house was in darkness as well.

Tingling like a criminal I took out the house keys I had failed to return and tried the back door. The lock resisted all probing and had obviously been changed. Enraged I charged back to the front. Again! Clifford has struck again! There was, in fact, an air of untendedness about the place I had failed to notice on my nervous entry. The lawn was shaggy. Dead fronds littered the grass beneath the palms. A window creaked inquisitively in the next house and I knew I was under observation. So I went back to the car and drove into the town centre where I phoned Flora from a call-box.

'The address,' I demand. 'Give me Laramie's address.'

'Julie,' Flora says placatingly and maddening me, 'are you sure you should be doing this?'

Her gentleness which I have always admired now merely infuriates. I can see her calm big-boned beautiful face flooded with charity, reproach, tenderness—all the virtues she makes me feel I lack. Well, almost all. Mostly lack.

'Please.'

'Oh, God,' she says. 'You won't make a scene? Who am I to come between mother and children?'

'That's better. Who indeed?'

Then she tells me and adds a repeated warning to cause no upset.

'I am the one upset.' I slam down the receiver.

It is fifteen miles to the small beach town and I do it in under twenty minutes, skimming through the tides of cane and onto the phosphorescent light line that is the sea. The moonlight is both beautiful and horrible, emblazoning the half dozen blocks of houses and it is a matter of minutes only to nose out the address extracted so reluctantly from my last friend. Impacted wisdom. Gum surrounding.

The house squats on an acre of esplanade, a newish place of timber and galvanised iron made popular by trendy architects who have taken as their prototype the primitive makeshift dwellings of early settlers and mixed the metaphor with all the laminated surfaces, easy-living gadgets and air-conditioning units those early settlers would have wept to possess. The house blazes with light, the television is jabbering at top volume and through the loutish racket I hear the voices of my children raised in good-humoured laughter.

I sit there in the car, the sea mumbling its same old ballad on my right, palm trees creaking brochure noises and feeling like an intruder as Flora's voice tells me above sea-sound, to leave well alone and me believing now that she is right, that to walk in at this moment would be selfish and insensitive.

The hell with that!

My natural longings override and I close the car door gently and tread misgivings down on carefully bush-scaped gardens all the way to the entrance porch, a kind of galvo igloo, and press the illuminated door button.

'Christ!' Clifford says when he opens the screen door. 'What the hell are you doing here?'

Unexpectedly I start crying.

'Oh God,' he says. 'Oh God.'

My supplanter, an organised brunette, appears behind him. Her face is unexpectedly resigned. She sums me and the situation and its concomitants up immediately.

'You'd better come in,' she offers over Clifford's stubborn shoulders.

My aggression has inexplicably become humility. I am looking for redemption. I ask if that will be all right. She winks at me. *Winks?* I can tell Clifford wants to flatten me. Any moment he could start hurling jardinières. 'Of course,' she says.

The two older children looked embarrassed when I am ushered into the living-room, a vast area punctuated by resting places of bamboo, leather and linen. Timothy gives me one brief glance and returns to television. 'Hi,' he says, watching the screen.

'Drink?' Laramie asks in a civilised way.

I nod my stoic skull.

There we are, one big happy family—father, mother, mistress, kids. I sip a whisky sour made with the expertise of an old barhand. Maybe Laramie *is* an old barhand. How to make an opening in this dumb-show except with phrases that would seem to whicker with complaint. Daniel and Etta have lost that carefree joy that involved them before my entrance, stage right. I have to ask them to come and give me a kiss. Abashed, awkward, after vestigial pecks they retreat to a distant divan to watch proceedings.

I clear my throat and croak. 'I would like the children to come back with me.'

This is too brash, too abrasive; but I am beyond finesse.

'You what?' Clifford roars.

I take another gulp of whisky. I repeat those words. I add riders. 'I've managed to get a reasonable sort of flat. It's big enough for all of them. Half a house, actually. Timmy could be full-time with me. There's a school close by. Daniel and Etta could come each weekend.'

I tail off. Where are the cries of joy, the wide smiles of relief? There is a fug of spiritual inertia enveloping the stage although Laramie's eyes, I notice, appear to have a new gleam of interest. The silence becomes the abyss into which I sink.

Cued, Clifford rises, tight with anger, and goes over to the bar, a prominent feature of the room, an extended prism of black glass and marble like an orgasm in *Vogue*. It would cost three years of my current salary. I am hoping Clifford might smash it in his naive way but instead he takes much time refilling his glass and I can see his back rigid with suppressed fury. Finally he turns round, leaning against the buffet to confront my idiot suggestion, his hands shaking. Laramie pretends indifference, picks up a magazine from a side table and begins a casual flicking through of pages. Maybe she is looking for another bar. I envy her. She is monstrously self-contained with her other-deluding eyes and mouth. She is wearing a recklessly brief sundress. There seems to be nothing but legs.

Clifford's mouth muscles make a lot of movement before he manages a choked cry. I translate. 'After what you bloody did!' he is accusing. 'Get to bed, kids. Abandonment. And you have the gall . . .'

Timothy snaps the television off and moves closer to listen. This will be a real-life soapie. 'I said *bed*.' Clifford glares at the kids in turn who give sly grins and sidle to the back of the vast room and a corridor leading to where? I imagine they will loiter at strategic shadow points. 'I cannot believe that I am hearing this. My God!'

That *dégagé* quality that sustained me through a decade and a half of marital turmoil has seeped away. I find I am contemplating my fingernails, kid in the corner, lost for that pert stridence I had believed would carry me through this situation.

Etta calls, safe from a sombre recess. 'Mum, we like it here. We're okay. You don't have to worry about us, truly.'

'Yes, really, Mum,' Daniel adds, 'We're right. Honest. Anyhow it would take forever getting up to your place at weekends. It must be four hours in the bus. We'd have to fly.'

'We can't afford for you to fly,' Clifford snarls.

The kids troop back into the room. They shuffle feet about. Their trendy grammar school has weekend activities they would miss stuck with Mother in the umbilicus of the state. From here, rancho Laramie, they are far more accessible to school pals, school shenanigans.

Timothy comes over and sits beside me. 'I'm a boarder now.'

'Oh darling,' I say and find myself hugging him suddenly, rubbing my face against his hair which smells deliciously of small boy grubbiness. 'Are you?' He is so small. 'Do you like it?'

He disengages himself, not wanting to hurt my feelings.

'Heaps. I like it heaps. The food's awful but we have a lot of fun about it. And there's a matron. I am the second youngest boarder.' He seems proud of this. 'And I'm in a higher grade than at the public.'

'Boy genius,' Daniel comments who has also slid back into the room and is smiling quite nicely at his runaway mum. 'The little prig tops his class. They all hate his guts.'

Timothy smirks with a glowering kind of radiance. 'The others are extremely dull.'

Laramie's expression of distaste at my son's innocent display of wunderkind powers registers. Her fingers appear to be torturing the margins of her magazine. This is her third or fourth weekend spent *en famille d'un autre*, I estimate. Can she take it?

Clifford, realising that I am not going to become hysterical, that my tears are snuffed and emotional violence unlikely, seats himself at last in a chair opposite and putting on his earnest face leans forward. 'We must think about selling the other place if you won't move back there. I've hung on to it hoping you'd come to your senses.'

'I *have* come to them.'

'I can do square roots,' Timothy remarks *à-propos* of what? 'No one else in my class can.'

'Jesus!' Laramie cries suddenly and goes out to the kitchen and begins rattling cups.

'I don't think you should do anything in a hurry, Clifford,' she flings back over a redwood room divider. I can see a stubborn set to her shoulders under the fluorescent blue in the cooking area where her hands keep punishing crockery. She and Clifford have more in common than I thought. Is she tiring of the set-up? She is not dramatically younger then either of us. Flora has told me of two marriages previously abandoned in Melbourne and Sydney. She is unused to children. Why then those happy cries that broke my heart as I waited for the doorbell to be answered? I guess, and later Daniel confirms my guess, that Clifford has raised each child's allowance in a love-loyalty buying orgy.

Laramie's words give Clifford pause, as they say. He appears trapped on the harmonics of that high-pitched utterance, caught quivering on a possibly collapsible situation. Laramie is far gutsier than he.

There is no point in prolonging this visit. The children have absorbed my presence and disgorged it. Mother and reduced circumstances are at point A. Father and increased riches are at point B. They are true children of the late twentieth century whose emotional geometry draws the shortest distance between two points—self and the piggy bank—without need of a ruler. I am filled, too, with *schadenfreude* as I note crackings and crumblings in the perilous relationship of lovers. I could almost smile. I do smile. Some inner voice assures me my turn will also come as I put down the glass no one has offered to refill.

I rise and taking a liberty move round the room divider to the kitchen where I glimpse Laramie standing for a brief moment at the back window, sucking greedily on a cigarette and staring into tropical blackness.

'Excuse me,' I say. 'I must be going now. There's no point. Thank you.'

She turns and makes stabbing motions at the sink with her cigarette. The room is a centre-fold dazzle of glittering surfaces, of polished wood and granite, tile and steel. She nods over the dead butt and her face is sheened with an indescribable patina of grief and sympathy in a down-turned smile. 'You're welcome,' she says. Her lips remain parted as if she intends more, much more, then they clamp shut. Inadmissibles. She winks at me. Clifford's bulk looms behind us both.

'Well?' he says. He often says 'Well!' A drawn-out replete sound, a fatness of decision made that brooks no debate.

Sparingly the children kiss me goodbye.

'See you soon,' they chant, the worn-out phrase confirming for them that Mother is decamping only briefly like the fast run-out of an overworn home movie that is an endless repeat. No one asks where I will be staying. No one cares. As I go back to the car I hear the joy shrieks break out again and I drive back north through the night, fuelled by the lead-free anger of rejection.

What have I gained out of all that?

What lost?

*   *   *

Baxter is working me to death.

I wonder why men dislike women so. Oh yes, I know about all those *bon viveurs, boulevardiers* and fags who cry: 'Some of my best friends are women!' Change women to Blacks, Jews, Asiatics ... You get what

I'm trying to say? I think about this quite a lot. Half the world's population has been brought up to be shit-scared of the other half. Don't speak to ... don't accept ... don't ask for ... On and on. And of course the warnings are generally well-founded. Pornographers show ways to hate. Why? Is it because overall women are passive, accepting? Does it drive men bonkers to see the little woman crouched over the stove when they reel in sloshed, meekly waiting to serve up the over-heated dinner? The submission? That overt dread of the raised beefy hand packing a punch that sends the little woman rocking back with the humbly proffered plate? Only to spill it, of course, and thereby really earn more swipes and clouts. Open her mouth to apologise and she'll have it shut for her pretty smartly with a hand and an explanation. 'Nagging bitch' is a favourite. Maybe passivity does feed aggression. There's nothing like turning the other cheek to infuriate. Is it only that? Is it the capacity women have for simply getting on with the basics of living? All those war-torn Middle Eastern countries gun-blasted each night and each morning—there they are, the girls, out sweeping up after the boys! It's a laugh.

Are women hateful because occasionally men need them? Well, they don't really. Every second male seems to be determined on homosexuality these days. There are always brothels and self-abuse for moments of necessity. What is it? What is it? I can find no answer.

I ask Baxter as we munch a sandwich together one sweating lunch hour. He regards me blankly, bleakly.

'If I were honest, which I'm not, love, I'd have to admit we envy you. I'm not honest. Men won't admit to envy. It belittles them. There. Is that answer enough?'

My spacious half house with its two empty bedrooms is patterned with heat stripes of sun. Veranda lattice carves the leaves of overpowering vines into shady squares that slide across the floor boards and I experience their carved shapes as if each moving shadow has been branded. Not on flesh. On some uncorporeal part of me.

Once I was fond of this town with its old pubs near the river, its dated stores, its central road planting of palms. There was sea smell and river smell and the senile friendliness of coastal trawlers blooting through the nights of childhood, the grimy milkbars and cafés where a kind of warm slovenliness reigned round the juke bokes and the pinball machines and the tired wives of the Greeks who ran them. Now, with governmental benedicti and the carnal ploys of entrepreneurs like Clifford, the lovable slatterns have been rejuvenated. The town has been malled to death and fake settler fronts shine with new acrylic paints; high-rise hostelries pierce tropic humidity and stare out to sea and the islands.

Weeks pass in a daze of sweat before the rains. Christmas and school holidays approach. I ring Flora. Don't help him, I order. Now they will need me. Now Clifford will learn the crucifying quality of what it is to lose cook nurse nanny. I am wrong. Clifford has hired a new live-in housekeeper, a reassuringly plain woman of unarguable middle years, chosen no doubt by Laramie. (My God! That name! Is it baptismal? Could the parents have been serious? Perhaps she was conceived during an ads break in a Western!) And he has moved back to the family home. So long, Laramie! To continue: everyone is happy. The housekeeper cooks like a dream, is tolerant but firm, has a driver's licence and neither drinks nor smokes. (Hearing that makes me light up immediately.) Her name is Bodil Kierkegaard.

Baxter, who is single again after a very nasty divorce, offers me a week away. With him. The assistant editor will be standing in to cope with all the excitement of picnic races, carols by cyclone and the seasonal mugging associated with the spirit of goodwill.

I decline.

Baxter is piqued.

I lie and pretend the children are coming to spend part of their vacation with me.

'Unwillingly, I bet.'

'What? What was that?'

'You heard me. God, Julie, I *know* about kids. They don't want to come to a two-horse town like this. Your nineties' kid wants glitz. No homespun pleasures for him.'

'You don't like the young, do you?'

'Oh God,' he says, breathing heavily, 'play Mummy then.'

It is on the tremulous eve of Christmas with early cyclonic rains pelting down in two-hour bursts, that Clifford rings me. The din on the iron roof is so tremendous I can hardly hear him. Through the open door beside the phone I watch trees prostrated by water, their

branches flattening towards earth. Like me. I am writing the single-
person's Christmas cook book: prawn *flambé* with stuffed mushroom,
to be followed by sausage wellington and sardine farcie. I'm kidding!
I rally and say coolly to my distant husband, 'What a surprise!'

His voice is so faint, so muffled by weather, I have to keep telling
him to speak up. Has his latest motel venture collapsed? (I hope.) Is
there a politician he is unable to buy?

'What? Who? What's separated?'

He does not elaborate.

'I'm ringing from home.'

'Where?'

'Home.'

'Where's that?'

'Don't smartass me, Julie. Don't be such a bitch. Our home. Thank
goodness we didn't sell it. The kids are settling in again as if ...' He
stops at that point. 'Mrs Kierkegaard is housekeeping. They love her.
Flora's rallying round. I do like Flora.'

Strangely I can hear all this with appalling clarity. You traitor,
Flora!

'I can't hear you,' I say.

'Julie!' He is screaming across wind-spun wires and latitudes. 'We
have to discuss this. *Rapprochement.* Something.'

'What? What was that? Look, I can't hear.'

He prays or blasphemes briefly and hangs up.

I sit in the dark listening to the rioting of wind and water and drink
one brandy, two. Why haven't the *children* rung? I sent them deliri-
ously expensive presents. Why haven't they rung? I know there is a
new illiteracy and innumeracy government-planned to create slave
forces, but Timothy is a child genius who has already broken into one
of the town's banks with his computer and rearranged a score of
accounts. For fun, he explained, when visited by a six-foot policeman.
Flora told me this. Timothy, surely, could dial me. I can only assume
they are bored with even the idea of me.

As the frenzy outside increases, I take my drink into the bedroom
and turn on the radio, waiting for Santa.

* * *

You win, Baxter.

Here I am pursuing my irascible boss, my nervy, cynical asp-tongued boss, to the joys of a Sydney beano. Do I have an excuse? This behaviour is unpardonable. I'm lonely, I argue with the inner accusing me. I'm lonely lonely lonely. I want to be held, comforted. Flora used to say in her youthful years that her secret wish was to be clasped carnally by a violinist who had just finished playing the Sibelius violin concerto with the same flair as Oistrakh. Then laid. That's how I feel. Almost anyone will do. Even Baxter. I know which hotel he is booked into. The paper required an emergency address. I fly down and book myself into the same place, order myself supper from room service and dial him on the intra house phone. A woman answers.

It's the story of my life.

Next day I am too disheartened even to ponder the equilibrium-inducing properties of shops, films, theatre, galleries. I take a cab to the airport, departure delayed for three hours because of storm damage at the northern end's landing strip. The airport has endless permutations of plastic food, plants and reading matter. It is a kind of dying.

Back in my house I listen to the rain that has settled into a hammering waterfall, watching the ripped leaves of banana trees in the garden thrash uneasily in the soak and turn off the radio whose static crackle unhinges me. Its crackle could obscure anything except my solitary state. I am absorbed by my own pointlessness. But in the last of the afternoon greylight during a pause in the rain as I mourn burnt bridges, mentally kicking out embers that still glow, there is a ring at the front door and I find myself racing to fling the house open to anyone, anyone at all.

＊　　＊　　＊

I don't think I've mentioned that when stressed, to use that fashionable adjective, I stutter. Not markedly but sufficiently to irritate myself. I'm not sure what it does to others. I will not attempt to reproduce the phenomenon here, for visually it is maddening. Also I wear glasses of formidable dioptres.

These are not attributes that could be regarded as winning.

Behind the glasses lurk not unattractive eyes. Even I will admit this. They are large, blue and with that vague dreaminess of the horrendously short-sighted. Clifford courted me with my glasses off. I made the most of astigmatic charm. Actually he found my helplessness extraordinarily feminine, near-blindness giving me a pliancy and a dependence that captivated him. I'm sure it must have been that. It also explains why before marriage I could not say I had really *seen* Clifford. Without my glasses everyone appeared beautiful. I live/lived with these failings and turned them into fun moments with my children who very early learnt to do hilarious parodies.

Why mention this now?

As I say, I race to the front door.

Huddled under the awning at the top of the veranda steps, Boxing Day notwithstanding, were two women with a collection bag. Were they looking for turkey leftovers? The fag ends of pudding? This in itself was surprising but these two women were nuns, I assessed, peering through my misting lenses, and sporting that sisterly tropic rig that has become a habit in itself. When I say habit, I speak conventually of course. They sported short sodden navy veils, practical blouses and modest mid-calf skirts. A small cross dangled on each blouse. On analysis there wasn't anything so different after all from the garb of the teaching sisters at the convent day school in town whose end-of-year concert I had recently reported. It was just that there were gumboots to the knee and slung carelessly over head and shoulders streaming yellow plastic raincapes. Despite the weather they were smiling sunnily. More than smiling. Laughing, all teeth and good-humouredly crinkled eyes.

I became stuck on a consonant of invitation and simply opened the lattice door, ushering them onto the veranda.

Were they really nuns?

I looked for traces of moustache or beard. (There has been a lot of crime here. I am wit-addled by loneliness.)

Were they cleverly disguised muggers come to clean up on Christmas presents?

Busily they removed raincapes, shaking them and hanging them to drip over the back of the old seagrass settee, all the while making delighted remarks about the weather.

Apologies. 'We're so sorry to trouble you, dear.' Separately and together. 'So sorry.'

We all stood smiling at each other.

Something should follow this.

I waited. I wait. I switch to present tense.

Their eyes are clear, calm, utterly unclouded. Ah, how I envy that.

'We're collecting for our little mission,' the older one explains. 'Saint Theresa's Aboriginal mission school at Bukki Bay.' Her companion nods the words into place. Behind them I see their Kombivan flinching under weather, its headlamps blazing steadily towards the north.

'You've left your lights on.'

'Well, we'll only be a moment, dear,' the shorter, plumper one says. 'Can you spare us a moment?'

I believe in their authenticity at once.

I must tell you: I have invented the weather. My personal weather. What I really, most urgently want to invent is the climate, a larger embracing caul/envelope to contain myself. Within that membrane I shall be able to press the emotional buttons of sun and shade and, let's admit it, fool myself.

My consonants struggle once more with the invitation to come in. I open the front door wide for them. They hesitate. Perhaps there is a mad gleam to my eye, gluttonous for company. I see them hesitate.

'Do me a favour,' I plead, 'this Christmas tide.'

'Of course,' the older one responds doubtfully, frightened by archaism. 'What is it, dear?'

'Come in. Please. *Please* come in.' That wretched 'c' finally gives respite. 'Break bread with me.' I start to cry.

Put like that, how could they refuse, those two women of good will? I am using unfair weapons.

They in their turn stand hopeful and squelching on the veranda while investigating my features for criminal traits. (Those thick lenses? That nervous stutter? That archaic mode?) Then, 'Run down and turn the lights off, Aloysius,' the older one says.

Sister Aloysius flings her cape back over her head, smiles encouragingly at me and heads back into the rain.

The other nun smiles in her turn. There is a frightening strength behind the gentleness. 'I am Sister Tancred.' A hand pats me momentarily on the shoulder. A voice says, 'There, dear. There. Now let's go inside and tell me who *you* are.'

And without hesitation I tell her. And more.

*   *   *

There is something about being touched in kindness, no matter how briefly, that acts on me with the shock of the unexpected. Humans should touch more. Flora tells me that. They need it. It was so long since Clifford had even patted me with flesh or word. I dismiss at once those sterile morning and evening salutation pecks flicked out as one heads for the car or returns coming by the kitchen. But even in the absence of Clifford's affection there had always been hugs from Flora and the kids.

Picture this: Sister Tancred has put the kettle on and is exploring the geography of my kitchen as if she has read this map before. Cups, saucers, spoons, rattle onto a tray; milk and sugar appear and there is only the smallest hiatus before she locates the tea. Sister Aloysius brings everything into the sitting-room where the wooden shutters flap and weeping heart-shaped leaves are pressed against glass. The world is damp. I am at the nadir.

And again one of them—which one?—says, 'There, there, dear.'

So I crouch sodden and heart-shaped and pressed against the arm of my chair while the two of them play host to me.

The comfort of strangers has a veracity all its own. I examine these strangers when my grief has spent itself into a grimy screw of handkerchief. Sister Tancred is a tall rangy looking woman with alert grey eyes and a crop of brisk grey curls—she had removed her sodden veil. Her smile is slightly askew. She plays mother with the teapot. Every movement is deft. She has the confidence of one who has traversed hostile countries and conquered unruly tribes. By now they have dragged off their gumboots which lie dribbling on the veranda and I am impressed by the sturdy confidence of their calves. Tancred's lips permanently tilted up at one corner give her the air of one repressing mirth. Her hands, locked in the ritual of tea ceremony, move with surgical precision from teapot to milk jug to cup.

'We're nurses in a way,' Sister Tancred says.

'And teachers,' Sister Aloysius adds. I guess at ages. Sixty? Fifty? Sister Aloysius must be the younger but her round soft face has been leached of colour by the Tropics. Her eyes are a steady and unblinking blue.

'Both,' says the other, nodding.

They look at me with widening smiles.

'But as missionaries,' Sister Tancred adds. 'If you understand what that implies.'

I assure them I understand.

I am sipping tea and repressing sniffles of waited-on self-sympathy. Flora is a Catholic now in some sudden post-university conversion, perhaps to placate her husband who is a member of the Holy Name Society as well as Rotary and is called Hamilton. I have often attended functions at the school her children attend. It is simply that the word 'missionary' has a dated flavour. It summons up frontiers of another century, priests clubbed down as they lurch from their boats to the black sands of Erromango; sly arrows rupturing Protestant skins; and as if I am struck, there I am back seventeen years and talking with the tiny French nun outside the mission church at Ebouli. She has just explained the popularity of Seventh Day Adventism to me. I am reporting on a revolution, a minor insurrection, for my paper under the aegis of an older watchdog journalist who has abandoned revolution for the hotel bar. The Adventists, she tells me forgetful of the forces of insurrection, are rivals in the field, in the unending soul-search.

'Vegetarians, you call them. The natives call them kai-kai grass. Emi kai kai grass.' And she had laughed delightedly against the chorus of riotously cheerful hymn singing that billowed out from the half-walled church with its palm thatched roof and its garishly coloured icons as all the islanders joined in a valedictory chorus when the Mass ended. Then she looked guilty and bit her lip prettily, penitent for lack of charity while her face composed itself into absurd lines of gravity for she was little more than a girl herself.

The two of us stood there and watched the rebel soldiers swing up the coral road to the church grounds and hesitate at the gateway. Immediately she had left me and run towards them clutching at skirt and veil and shouting, *Allez. Allez-vous-en! Allez! Allez! Le dieu, le premier!*

The lieutenant in charge of the ragtag group was wearing a fatigue jacket three sizes too large, old army shorts and thongs. He was carrying a rifle which he swung towards her as she raced down the path between the burao trees. '*Bêtise!*' she had snapped, grabbing the rifle by the barrel and pushing it to one side. '*Telle bêtise!*' In the tussle the gun exploded skywards and brought down a small branch of flamboyant loaded with scarlet flowers. Both of them stared at it startled as the blooms fell on and between them and the men behind the lieutenant started to giggle. '*Tel sang*,' the little nun said, grinning to herself. '*Vous avez puisé du sang*! You've drawn blood.'

Behind us the singing had ended and the congregation began to come through the open doorway out into the draining sunlight and the mirror blue glitter of the sea. Their eyes were widened by the gunshot, the sight of the ragged platoon. 'Go now,' the little nun was saying. She raised her hand and made the sign of the cross. 'Go in peace. There is nothing here subversive. Only people who came to pray for peace. We pray for you and all of us.'

The soldiers were shuffling feet. They were hardly older than the little French nun who stood there defying them. That a woman should defy was an outrage. But this was not a woman as they knew it. She was one of a group who lived without men. Perhaps they were not women. And the totem each wore, the crucifix on the breast, though it was familiar to them, still had its own puripuri, its own magic they could never really comprehend: the man nailed out.

The crucifix shimmered with light on the edges of their dark places, that hanging man with arms outstretched, the sadness of the agonised face.

I was there to report revolution. That was my part of it and I came back and wrote what I'd seen and Clifford whom I had met by then, read my piece and rang me and said, 'You need a man to take care of you.'

*   *   *

Sister Tancred tells me about their work.

There are three of them running a cottage hospital-cum-dispensary, and a school. 'We're collecting money to buy equipment, dear. The most basic equipment. You can hardly believe how basic. Not supplies of the latest drugs. Oh no. Aspirin even. Lomotil. Disinfectant. Eyedrops. Supermarket medicine.' She explains that Sister Luke who had been left behind to run the tiny hospital ward is a qualified nurse. It is holiday time, she goes on, and she and Aloysius are free to do this. 'We feel very selfish,' she admits, 'taking time off when Luke might need us. More tea, dear?'

I am staring through the blurred window of my own misery and am conscious of shame.

With that impetuous mindlessness of tropic weather, the rain stops belting and the sun blazes on the mouldering garden. Sister Tancred observes these last orange streamers of sun and says they must be getting on. At Sister Aloysius' nodded agreement I want to cry out to them not to leave. I want to whimper please, not right now, as if I am a child being denied a last glimpse of pantomime, the curtains bucketing down then rising once more on the lit village green, the actors lined up hand in hand, taking bows, hat-doffing, sweeping their obeisances to the simpleton audience.

My proffered donation elicits a ruffled duck response. 'No. No. Thank you all the same. No. We couldn't now. Not now. God bless you,' they say. And their eyes are the translucent waters of oceans beyond the planet, of unmired depth. They go out to the veranda and wrestle once more with their gumboots, carry their sodden veils neatly over an arm and make their way down the steps under their plastic slickers to their van while I follow, a chastened child, fumbling with unsaid pleas, trying to muster up any reason to detain this comfort.

Their faces look out at me brightly from the van. They are on the homeward run now and will be going straight through, wanting, sentimentally they excuse themselves, to be back with their people— their children—spiritually, at least, for the days before New Year.

'God bless you,' they cry as the van splashes off. 'God bless you.'

＊　＊　＊

Within the month, unable to obliterate the memory of their enchanted personal climate and the calm weather of their faces, I have written to them. Is this as useless as sending a cry for help by bottle? Some truck, boat, bush pilot's plane will drop my letter off.

There is a worm in my mind, a maggot nibbling, an envious lust.

I want to share their weather.

I work zealously on Baxter who has returned relaxed and possibly surfeited by southern fleshpots, urging him to allow me to do a series on Aboriginal reserves.

'You're mad,' he says, lighting this tenth cigarette for the morning. It is barely eleven. He has a notice affixed to the wall behind his desk:

There will be no non-smoking in this office. 'That's a very sensitive area. You'll have to get special permits to enter and if you blow the top off them, there'll be a government mafia breathing down my neck.'

'*Is* there a government mafia?'

'Silly child,' he says.

I drive south again to what was once home, choosing a weekend when I know the children will be there. Communications have resumed after an explanatory letter from Etta and Daniel, accompanying a battered box of chocolates, that father had taken all of them to the Gold Coast for a fortnight in the Christmas break. 'We tried to ring you,' her letter complained, 'but you weren't there.'

I arrive in the late afternoon.

'Mummy!' they all shrill with varying shades of enthusiasm. I have not warned them of my arrival. Timothy has grown a foot. Etta has discovered boys. Daniel has discovered girls. Clifford, who might have discovered anything at all, is away in Brisbane at a meeting of company shareholders whose board plans to turn the entire western seaboard of the Cape into a fun park with condominiums.

Bodil Kierkegaard whom I meet for the first time is indeed everything Flora has led me to believe—height, girth, looks. 'Call me Bodil,' she says. She wears her heavy swag of hair in an impeccable bun. Her face is round, good-humoured and confident. She is not as old as I had assumed. The house has a gloss it never experienced under me. She serves me afternoon tea with delicious savoury tartlets. Even as I munch I can smell something more delicious cooking quietly in the kitchen.

'Early dinner,' she explains noticing the turn of my head. The kids are sitting in an orderly way listening absorbed to a male singer whose voice production is halfway between vomiting and the grunts of a talented constipate. 'The two older ones are off to a school dance. Timothy and I are going to play chess on his computer.'

My God! What can't she do? I don't even know the moves.

'Don't worry.' She gives me a reassuring smile that is genuinely all heart. 'I'll be picking Dan and Etta up by eleven.'

Where did Clifford find this treasure? She must cost a fortune. I notice that when she instructs the children to do or not to do something, they obey instantly with a good-humoured okay Kirky or sorry Kirky.

This is nightmare country Clifford has invented for me.

I had only ever to give a positive direction to find we moved instantly into a battlefield of negative bargaining.

Saint Kierkegaard suggests I stay overnight. (There will be a lavender sachet under the pillow, I know.) Clifford will not be back till late Sunday.

'You won't tell him?' I beg.

'Trust me,' she says.

It is a mistake.

For two hours after dinner (*boeuf en croûte, bonne bouche* potatoes, tossed salad, caramelised pawpaw—Jesus Heaven!) she and Timothy play chess. I am redundant. He beats her once. She beats him twice. He loses with charm and good grace. She drives off expertly and promptly to pick up the older children and I imagine I will have Timothy to myself if only for ten minutes but he yawns, switches off switches, disconnects terminals, tidies up and says, 'See you. I'm really tired, Mum,' and has showered and pyjama'd himself before I can take a breath. He suffers my goodnight hug, pats me and says, 'There!'

At eleven fifteen sharp Saint Kierkegaard returns with the other two. I hear their laughter as they troop up the steps. Both are at that stage of adolescence where their beauty is so stunning it catches the heart because it is so ephemeral. Look a minute later and you'll have missed it.

'Still up?' they ask me, not accusingly, but surprised by the old girl's stamina.

'I haven't had a chance to talk with you,' I say. 'Tell me all about it.'

Their eyes slide across each other.

'In the morning, Mum,' Etta says. 'We'll tell you all about it in the morning. Kirky gets cross if we're not asleep by midnight at the very latest on our nights home.' She giggles.

Does she indeed?

'Goodnight, kids,' I say hopelessly. It is as if my heart as well as my head has been bruised.

Saint Kierkegaard bustles in from the kitchen with a snack. It is some delicacy compounded of smoked salmon and sour cream. It is beautifully served, a landscape too lovely to fracture. I think I hate her. When I decline she says, Never mind. She will. She feels peckish.

I trail off to bed made up in the spare room. There's not only the lavender sachet; she has put a posy in a small jar by my reading lamp, two paperback editions, Márquez and Vonnegut—God! she's a reader as well!—and a glass of hot milk with a cover on it to keep it warm.

In the morning when I potter out (Guiltily? Of course, guiltily) to make myself a black and lacerating coffee, I hear Timothy romping and chuckling in Saint Kierkegaard's bed. The final thrust! I am definitely not needed and I muse on the redundancy of natural parents. Parents are required as incubators only.

The rest of the household saunters in as I am rinsing my coffee cup.

'So you're off then?' Saint Kierkegaard is rosy from sleep and large with good humour. The kids are pestering about her, calling her Kirky and failing to dislodge her imperturbable calm. Observed in the bright light of morning she appears as a handsome den mother. The kids barely notice me. I think I may have developed a cringing habit in their presence.

Stateless.

'Yes, I'm afraid so.' I look at my children and ache. 'Lovely to see you so well and happy, kids.'

They give dutiful pecks and hugs. I am the one who clings hardest.

'See your mother off to the car,' Bodil Kierkegaard says. 'And I'll get some breakfast going. How about griddle cakes?'

What a psychologist! My feet unglue from the living-room floor and trudge away, leaden-soled across the veranda and down the steps and out to the road. Even the garden has a burnish. The bougainvillea hangs in manageable blazing swags of hot pink and purple. The flamboyants riot along the fence line. I look back at the house and it is white and warm and filled with good smells and good will. And I have lost it.

As I open the car door, rain falls with terrible February immediacy.

'Don't get wet, kids,' I urge, a last motherly attempt.

They seem glad or relieved with the dismissal.

'See you soon,' they chorus, uttering that most insincere phrase of social vernacular. 'See you soon.'

In my driving mirror I see them scuttle houseward through rain, dressing-gowns flapping.

They don't look back once.

*   *   *

Sending that letter to Sisters Tancred and Aloysius, care of Bukki Bay Mission had seemed a hit-and-miss affair, rather like flinging a note to the wind. Nevertheless, I had tossed.

By the end of the Wet I have half persuaded Baxter who at heart is a stirrer and who was once trampled by a Brisbane police horse during the heady protest days of the seventies and is one who struggles gamely to shock the local bourgeoisie within the limits imposed by a not altogether liberal southern newspaper owner, that the current climate of colonial shame would be receptive to a series of articles on the appalling conditions in some of the government reserves and fringe communities of the sunny state.

A southern judge has even admitted weeping among the shanties of Moree.

'All right,' he concedes finally and ungraciously. 'All bloody right. You do the legwork and the paperwork. I suppose you'll want expenses as well, eh? Who the hell up here is going to read these articles with any sympathy?'

'You might be surprised.'

'I'd better be.'

'Look, Baxter, there's a new government now. They at least will be delighted by anything that exposes the failings of the previous one. I'll slant the stuff that way. I won't even have to slant it. The degradation of Aboriginal living conditions has been going on for decades. Decades. Let's make a buzz.'

'This new lot are as rotten as the last,' Baxter says gloomily. 'I guess I have only my job to lose.' Then he grins. Perhaps at the thought of tail-twisting. 'Anyway, I lie, love. I'm getting sick of the north. It's filling up with bloody southerners. I've got me a patch in a totally undiscovered section of the coast several hundred miles south of here. No power. No water. And best of all, no people. No nothing.'

'Clifford discovers everything.'

He ignores that. 'It's time I thought of getting out, anyhow. I shall rewrite *The Compleat Angler* and relocate Walden Pond.'

'And where's that?'

'I shan't say. You think I'm crazy? In a flash Clifford and his minions would be carving it to pieces, ripping out the trees, shoving up the concrete and stuffing the ecology. I do believe, Julie, that that bastard husband of yours has surveyor grids on his specs.'

This semi-amiable exchange is Baxter's formal blessing.

Yes, I am devious.

Yes, I am building a tricky fabrication, a guise of work zealotry, when really I will be travelling to recapture that elusive pat on the shoulder, the steady gaze of unperturbed eyes that regard my selfish problems with sympathy but as so trivial they are placed in correct perspective.

At that ultimate vanishing point I will find the meaning, the nub. I will be reduced from the awful loneliness of space by the inevitable merging of those distant lines.

In another climate.

* * *

I begin at the tip of the Cape.

I travel on small Cessnas taking frozen meat and grocery crates to impossible places. My memory of the next three days is constantly ruptured by the vision of a frozen piglet, trotters rimy with frost, a metre from my own. 'You comfy back there?' the pilot had asked before adjusting his earphones. 'Great!' I had said. 'Great!' I would dread a forced landing. The coastline is alive with crocodiles. I mention this to the pilot who says, 'Don't worry. They'd go for the meat first.'

Three days of it, catching feeder planes to dots on the map. I wave my permits and talk to tribal elders. I manage to speak with the women at these reserves. There is discontent about land rights and even more discontent about the effects of liquor, crates of which are smuggled into the 'dry' settlements by truck or dropped off in secret clearings by private pilots on the make. Well, not so private. I take fourteen pages of notes and fill half a dozen tapes. I must be careful. Baxter doesn't want to be sued.

This is redneck country.

There is so much resentment from whites who seem to regard even the sight of a blackskin as a personal affront. I get talking with a fried blonde at a motel in Reeftown on the third night and cannot resist postulating colonial treatment of Aborigines as a dinner topic.

She barely looks up from her de-thawed slab of barramundi.

'I believe in slaves.'

I rise and carry my dinner to another table and when the waitress starts to become agitated and interfere, I march back to my room holding my plate, protecting my food from an excited head waiter determined to take it from me.

With the air-conditioning on high I spend half the night converting my notes and tapes into some sort of formal order, fold the result into an envelope and walk out into midnight to drop my first article in the mail.

The town has a hot dead feel to it, the cooler air from the seafront blocked off by the cement towers along the esplanade. Hoons roil around intersections on motor bikes, buzz groups of seedy young loiterers in arcade entrances, drunks and druggies sleeping it off on benches doused in frangipani. It's not safe to be out at this hour and when I spot three youths making a diagonal crossing designed to intercept me some hundred yards from my motel, I am forced into a run. We are alone savouring the tropic fug. No police. Only lone cars looking for action or leaving the massage parlour belt, and the flat silver of reef waters stretching out on my right beyond the palms.

My flight is followed by catcalls, obscenities that hover in the dark air. Inside the reception lounge I tremble beneath the uninterested eye of the night clerk. 'Getting rough, this town,' he says. 'You should have known better than go out at this time.'

Victims are always wrong.

*   *   *

The plane I catch next morning is a mail run flying to a number of station properties in the central Cape. I'm out at the airport with three hours' sleep behind my red and jumpy eyelids, the pilot already foot-tapping impatiently on the tarmac for his only passenger. As we walk across to the Piper Cherokee he explains his route briefly and without enthusiasm.

'Up to Coen first, then Wenlock and Iron Range. I'll drop you off at the Range before I fly up to Weipa. I'll be stopping over a night there, so I'll pick you up tomorrow, late afternoon. Okay?'

I nod.

He looks at me curiously before he straps himself in.

'Anyway, what's the big deal? You got friends up there?'

'I might have. I hope I have.' A few days before I left Sister Tancred had replied with the warmest of invitations. Could I bring mosquito coils? They had run out. I had packed a dozen boxes. 'I'm doing a story on the reserves and fringe camps.'

He looks at me thoughtfully. 'I could give you a few. Save you the trip. I get in to all these places. I've seen the conditions up on the Tableland, over at Bessie Bay, round the Cape. Have you seen them?

'I've spent the last few days.'

'Well, I hope you had a good damn look. They're a bloody disgrace. Kids with eye infections and Biafran stomachs. Permanently dripping noses. Half the adults rotten with DTs or TB. Most of them with syph. We're great colonisers, aren't we? There's even Aids at a couple of places. The town whites go out and sodomise the gins. They pass it on.'

I am surprised to hear such empathy, such self-criticism of the lucky country from a freckled redhead who would, I imagine, have been the last to give them a thought.

My children. Those children.

'You know those places pretty well, then? I'm hampered by time. The paper's given me the bare week.'

'Lady,' he says, 'I've lived on some of those reserves when I've been caught by the weather. They're good people fundamentally. They want to help. They're naturally gentle. All the virtues we claim for ourselves. They've saved my life more than once. And no, I'm not being sentimental. Hold tight now. I'm taking the old girl up.'

The plane taxis down the runway, swings about and roars off along the strip, rising easily into the early morning air flying north-west over the Divide. On my right I watch the last of the tourist clutter vanish, the reef shallows fade. In a half doze for forty minutes I snap to as the plane begins to dip. The pilot is yelling back to me, 'Parcel for Yarraden. Nearly forgot.' He brings the plane down neatly on a makeshift strip at a station homestead where I can see someone waiting with a four-wheel-drive. Smooth as syrup. The plane is stopped practically beside the car and the pilot comes back towards me and begins rummaging, hauling out a sack which he lugs over to the doorway. 'Time for a cuppa?' the station hand asks as he helps the pilot ease the sack down. The pilot shakes his head. 'Maybe on the way back, mate.'

'Any time,' the other says easy and casual. Then we are away again and flying steadily north to Coen, half a place, half a town.

Two steers scatter as we land on the strip just out beyond the last of the houses, racing madly for the fence. I take a look at the pilot's face expecting anger but he's a cool man, a northerner, and must have taken dozens of hazards like this in his stride. The plane taxis back down the runway to the shed that doubles as office and weather shelter. The pilot cuts the engine, clambers down, hauls me out for a leg stretch and begins unloading sacks from the plane's gut. A young man who has driven out into the paddock with a semi walks across grinning.

'Move your fucking cows next time,' the pilot says amiably. 'Or you can do without your mail.'

Airborne. North-east to Wenlock and twenty minutes later we touch down on a grass paddock a mile from the homestead. 'Civilised,' the pilot murmurs as he heaves mailbags over the side. 'Not a steer in sight.' He waves briefly to the station manager driving out to collect. 'I need a co-pilot on this run and then I could shoot the bastards. The steers, that is.' Is he serious? He's grinning like a goat. The farther north, the tougher. And I don't dislike it. We are a frontier away from those morning coffee sessions with the school mothers' group, the carefully staged dinner parties for Clifford's dubious buddies, the trimmed grass strips of the suburbs and the stutter of garden sprinklers.

Another world. Another climate. Different weather.

*   *   *

No one is waiting for me at Iron Range. No anxious face peers out the side of a road-battered Kombi. I hike my bag into the shade of the nearest tree on the strip fence, light a cigarette and settle down to wait.

The plane is a speck of noise rupturing the blue. We're casual up here. Laid back. 'See you tomorrow then,' the pilot had said, slapping my bag familiarly. But the engine drone has long faded and I become aware of insect click, the mutter of leaf arguing with wind, the infinitesimal movements of dust in landscape whose endless permutations of grey, blue, green, fawn, olive, khaki swamp me in a world of resentful trees that twist and writhe away in a stage-set unplushed except for the velvet of dust.

I take out my camera and snap desolation. Its ribs and mine are braced against the assaults of isolation where fright stalks the emptiness. It is fifteen miles from here to Bukki. Should I begin to walk? All morning I have been suffused with intangible sensations of arrival as if the plane, the pick-up trucks, were merely forerunners to an inevitable last journey into north. Omit the article. North.

I snap desolation again and remember a little pub Cloncurry way on an assignment three months before. In the bar I bought myself a beer so achingly cold it split my skull. Half a dozen old-timers propped up the bar, all gums and skin cancer, and they turned resentful wizened faces in my direction, glaring at this stranger in town, this female crashing their domain. They looked, they assessed (saved by my thick lenses!), they turned away. My glasses are a great assuager, conveying orthodoxy and respectability. They have pale pink frames that don't really suit me and I had glanced then at my reflection in the bar mirror, caught it unexpectedly for that horrendous second of non-recognition to puzzle over sad earnest features that were worryingly familiar.

Exactly. I have such a vision of myself, some poet wrote (Who? It will nag me for hours!), as the self hardly understands.

I wait.

A whole decade passes by me on paddock dirt. Overhead a hawk charts the coastline, mapping the bays. But even as I attempt to chart with him and realise at the same moment the misquotation in my personal assessment file—not 'self'. The word was 'street'. 'A vision of the street'—the noise of a car engine cuts through the scrub, uncoils a turn in the road and pulls up beside me and my dumped bag.

Aloysius. Her smile on full beam. The lightest of welcoming kisses on my cheek and a flurry of apologies for being late. Well, not so late. She was worried I might have thought she wasn't coming at all. An unexpected obligation, she is explaining as I settle into the van. She had to visit a sick friend on a property near Wenlock and had been on the road four hours already. Despite the drive there and back, despite the thermometer standing steady at thirty-four degrees, she is cool and unruffled. I compare my sweating anxious self with this nun-magic as she gets back behind the wheel. Her pale blue skirt and shirt appear freshly starched. Her veil still bears the knife-edgings of the iron. Her face is a map of every kind of kindness in the world.

'And how are you dear?' she asks, patting my hand. 'The weather's different from when we last met, isn't it?'

I am laughing at our contrast.

'Oh yes,' I tell her. 'Yes yes yes.'

*   *   *

The van has taken a track off the main road and heads north, to the north that pulls like a lodestar. Sister Aloysius handles the van like a truckie, a sainted long-distance haulier and I sneak glances at the grey locks tousled beneath the veil, at her face lined with years of benevolence and goodwill, her mouth forever holding the up-curve of a well-tempered smile. Being is her only reward. I had never before met anyone, Flora included, apart from Tancred, who gave out so fully the confidence of being rich, rich in the best sense, a kind of unplumbable well of spiritual wealth that sustained. 'You see, dear,' she was to say to me later, 'you have to love your work. Job satisfaction, isn't that what you young people out there are looking for?' She had spent all her life working in one mission field or another. Wealth amid the pus, the vomit, the drunken screeches, the thud of flesh on flesh. The same hour she uttered those words to me I heard her mildly rebuke Billy Thursday who worked in the Bukki Bay vegetable gardens for saying 'shit'. 'I'll teach you another word, Billy,' she said. 'No one will know what it means so it won't offend, eh?' Say *merde alors*! That's French and it means the same thing. Then the police won't be able to arrest you for obscene language next time you're down in Charco. Now, dear, say it after me. *Merde alors!*'

'Doesn't sound no good, Sister,' Billy Thursday had said.

'Only if you're French,' Sister Aloysius advised. 'You work at it. If you like, leave out the *alors*. Very effective.'

She had looked sideways at me and giggled. Sister Aloysius, I love you.

There were only fifteen miles to go I had been assured. And as we drove I kept asking myself why my tragedy was not a tragedy. True, up here, in this desperate landscape. But why not? Should I measure the maritally endowed plight of my children against that of all those black ones I had recently seen? How did my kids' lot emerge in comparison with theirs? Where does tragedy lie? With women? Ah, I tell myself as the van rattles me seaward, only men may receive the nobility-enrichment of tragedy. Only men can become tragic figures. I try to think of any woman who has exerted that same tear-jerking quality of a Lear. I can think of none. Bovary, Karenina, Cleopatra— *putaines*, the lot! Who's moved by them? No one. *Absolutamente!* I mentally quote, remembering Lowry's Consul squatting beneath his volcano of mescal. God, if the Consul had been the Consul's lady, no one would have detected the slightest element of tragedy—except for him. Drunken old cow, I can hear. Stupid drunken bitch. But ah, the Consul, struggling with the unstrugglable with. What what what heart-rending stuff, even when he is *perfectamente borracho*!

Oh my God, I wonder, why? *Why?* He's a drunken old sot as much as his imagined female counterpart; but male sottishness is tragic, a waste of shame. Female sottishness is bestial. Who cares if Queen Lear had three ungrateful daughters?

I could do with a drink.

And as we skirt the potholes soft with bulldust and I look back at the parachute of grit we are trailing, I think I have a pointer. Women are bestial, subhuman so we have been taught to believe. Aquinas wondered about us. Who am I to chop logic with a guy like that! How, therefore, can they ever be tragic, for tragedy has been defined as the inevitable downfall of greatness in the face of uncontrollable odds? You win, Thomas, you win.

Is that it?

Sister Aloysius leans an ear towards me.

'Is that what?'

'Nothing. Nothing. I was thinking aloud.'

'We all get a bit that way up here. It's the heat. They used to call it being troppo when I was a girl. Now I think it's fried brains. Or spaced out. Or is that drugs?'

I love her simplicity, her innocence.

I have prodded something. She begins to tell me about her youth as she drives. But she *has* the aura of youth. She must sense my querying arithmetical interest. 'I will be seventy next birthday,' she says. It is hard to believe. 'I grew up near Coen.' She smiles her reminiscence. Her grandfather, she tells me, originally came north as an engineer for a putative gold-strike and married the third daughter of a cattle station owner. They had only one child, Sister Aloysius' mother, who grew up in Coen and in turn married a storekeeper in the little town. 'Ah,' Sister Aloysius says, peering momentarily sideways at me and down a long uncluttered corridor of decades. I pursue her nostalgic 'Ah' as she rides horse with her sister for over one hundred miles to Laura, boards the rail-motor to Cooktown, takes a coastal steamer to Cairns and then travels another eighty miles by the slow clambering train into the hills of the tableland.

'We were boarders at the convent,' she explains. 'We only got home twice a year, August and Christmas. It was quite a journey.'

I see Daniel, Etta and Timothy carelessly slamming the doors of Clifford's latest model Citroen, Peugeot, Rover, in their day-pupil stage as they are dropped off safely at school gates that suck them inwards to the spoils of capitalist fees. Clifford, big spender! *The minute he walked out the door*, I hum sourly ... Not that he was always a big spender. After two years of marriage and niggard saving we followed the Kharma trail that long-gone Christmas from India down through Malaysia, Indonesia and across to Hong Kong. Nowadays I don't like to think of those dreary youth hostels with their drearier clientele, all hard-rock egos like us, the cheap lodging in unplumbed houses, the diarrhoea, the skin infections and the unending yobbo pack of Australians on the beach at Kuta. The beggars didn't stand a chance with Clifford. He had learnt to say 'Piss off' in ten dialects. In Hong Kong he wanted to do the tourist thing and go up The Peak.

'Pretend you're blind,' he hissed at me, 'and then you'll be able to go up free. Go on, fake it.'

Now I know I'm short-sighted. I know I carry a swag of dioptres. But it's not as bad as that.

'For God's sake!'

'Do it!' Clifford ordered. 'The money's running out. They'll let me up free as your minder.'

Clifford wanted to be able to say later to his buddies, 'We took one thousand in travellers' cheques and came back with nine hundred!'

My God!

So I did a stumble-clutch act and it worked and when we got to the top there was so much smog I might as well have been blind. Hi there, Cliff! Prosit! And, my dear, if you'll forgive the crudity, up your tiny wallet!

Clifford, I see you, I see you. I cannot stop seeing you on that trip in your post-hippie gear, your nasty little woven grubby shoulder bag and those terrible loose pants letting your parts swing free. Halfway through that trip you had teamed up with a Melbourne kharma bum, a macro vegetarian who prided himself on his well-being and his youth. Gull (Call me Gull, mate!) later drifted to Queensland where all the returned fakirs were settling and we would run into him over the years in his rural bohemia, aging far more rapidly than a meat-eater but still obsessed with juvenescence. By this time, of course, Clifford had rejected low-life acquaintances as he took to white shoes and share folios, his own course diametric to Gull's. Each random encounter brought the same avid enquiry: Come on, how old do you think I am, hey? How old?

The last time I saw Gull there had been a seven-year gap. Our supermarket trolleys locked wheels near the doggy-bite section. He still had the same shoulder bag and a no-longer-tender hippie partner who ran a hairdressing salon called On the Fringe.

There was that terrible fifteen-second pause while we fought to recall names, examining altered facial lineaments. 'Julie,' he finally managed. 'Hey, Julie! How you doing?'

He didn't wait for my reply. 'Hey, Julie,' he asked enthusiastically, 'How old do you think I am, hey?' There was a wrenching and dragging of trolleys. 'Come on, Julie. How old?'

I looked at that shoulder bag, the loose cheap batik shirt, the stained cotton pants, the leather thongs, one strap chewed and swinging loose.

'Judging by your style,' I said in a measured way, 'you've got to be still in your fifties.'

Mutual acquaintances tell me he has never asked that question since.

I'm digressing, I know, but the vagaries of living constantly stun me. I compare the narrows of all our putrid suburban lives with the giant swinging ellipse of forest sky cloud and know I am nothing. Nothing. And my meanness to Gull comes up and whacks me across the face.

I know in the pith of me that Sister Aloysius is never mean.

'You aren't, are you?' I ask.

'Aren't what, dear?'

'Nothing,' I say. 'Nothing.'

We've known some oddballs, Clifford and I. But I was always the only one amused.

When Daniel was born—take this as an example—the doctor who attended me was notorious in Sugarville for having a mistress whom he later shot as she stumped off out of his front gate after a nasty verbal exchange brought on by the heat and the probing of his fed-up wife. He pleaded not guilty. 'I was cleaning my gun,' he told a fascinated jury, 'and we had been arguing about the pull-through. As she walked away I pointed it playfully at her.' Playfully? 'Come back,' I told her. 'It was all an accident.'

He was convicted but after he was gaoled the Sugarville police could not cope with the flood of cards, flowers and hot meals delivered by loving patients, other ex-mistresses, doting friends and still loyal wife. They moved him to a prison two hundred miles down the line.

Clifford was inclined to be sympathetic.

'He was a very attractive man,' he kept insisting. (Do men know, really know, when other men are attractive, in a heterosexual sense?) I suspect that Clifford, during his decade of infidelities, must have seen himself in a similar position.

The landscape has switched from drunkenly reeling eucalypt scrub each side of the gravel road into clotted tropical forest. Sister Aloysius wears a small moustache of sweat on her upper lip; sweat runs from her hairline down her cheeks. Her soft pale skin is glazed with water. She fumbles with the top button of her shirt and daringly unbuttons as the van lurches brutishly over the rutted track. Prescribed point B must be close, now, as the road uncurls its tight corkscrew towards the sea.

I think of my children and try not to think of them, feeling like some astronaut struggling to regain the capsule west of Aldebaran, hampered by weightlessness, my weightlessness being that lack of importance I exercise in their lives.

We bucket over range runnels, cross creeks and gouge our way into darker forest in a mini-Calvary.

'Nearly there,' Sister Aloysius offers comfortingly.

She swings the van off the main track into a pair of rutted furrows heading east. On my map it is the broken marking of a faint pencil line. It is no longer a road. It is merely a set of roughly parallel trenches drilled into position by the few cars that come in and out of the mission or the fluted spoor of curious drifters.

'We're not really a mission,' she explains, tuned in to me inexplicably. 'Not an official mission, either government or church. We're just a trio of renegades running a health clinic and a very basic school outside the official Murri settlement. *Sub rosa.*'

'No government aid?'

'None.'

'But does the government know you're here?'

She hesitates perceptibly.

'There's an unofficial tolerance of our presence—listen!' She interrupts herself. Over the dragging sound of the motor come the high-scale notes of a waterfall. 'You'll see it in a minute. You see, we're not actually on the reserve. They could throw us off tomorrow if they wanted. We're on an adjoining leasehold. The people give us permission to go in and out and that's all that matters. We don't interfere, unless you call help interfering. We're not really proselytising. Now look. Look at that!'

Ahead of the van a great lance of silver dazzles out from the rocks a hundred feet above the track, shafts through the canopy and burrows into a boulder-ringed pool below. 'It never seems to stop running,' Sister Aloysius says. 'Not even in the Dry. It's like a miracle.'

I should be taking notes of all this for Baxter but Baxter, too, has become a distant shape blurred by the mist of the falls, vanished into a greener and greener landscape, the ghost figure at the heart of Rousseau's jungle.

Refreshed, Sister Aloysius puts her foot down in a reckless way. She has God on her side. I hope he is on mine as we rocket over-fast down towards the coast. I can smell the sea though I can see nothing through the density of leaf trellis we are penetrating. There's an intimacy about the track as it twists to the curves of the range, climbing down into chimings of water from summer springs. A world of leaf and water.

'Nice, isn't it?' Sister Aloysius mops more sweat from her face. 'That's national park to the south. I love this part of the drive. Two more jump-ups and we'll be coming down home.'

She says home with all the casual authority in the world.

It pricks me.

The van takes a last loop and enters a long straight run into glittering blue. 'Here!' she cries, enthusiastic as a child. 'Look! We're here.'

A peacock silk spread, a shock of aquamarine.

There is a beach between headlands, a perfect wide-sweeping half moon between tumblings of granite, thickets of palms and a huddle of rotting shanties, tin lean-tos, old trucks roofed with plastic at the heart of perfection.

Sister Aloysius does not bite her lip as I bite mine.

She is easing the van into a central clearing, dodging a cluster of small children and dogs. 'We don't have power at the moment,' she says cheerfully. 'Well, very sketchy power. We're saving up for a new generator. Our present one is ready to collapse any time. We have to be very careful. Skinflint!' She waves to the kids, calls names and hellos, her face transformed by a huge smile.

There has been an attempt at streets, I see now. Between the shacks and the sea a wide pounded dirt road runs parallel to the beach and at one point, the point where Sister Aloysius has parked the van, another dirt road intersects, running straight towards the water as if about to plunge in. There are scattered groves of banana trees, the dense cumulus of mangoes.

'Home,' Sister Aloysius repeats, giving the syllable its roundness, a satisfied fullness that has the inevitability of all arrivals, repeats, with her bright unbaffled unironic smile into the sunniness of which Sister Tancred surrounded by half a dozen of the old people steps beaming. There are small bags of boiled sweets to be handed out to a dozen tiny black hands. Sister Aloysius cannot give enough. Sister Tancred has helped me down from the van and nodding towards a pair of buildings just visible behind the pawpaw groves at the end of the road, 'That's us,' she tells me. 'Welcome.' Names and introductions flutter round my head. A young boy in a T-shirt emblazoned Paradise Is Where You Find It, jeans through at the knees, is grinning at Sister Aloysius. 'Billy,' she says, 'you can help unload now. Get your brother to give you a hand. You can take everything into the store. Millie and Anne will handle it.'

'All time work!' Billy Thursday says giggling.

'Now, Billy,' Sister Aloysius says reprovingly and bestowing a sisterly kiss on Tancred's cheek.

Someone, please, place one on mine.

Someone, please, give me importance, even the most minimal.

*   *   *

They have made up a bed for me in the convent sitting-room. Sister
Luke is over at the school building. I shall meet her later. They don't
wish me to use the word convent, despite the cross on the eaves, the
icons in the sitting-room, because, as Tancred explains, they are a
ginger group, three breakaways perched on a mining lease acreage that
nuzzles the boundary of the government reserve. In this way they can
rebut charges of intrusion from departmental bureaucracy.

Three tiny bedrooms, a kitchen, a washroom and this larger section
along one wall of which is my fold-down stretcher. Apart from two
framed colour renditions of the Virgin and the Sacred Heart, a small
crucifix, and a set of shelves crammed with books (I will nose out their
reading tastes later!) there are no decorations. Sister Tancred guiltily
admits she has a Gauguin print in her room. I ask to see it and we
stand together absorbing the burnt browns and pinks and the wind off
the reef outside this dwelling comes in sliced by glass louvres, and
blows the palm trees on the beach at Hiva Oa.

Sister Aloysius has come up to stand behind.

'Ah well,' Tancred says.

Is her breathy expulsion part of the ritual of loss?

I have nothing to unpack. Nothing of importance. Sitting on the
veranda of this old cottage that had been purchased in Charco and
road-hauled to these gasping acres, we drink tea and look out through
the gardens at the other building, a two-roomed affair, one of which is
a small dispensary, the other a ward of six beds. Sister Luke bustles
over for a brisk five minutes, a stoutish woman of jokey efficiency
who, again I estimate, is younger than the other two. But then, I have
been wrong before. Muffled by croton and hibiscus shrieks of
playtime laughter come from the open-air schoolroom on the edge
of the beach.

These women constantly astonish me. Tancred, I learn, is a doctor
and licensed to practise. 'Common sense and practical first aid,' she
tells me, her lip paused on that of her cup, 'are more important, more
use.' In the seven years they have been here she has performed
appendectomies and delivered fifteen babies, set broken limbs and
stitched up innumerable gashes. If things prove too difficult, they
radio Charco for help. The flying doctor service has landed a chopper
half a dozen times in the central square where the roads cross.

'We do our best.'

'And what do you get out of it?'

I could bite my tongue off.

Tancred regards me as if I'm a fool and a rude one at that. My words have punched a hole in the fabric of the day.

'Everything.'

And Aloysius? A qualified teacher who has worked in Burma, the highlands of New Guinea. She has nursing certificates as well. But there are no certificates for love or self-abnegation which they possess and I am humbled over my tea and my cup trembles its own apologies in its saucer.

They walk me across to the schoolroom along a path hedged with shouting masses of colour, open-throated hibiscuses yawning into the afternoon. The airy building, a one-walled roofed shed, really, stands on the nuns' land just off the reserve. Over the years they have furnished it with gifts of small tables and chairs, an easel blackboard, painting materials, modelling clay, a cupboard of readers. Although the children have gone for the afternoon, their presence lingers in this breezy learning centre where Aloysius has managed to entice a dozen or so of the younger children to come five mornings a week.

The tables and chairs have been painted, the pathetic little stock of readers is stacked neatly on a shelf of the locker.

'Not that it needs,' Sister Luke says smiling benignly, 'all this. Not to teach basics. A firm stretch of sand. A pointed stick. But it helps.'

Fathom deep in flowers I pause outside the classroom. A short distance away beneath a mango tree, someone has erected bush benches and tables so the children can eat there between classes.

'*If* they have a playlunch,' Luke says. 'The kids would rather run home. But we use it as an excuse to get some milk into them, fruit. Whatever we can spare. We've tried to make it as pretty for them as we can. As ... well ... gentle. We're happy when they learn to read enough to get by with shopping if they go down to Charco, to fill in forms and so on.' She sighs. 'Most of the people at Bukki are outcasts in a way, fringe dwellers from Charco. They've forgotten their own dialect. We'd like to work in language, of course, and yes they should be learning that in an ideal world. But it isn't an ideal world, is it, so we try to teach them what we feel will help most and at weekends we run reading classes for the adults, those who want it. It's mainly the women.'

'Something's working,' Tancred interrupts cheerfully. 'Even if the way the children keep this place helps make them want to make their own homes better, we'll have done something. You don't know a millionaire, do you?'

We turn and walk back.

For part of that weighty afternoon I sit on the convent veranda and lay out the bones of an article that will never, not ever flesh out the purpose of this place. My heart is no longer in description. It is somehow in being. I put my papers aside and wander alone through the settlement to the beach, knowing for the first time what it is to be the wrong colour, becoming the intruder for whom the rags, the dirt, the milky eyes of old men and women listless outside the leaning walls of their huts are not offensiveness directed against my narrow over-zealous first-world smiles and niceness, but badges they sport with acceptance. Indifference almost.

They simply are.

*   *   *

The trouble with Clifford was that he had no sense of humour. No humour and a tin ear, I say, adding a gratuitous piece of carping.

One evening when we were watching a television documentary on domestic violence the reporter began interviewing a cabinet minister, a handsome blonde with expensive hair and boutique clothes, who sported a remarkable black eye. Neither interviewer nor minister made reference to this. 'What we are looking at,' she began with impeccable poise, 'is the implementation of new attitudes within the legislature.' Already I had begun screeching with laughter. 'You think you can do this soon, Minister?' the interviewer asked respectfully. The Minister, smiling brilliantly, had brushed an immaculately groomed hand through the blonde cap. 'Indeed. We have already set up a task force to investigate, collate and assess. You must realise that this problem affects an enormous percentage of families, not merely in the depressed areas but across the spectrum, from the wealthiest to the poorest.' 'And why is this so, Minister?' the interviewer asked. He appeared unaware of the purple shiner confronting him though the camera probed. 'You may well ask this,' she said smiling again. 'It is one of the imponderables ...' I almost fell off the settee as I rocked back and forth, hugging my mirth. 'Get that stupid bitch off!' Clifford snarled, grabbing for the remote control. (It was only a week since he had destroyed a treasured teapot.) But I waved it in the air out of his reach. I think this was the funniest thing I had seen on television for years. 'It's make-up,' Clifford hissed. 'Bloody make-up.' 'No no,' I insisted. 'There's a great swelling running right across her cheekbone.' 'Oh God!' Clifford cried and stalked off. I could hear him clashing pans in the kitchen to the crisp goodbyes of journalist and politician. 'Thank you Minister, for discussing this problem.' 'My pleasure,' the Minister said.

An affable digression beside an affable sea whose unending movement scours the mind of importunate anxieties. I have left behind the squawks and shouts from drunken lean-tos, the quacking cries of the women and the drunken gabble of the men and am streteched out on a beach of such lambency, my ear cocked to the ocean's old folktales, that the squalor through which I have just walked might be a thousand miles away instead of a few hundred yards. My impertinent stroll had been met with passivity, eyes looking curiously for the moment then rejecting. Some answered my greetings. Others turned away in their abjectness. Do they feel the little convent intrudes?

I ask them later that evening as we sit over a meal. It is the most basic and delightful of meals: banana, cheese, bread and sliced mangoes. Tomorrow, they assure me, there will be fish. Billy Thursday will be taking his boat out. That was Billy helping today and it wasn't possible by the time he had the stores sorted out and helped the women pack them away. Billy is one of the few able-bodied men here and he is the youngest. They tell me more. There are fifty people altogether, at least three-quarters of that number old and in need of care. And yes, they reply to my unasked question, the other young men could have caught fish. In fact they did catch fish but there wasn't enough to go round. It was a bad day. They wanted to share but Tancred wouldn't hear of it.

'We're here to give, not take,' she says, smiling over her bread and cheese, her smile flitting through the open doorway into the sealight of dusk. 'Though being here is a form of taking.'

* * *

I sleep badly.

Mosquitoes keep droning in against waves of citronella and the smoke from my mosquito coil. I crawl from my stretcher and tiptoe to their kitchen where by torchlight I heat myself some coffee on the gas stove. The refrigerator, also runs on gas, is their only indulgence and I recall that in the store there is a freezer unit powered by the rachitic generator where the community stores dairy products and fresh meat, most of it donated by the nuns. How does the convent afford to make these gestures? They were handing out oranges to the kids after lunch.

Above the sink is a wall plaque I read by torchlight. 'Where there is no love,' it informs me in plain roman, 'put love and there you will find love.' The words crush my pip of a heart.

I take my coffee out of the house and onto the cold soft sand under the mango trees where the bush benches and tables are chunky punctuation in the starlight. Peace is explicable. It is inexplicable. Luxuriating in something more than silence and sea stir, I want to stay here. I want to stay. The grove is filled with good will.

Behind me comes the sound of a polite interrogatory cough.

Sister Tancred, also holding a mug, scuffs through the sand to join me. 'I couldn't sleep either.'

'You need new screens. I'll run a fund for you when I get back.'

'Will you?' Her eyes in the silver-streaked air appear amused. Her grey hair flutters small wings in the breeze from the water. She is wearing a billowing kind of cotton wrap and at her neck her cross picks up starlight, blazing briefly with each movement she makes. 'We need lots of things. Things,' she repeats, injecting contempt. 'Wanting things is a disgusting business. But! I'd like to see every family here with the right kind of shelter. Theirs. But strong. Durable. We need a communal laundry, toilet block. It's started, of course, but like every-thing else . . .' Her voice trails out over the small dunes hunting the sea and becomes part of the endless pulse of water chatter, hoists sail and drifts away.

How do they manage? How?

'We're dole bludgers,' Tancred says laughing quietly. 'Unashamed. We're here—working on the reserve that is—not quite illegally though the land our buildings are on is legal enough. The order purchased the lease before they—well, as it were—wiped their hands of us. Our presence caused government upset for a while. Politicians pried then accepted gratefully what we were trying to do. The mother house decided to deny our presence and lied—only a little lie mark you—and insisted we were a group of eccentrics to whom they had leased the property in their turn and were in no way connected. A ginger group. Of course as unemployed nurses and teachers we get benefits. But they are all ploughed back in care. There used to be four of us.'

Four. Why do I find that statement ominous? Is it the imperfect form of the verb? Is it the cardinal number? Used to be. Here am I. Are they. Three plus one. But I have not planned a plunge into the dubious waters of self-abnegation. Wasn't marriage that?

I query number four.

She was young, they tell me, only recently professed, with all the monstrous idealism of the young. Reality had cracked her open. She could not cope with mucus, vomit, poverty that expressed itself in the possession of two rags only of clothing. Of drunken rages, broken heads. But most of all she could not cope with the sheer stoicism of the unfortunates who burrowed beneath their bits of tin and packing case and could emerge grinning into new mornings. For she couldn't.

'New mornings stab,' Sister Tancred said. 'In different ways.'

When the three of them had arrived at Bukki there had been five houses relocated in their white-anted splendour from abandoned mining settlements, seven makeshift gunyahs of bough and iron, a couple of slattern caravans hauled in by a truck now lying dead in the scrub on the through road and a rotting shed. There was one tap to service the community, the water piped in from the creek in a guilty moment when a shire councillor tried for absolution, earth closets and a second-hand generator servicing a pole from which electricity wires in spaghetti loops swung out to each dwelling of substance. 'Substance!' cried Sister Tancred, her voice unnaturally loud in the dawn hours. Most of the time they used kerosene lamps, themselves a hazard.

Their intrusion—they felt it to be that—was a delicate affair, the gentlest of invasions that took month upon month to overcome the shyness and the resentment of the little settlement by tender persistence, by offers to ease ulcerated legs and pus-rotten eyes in the handful of children. Daily they had visited the bedraggled shacks, picking up babies, cuddling and coaxing the bigger children into visiting the little cure room. The mothers, fearful and suspicious, came too, reluctant to let their children out of their sight.

'Watch me,' Tancred had said. 'Watch me now. See what I do. I'll make this better.'

And swiftly she would clean up a sore, apply ointment or dressing or put drops in an infected eye or bandage a bloody gashed foot saying, 'You must come every day.'

But they forgot and tireless she would visit them, three times a day if that was what the treatment required and became as jubilant as they when the medicine worked.

'They trust us now,' Tancred said. 'They'll come to us. It took a year to achieve that. And two years to build them the wash block. It's the women you have to work with. If you can win the women over, you can do wonders.'

I thought of Clifford and Saint Kierkegaard, of Daniel and Etta and Timothy wallowing in the comfort of things and my eyes stung.

Sister Tancred is peering at me through the grainy air.

'You see?' she asks. 'You see?'

*   *   *

With the expertise of a Walton who never, not ever, fished waters like these, Sister Luke is cracking out a line.

She's wearing gumboots and her skirts are hoicked up but modestly tucked into over-large army shorts she has dragged on over the skirt. Her strong features are baffled, squinting into sun as it rears up scalding above the rim. It is not the best time, she explains, but she has hopes. Briefly she touches the cross at her neck. I understand talismen.

I stand on the wet sand with her. Sister Tancred has gone back to the convent to begin another day.

Sister Luke is French. From where?

Dijon, she tells me. Her accent is barely noticeable now.

'Fifty next July,' she admits. 'Out here for eight of those years.' As her line suddenly buckles, whizzes and speeds away towards the reef she yelps with pleasure. I watch her play it in; skilfully hauling, paying out, winding and finally bringing a flashing foot of quicksilver in to the shallows. Her fingers move deftly. In seconds she has unhooked it, stabbed it neatly with a small pocket knife and dropped it into a bucket of saltwater. Rebaiting her hook she casts again, the line singing out over the water as easy as summer. 'You're good,' I say awkwardly. 'I try to be,' she replies, deliberately misinterpreting. And then she laughs, her face crinkling in sun dyes.

'Where were you before this?'

India, she tells me. Oocatamund. Ten years there. Four in the New Guinea Highlands where she met Sister Aloysius.

Dare I ask if she feels it has been worth it?

She replies before I can formulate the question. 'I haven't regretted a minute. There was someone, though, a consular official in Moresby said to me, Wouldn't you be had, Sister, if there were no hereafter?'

'And what did you say?'

She turns and looks at me, amused, then out across the water, laughing to herself. 'Whatever. It's been a satisfying life. I've tried to do something with it, you understand. That's all one can do. I've tried.'

'And what did he say?'

'Oh, I didn't tell him that. I simply looked enigmatic.'

After ten more minutes she reels in her line. I pick up the bucket with the fish now lying in water turned rose and together we walk back over the dune slope to the small house huddled on the rise.

Tancred invites me to accompany her on her rounds. I watch as she packs her bag. It's not much that sad assortment of painkillers, gauze bandages, disinfectants. 'There is,' she tells me, 'a variety of antibiotics locked in the clinic store. I'm afraid I have to dole them out myself. They forget to take them and I can't afford to waste a cure.' In the tiny ward Sister Luke is already busy with thermometer and charts. There are two patients, a woman who has just given birth three days before and an old woman with a badly gashed foot.

Tancred redresses the dark wrinkled flesh. The old woman lies limp as a browned and dying flower, her face twisted into a smile as Tancred bends over her.

'That's coming along nicely, Tillie. You'll soon be up, digging pippis, eh?'

'When I go home?' the old lady asks.

'Soon,' Tancred says. 'Soon.' She introduces us. 'This is Tillie

Thursday, Billy's grandmother.' I take the thin brown fluttering hand into mine and I take, too, the wide gummy smile of inexpressible sweetness that flutters to me from the pillow. 'Tillie's Wujal Wujal tribe, aren't you Tillie? There are four different groups here, all left over from Palm and Yarrabah. Perhaps I shouldn't say left over. They had exemptions in the fifties and they came to Cooktown where their parents had been abducted by the Government. Now they want to be back near their own place, you see. Just be near. They don't even talk language any more. We've killed that for them in our kindly way.'

Tancred pours a glass of water from the jug on the bedside table, produces a tablet from her bag and slips the medicine onto the old woman's tongue. It is like giving communion. Then she eases the old lady up, one arm supporting her back and puts the tumbler of water to her lips. 'There,' she says as the old lips sip and the throat swallows. 'There now. I'll be back at lunchtime. You'll be even better.'

'What was that? Not aspro?' I ask as we turn to the other bed.

'Don't be silly, dear. That was a terrible gash. Penicillin. But I have to make sure she has the whole course and the wound is properly healed before I let her home.'

The other patient is young, no more than sixteen. She is suckling her baby and smiling over the tiny skull on which the lines of black fuzz scrawl intricate maps. Sister Trancred waits until the baby has finished nursing, takes it gently and pops it into the scales basket. 'Three kilograms,' she announces. 'He's getting a real fat one, this.' The young woman grins and examines me with bright eyes while Tancred walks off to the end of the room cuddling the baby, expertly burping it, rubbing its back and then returning to the bedside.

'When I go home, Sister?' Glory Fourmile asks.

'Go! Go!' Tancred chides, mock cross. 'You all want to go. Aren't we nice, eh?' The old lady giggles delightedly. 'Four days, Glory. Maybe five. We'll see.' She asks me to wait outside. She has to swab and clean Glory's genitals. 'Just a precaution. She had a little tear.'

Outside it is full morning. Leaves water sky contain such affirmations of goodly intent. They contain such affirmations of self-involved uninterest. I could howl for the paradox. Behind me can be heard the drumming of water into a basin, the clank of instruments being laid down, the confident voice of Tancred and one tiny whimper from Glory Fourmile. Sister Luke strides across the grass strip, her convent chores done, waves briskly and goes into the little hospital to take over.

*   *   *

I am struggling with tribal names in my notebook. *Ganyju. Gungganyji. Yidinyji. Kuku-yalanji.* Sister Tancred calls her doctor's bag her *bundu.* 'I'm speaking language,' she says with a smile.

That morning while she does her house-calls I stroll south along the beach towards the dark clotted tangle of the southern hill.

Landscape affects the emotions so indelibly, so permanently. It is difficult to feel grief, loss, the components of sadness under chirpy blue and saffron. Rain is needed to stimulate the tear ducts, not those blasting tropic falls that assail each year, but the drizzle of northern hemisphere grey where roads gleam with water slick and trees weep, hills weep, gutters shed sodden bus tickets and wrappers and the world holds its tensions tight under the carapace of umbrellas.

Is this the result of the poetic metaphors that have been hammered into us? Must we forever associate heaven's tears with human ones? Is it a natural sorites? Could Wordsworth or Shelley or Keats have written their more extravagantly maudlin bits under a sky of ripe cobalt, temperature one hundred degrees in the shade? How can one feel that sublime rending in the heart when everywhere, everywhere, sunniness, blueness, a glistening succulence of leaves present a front of the most bored indifference? There is a greater eternality about tropic places. They flaunt a superiority to human endeavour that is crushing.

I sit on the sand of Bukki Beach and draw squirls and squares I instantly erase with the side of my hand.

I write up my notebook.

I draw a sketch of the beach looking towards the north. I draw another looking towards the south whose thickly forested ridge I have not yet investigated. Jeannie Thursday scampers down from the schoolroom, released for lunch. Her brother Jimmie slows up when he sees me and circles widely, his sister tagging behind. Already I know the names of most of the children. The two of them stand knock-kneed and awkward, running splayed toes through the sand, giggling.

Jeannie is seven or so. She come over and props one skinny leg for my inspection. Sister Aloysius has bandaged the knee and strapped the dressing into place with sticking plaster.

'What did you do to it?' I ask.

Jeannie is overcome with shyness. She wants to but cannot answer.

Her brother's great brown eyes flash. 'Fell on rocks. Them!' He points towards the north headland. 'Getting *wirul*.'

'What's that?'

'Shellfish.'

I am learning to speak language.

I am learning other things, too, this day.

I wave to the children and begin trudging along the beach to the northern scarp. Out on the water islands float above the horizon. I climb the lower outcrops of rock and turn my eyes south to look back at this paradise slum and have the most incandescent sense of being home, a sense so invasive and total I can barely make my feet move across this sunwarmed granite and return to the convent.

When I do there is a radio message for me. My pilot has been held up at Weipa with engine trouble and won't be in for two more days.

I am a burden, an intruder.

I am over-joyed.

Sister Luke operates the radio. This place is full of surprises. She is a trained telegraphist, has an electrician's ticket and can handle the generator with aplomb. Over dinner that night she assures me it is nothing. Born in Dijon, she reminds me, but raised on the plains of Quebec, only daughter to a sonless farmer who was determined to make her self-sufficient. Her face wrinkles with amusement at my awe. Anyone could do it, she tells me, with training. She is teaching Billy Thursday. She enlarges on the pumping system she wants to install at the headwaters of one of the creeks so that the settlement tanks need never run dry. We are eating a kind of curry. There is far more rice than fish. They have said Grace with all the enthusiasm of diners at a gargantuan feast.

They are not waiting for living. They are living.

In a world of poverty and ugly wealth, criminality and the stink of moral decay, they wait with bliss lips for the ultimate birth.

After dinner the three women go into Tancred's small room which doubles as chapel and I hear their voices—combined ages far more than a century and a half—singing their Office.

They sound so young.

I am the ancient, crawling along the edges of the dark where a wind is slashing palm branches and shaking paper florets of bougainvillea near the door, scarlet bracts flinging colour momentarily as they flutter past the light.

*   *   *

As I flutter.

From that anarchic outside world I appear to have stumbled upon a centre of calm. The little convent of Bukki Beach is the eye of the storm.

So much time and space now are devoted to a meat hunt fostered by pornbrokers eager for bucks. I am getting tired of the unconcealed interest in female genitalia. Why don't people just go for the medical text? With diagrams? Nipples, labiae, the secret places to the uterus— all done over with lick-lipping (I should say lip-licking) meticulousness. Why can't the male animal take the female bits and pieces for granted as females do? They're there. They have as much significance as noses ears eyes. Is it uterine envy? Sigmund didn't know the half of it! A fool of a man. That literary absorption with buttocks!

The sisters' voices cool the enraged spots of my heart.

I think of Flora. She was different once. Years and years ago she commented as we sat on the grass outside the lecture theatre after a therapeutic dose of Pepys, 'You know, I'm bloody tired of absorbing male attitudes, let alone studying them for God's sake! Wow! There's a servant girl down on her haunches! I'll just take her from behind. *En passant*, my dear. *En passant*. Or another hanging drapes or taking out the garbage or simply walking down a side area to the basement steps and the servants' quarters. She's the one! She has a hole! Excuse me while I just fill it.'

She lit a cigarette and sucked furiously. 'Meat!' she said. 'Meat meat meat.'

Flora was even more beautiful in those days. She had this virginal look that acted as a red-ragged challenge to the rugger hoons on campus. To me she theorised about a new culture, a literature that examined the male body with the same offensive precision, inspected their dangling participles and pieces of marginalia with a thesis writer's eye.

She wanted the male left nameless, dissected, used and forgotten.

She evolved a method. Beginning in a small way she would question any male who approached her for a dance at one of the numerous campus hops. 'What have you got to offer?' she would ask, blinking her enormous eyes. 'Vital statistics, huh? Length, circumference?' Young men flinched and wavered away. She began deliberately picking men up outside TAFE colleges after late evening lectures. 'Watch me,' she challenged. I watched. 'Not you,' she would say looking a prospective customer over and dismissing. 'You.' They couldn't believe their luck until she took them home to the flat, flung them into a brisk performance and then threw them out, pressing a dollar, or occasionally two into their hands. When she paid them they became furious. Humiliation, rage, violence to follow. She had her eyes blackened by affronted males and took in a protector, a huge rugby fairy 'who has,' said Flora, 'that very thing about sodomites Freud missed. Vagina envy.' His bulk frightened off wounded vanity. 'Client isn't the word,' Flora puzzled, filled with a semantic irritation. 'The only thing I can think of is serving boys.' It became her phrase. 'I'm off to pick up a serving boy,' she would say and bang the flat door to. 'Give me space,' she would shout back against closed wood. 'I'll need the merest five minutes.'

The rugby fairy was sympathetic in as far as he could understand Flora's cultural protest. He had the gentleness of a baby and the shambling musculature of an elephant.

The first time Flora sauntered past the technical college gates, lingering aimlessly under the shadow of a jacaranda, the prospective client made the mistake of asking the price.

'Price?' Flora said, 'I don't understand.'

'How much do you charge, darling?'

'I don't charge. I pay you.'

'Jesus,' the man said. 'Don't fucking give me that. You some kind of nut?'

'You want it or not?' Flora said. 'Frankly I couldn't care less. Plenty more where you come from, buster.'

'Fuck off, lady,' he said and vanished into the George Street dark.

She persisted in this approach. Men were insulted, intrigued, enraged. Several threatened to call cops. The more offensive ones she took home and waited until they stripped. 'Too small,' she would comment dismissively. And 'Kezza!' she would call authoritatively to the next room and on the cry, Kezza would appear, muscles gleaming with oil, the whole six feet five of him powered for assault to bounce the serving boy through the door.

We changed flats often. There had been threats of return. The humiliation bit deep.

Those were the days! Listening through chipboard walls to clients asking 'What's your name, love' and giggling softly to Flora's response-use of that old male cliché, 'No names, no pack drill.'

'Don't you want to know mine?' a couple of them had demanded aggrievedly.

'Why?'

Affront!

'The money's on the mantelpiece,' I would hear Flora suggest as they left. A whole fifty-cent piece.

'Why, you screaming little slag! I'll . . .'

'Kezza!'

Flora stopped her operation as suddenly as she had begun.

She had, she explained, seen briefly what it felt like to treat other humans as meat. She admitted to self-disgust.

'But men don't feel that.'

'I know. That's why I'm stopping. It's a no-win situation. If I've just made a few pause and think, well that's something. If they can think.'

She finished her degree celibate and went teaching and within the year had married an avocado farmer who courted her with roughly plucked handfuls of garden flowers, bouquets that tumbled apart in their honesty. On their third outing to a waterfront fish café in Townsville he proposed marriage. 'I give in,' she wrote to me. 'There's no other way.'

Of course Flora's tentative crusader openers, those casual strolls past the staglines, examining, staring into faces, allowing her eyes to wander up and down with a pause midway in much the same way the men were accustomed to examining and dismissing a line-up of girls were moves in sexual chess the rest of us cowardly ones envied. I envy her still. But as she explained before taking the ultimate step and plunging into obscurity with Hamilton to fight avocado mould, 'There would have to be hundreds of us doing it. Thousands. A global movement. I can't take on the world!'

True. And neither can I. But I might have chosen better.

Clifford was unfaithful to me in a dazzling arithmetic progression of adulterous activity. Once in the second year, twice in the third, three times in the fourth and so on. As natural as breathing. 'But you're my wife,' he would excuse himself. 'That's different. That's something special. I have a deep regard for the sanctity of the marriage relationship.'

Get knotted, Clifford.

*　　*　　*

How does one describe the panic of stillness?

At the southern end of the bay, some small distance west of the beach, the rainforest appeared to have recovered and recovered itself in a drench of leaf and vine. I had strolled up from the water well beyond the little settlement to be confronted by what appeared to be an impenetrable interweaving of trees plaited into other trees, a five-foot forest as they might call it in Honduras where forest density is assessed by the distance the eye can penetrate.

Less.

I came to a stop, examining possibilities.

The settlement was north of me and a mile away.

This was bright mid-afternoon on my day of reprieve, the hottest time of the day, but there was, as I drew nearer this barricade of green, a silence thick as porridge, a clogging soundlessness that crippled as it enfolded. Nothing. No wingflap. No insect scrape. Not even the papery scratch of lizard or snake. No twitch of leaf.

For a moment I stood and watched this enormous hump of green, then moved closer. Riotings of lawyer vine hitched themselves onto limbs of giant ficus, groped outward and clutched at other trees. I was more curious than frightened and began walking south along the perimeter, swinging inland as the clotted growth swung away from the sea until at last I was rewarded with the smallest of breaks in the wall, a glimpse of light between thinning trees. Despite the stillness, despite a ticking in my blood, I groped past the clutchings of vine and fern until I came to what had once been a clearing, a space where the regrowth had not yet reached the crazy height of the surrounding forest and where, centred amongst all this was what I can only describe as a house shape, a vegetable humpy guzzled up by forest but retaining its essential outline under blottings of leaf and creeper. It was apparent that underneath the density, the horrible fecundity, had been a shelter of sorts whose timbers had rotted and become a fertilising element of the green mass it supported. There were suggestions of windows, doors, a roof shape, but nothing else.

Standing there, sweating in the mid-afternoon, my body ran more with a watery fright than with heat. In the stillness I believed I could hear my pulse tocking against the air, tock, tock.

Yet I forced myself across the remnant of clearing until I was standing beside the hump searching its exterior wall of leaf for some opening, some micro-aperture through which I might penetrate the heart. At the landward end vine had clawed apart what once must have been steps to an upper storey and just to one side of this was a space where a door had been. It was as if I were being impelled to move onward and in. I wedged myself through and discovered a kind of room, the floor of which was now thick with forest litter, in which stood two mossy banquettes of leaves, twin beds as the furniture operatives describe them but now reduced to the lichen-dense mounds of a Shakespearian mid-summer's nightmare. At the far end under the rotted uprights of a wall divider was another doorframe festooned with mould. I was drawn to the cavern beyond, gripped but propelled by the total stillness and found in the green twilight table and chair shapes rejecting their man-made usage in a ferocious clutter of fern. I knew that if I probed beneath greenery I would uncover the abandoned cup, the abandoned kettle. I stood barely breathing on the upholstery of leaves.

It was the silence. The din of silence.

Suddenly panic took me crashing back through the doorhole to the first room and out beyond the lost stairway to the clearing and the inward vision I carried of the beach and its open sea-glazed eye. Running, scrabbling, scratched and mauled by restraining branches. Running, my breath gasping dry through a sand-papered throat, back through the matted walls of forest until I emerged, torn and bleeding on the sand strip south of the settlement. Where I still ran, stumbling crazily through shingle until I came up with one of the old men fishing and saw two of the settlement dogs hurling themselves crazily along the beach, ripping the air apart with their sharp yelps.

I fled towards them, beyond, pursued by the horror of nothing at all.

That night at dinner I ask.

Sister Aloysius looks up from her meal, throws a tiny glance at Tancred and hesitates.

'Was there a house? It felt like a house. It looked like one. Should I not have gone?'

'Don't mention it to the children,' she says. 'But yes, it was a house. A school house. Twenty years ago. Long before our time.'

How could the scrub have taken it the way it did? Had it been planted out of existence deliberately?

Not from what I hear.

They had come there, those two, filled with the trembling missionary ideals young teachers often have, newly married, eager to bring literacy to the isolated group. He was only a few years out of college, still zealous to spread light light light. She was even younger, untrained for anything and certainly not for the sort of isolation this part of the Cape meant. For a year she endured while the loneliness penetrated the marrow of her. More and more frequently she made excuses to get down to Charco or Reeftown or even Brisbane where her family were. She begged lifts from trucks, yachts, supply planes—whatever came through. And each absence she prolonged while her husband sweating through sultry evenings, sandwiched between leaves, with only a static-riddled radio for comfort, began drinking his solitariness as if he might drink himself into oblivion. Sodden from the night before he would stumble into his classroom, muddle through for an hour and then slip back to the house for another drink. Some mornings it was impossible to rouse him from his drunken stupor.

It all came to a head one week in the middle of the year. His wife was back with him, discontented and desperate. There were domestic shouts and screams, the thuds and blows and blubbering noises of female terror and then a deadly pause before the roar of the teacher's beat-up car started and the snarl of it rocketing out of the settlement driven at reckless speed towards the trunk road. He was incapable of teaching the next day. And the next and the next. His wife didn't return. They all waited in the little settlement for the teacher to give a sign but he closed the doors of the classroom in the clearing and shut himself in with the last of his remaining bottles. At the end of that fortnight he shot himself. The settlement heard the crack of the gun but would not go near. Finally two of the elders went down to the clearing but warned by the stench, fled back to their people. Someone got help. A pilot on the mail run, a supply truckie. Someone. The government tried sending other teachers there but the natives would no longer go near the place and eventually even the memory of the school foundered in files, the department ceased appointing teachers, forgot Bukki Bay and let the school house and school fall into decay.

'But what if they bulldozed the whole area?'

Tancred shakes her head. 'It wouldn't make any difference. The place has a sort of taboo on it. Their memories are long. Most of them remember when it happened. Some of them were pupils then. They're afraid.'

'But they're still so close. It's only a mile away.'

'I know. It makes no difference. We had a priest here some years back who blessed the place, said prayers over it. They knew all about it but none of them would attend. Still, it helped in a way. As if it had been sterilised. But not entirely cured.'

Tancred's fingers play with the cross she wears on a chain about her neck. Beyond, under moonlight, the sea is a scribble of grey and silver, tormented hieroglyphs as unreadable as the fears of the settlement or my own. Sitting there, sitting there, I am filled with melancholy, the sort of nostalgic tide that comes with music, only now I am hearing a multiplicity of airs that lead separately and instinctively to portions of my past, the high summers of youth when I believed I might fracture the mundane: a café here, a dance floor there, holidays by backwater creeks the colour of tea, car rides with scarves and hair flung back by wind writing their own statements of being young.

This is the moment I begin to feel torn by a mess of debauched applications that spread a patina of busyness across my existence and have no density. In anything, I decide. Except for the children. Had I achieved my destiny there or here?

✳   ✳   ✳

I want to stay here. It is a place with history and without. At the same time. There is a stasis to living—as I know it.

Clifford is a man for whom the outside grubbings of the globe mean little. Actually, I could date his infidelities by world events. During the collapse of the Berlin Wall, Tienanmen Square, the Gulf War and the collapse of the communist party in Russia, Clifford was away conferencing. Actually he was away with his current secretary who changed as frequently as the tourists in these parts. He was absorbed with his new island resort and could barely think beyond tourist culture. Returned exhausted from something, he would say to my tendered comments on current events: 'What? What? I don't know what you're talking about.' I must admit this total indifference to world suffering infuriated me more than his adultery. He is such a silly man. I mean, he can *read*. But newspapers fail to interest except for the real estate section. He listens to radio, true, but turns down the volume until the stock exchange report comes on. It's as if he has cut off completely from fundamentals.

I want to stay here.

I want never to return to the fabrication of twelve dozen madeleines or even the frictions created by Baxter who, although he is a fair boss, is a cranky and demanding one.

I am due to leave in the morning.

Any relationship has its barbs, I must confess, having observed that very evening the smallest of silent power struggles between Tancred and Aloysius as they dished up dinner. There was a brief tussle over a dish of stew that had been simmering for hours. Tancred won. There were tightened lips, for the smallest of moments, and I looked away pretending I hadn't seen.

When they drive me out to the airstrip in the morning I can barely see the landscape for tears.

*   *   *

Baxter. Baxter.

The radio has been bashing to death a little number called 'The Way We Were'.

I enter the office humming it, chucking in the occasional phrase.

Baxter is angry because I have returned two days later than arranged. His office stinks of sweat, furtive whiskies, cigarettes and late nights, a stench that surrounds him like the light around the body, the aureole of the doomed.

'Oh,' Baxter says, looking up over his bifocals, a nasty twist to his mouth, 'you mean unlined, flat stomach, continent, regular bowel movements? All that, eh?'

He can kill a mood flat.

The word 'deadlines' keeps cropping up. That's a great word, I tell him. What? he snarls. What's a great word? Dead lines. I give the full spondee. He hasn't a clue, the old Baxter. He needs the youthful unregenerate Flora to knock him into some sort of spiritual shape. Lessons in self-recognition.

While I sit pounding out my copy for the local crime file that, incidentally, grows every week into something resembling proportionately the mugging figures for Harlem, the phone shrills at my elbow.

'Where have you been?' Clifford demands. No preamble. No little courtesies of foreplay. He was always like that.

'On an assignment.'

'But where?'

'I can't see that is any of your business.'

'Okay. Now you've made that point, where?'

'Checking out Aboriginal settlements if you must know. Something that has never interested you, Clifford, unless you thought you could speculate.'

'Could you tell me exactly where?'

'No, I could not.'

'I'll find out anyway, Julie. So why waste time! I want a divorce.'

'That's what we all want.'

'Don't be a smartarse. I want one.'

'For your sake or the kids?'

'That's beside the point. I'm just giving you warning. I want to start proceedings straight away.'

Yes. This weather, this climate, this perfection is made for rage, hatred, recrimination. It is the sheer peerlessness that drives one crazy. It reveals by a process of underscored opposition the very ugliness of human nature. I can't blame Clifford. I can't blame me.

'That's okay,' I say.

'You're impossible,' he says. 'Do you know that?'

So he had again wanted tears and final pleadings, me clutching at the hem of his conversation, babbling for forgiveness.

'It's the landscape that's impossible,' I tell him. 'The weather. The lack of it. The climate. By the way, Clifford, I'm inventing the weather. My weather.'

'You're bloody mad,' he says, and hangs up.

The phone rings instantly and Flora tells my cocked telephone ear that she suspects Clifford of planning remarriage. Laramie has gone. She discovered a wealthy invalid ripe for picking at Surfers Paradise. *There can only be Saint Kierkegaard*, Flora guesses. *It's kind of insane, isn't it?*

Oh, I don't know, I think later. I don't know what Saint Kierkegaard wants. I make enquiries. In my nosey way I can discover a lot, even at this distance. Computers are wonderful things. It takes me two days to winkle out a place of birth, Denmark; place of upbringing, Sweden, where Daddy had a post at Goteborg University, and previous marital status. She has no offspring and no criminal record beyond parking infringements. I'm surprised to discover anything at all. I would have supposed she had simply dropped off a plane. The north is crammed with people who simply drop off planes. I think of a Dutch pal of Clifford who has been in the country forty years and has never put in one tax return. 'I can't,' he had explained simply. 'They'll know I'm here if I do that.' He lives well. Some are wealthy. Some live off social security having enrolled in the days when few enquiries were made, statements unchecked and politicians keen not to rock the vote. We're the soft cop. The sweet touch. But not Saint Kierkegaard. That is her maiden name, forsooth. And she is ten years younger than I suspected which brings her more or less into line with Clifford. She has been married once to a transport driver who failed to give transports, for the union was the briefest known to man. Six weeks on the clock! Mrs Bodil Clancy. For God's sake! He went away on one trip and she was gone by the time he got back. That's style for you. She migrated here from Sweden in the seventies, crammed with degrees from Goteborg and flung herself whole-heartedly into domestic service after a short look at the public school system. (I can see her lip curl!) She and Clifford will have lots to talk about. She has managed a motel, a restaurant, three boutiques and has been a housekeeper on an out-station beyond Winton. The heat! The flies!

Saint Kierkegaard will wow the family court. Maybe she will even serve them a *bonne bouche* they will be unable to resist. *Gott?* she will demand, all confident smiles. *Gott? Är det gott? Skulle ni vilja ha lite mera?* Is that good? Would you like a little more?

Oh hell hell hell.

This is going to be one of those confessional pieces where I refuse, absolutely refuse to write one word about my under-privileged childhood, sexual discovery behind the toilet block, religious trauma. Not one word. It didn't happen. I was middle-class secure. My parents had three other children about whom I have not the faintest intention of writing who were all successful and who scattered their talents in Perth, Adelaide, Melbourne. None of us writes much. But we get together in Brisbane for scarless family events, separate genially and go about our lives. Quietly.

I'm the noisy one. Noisy about my own set-up. But I refuse to lumber the rest of the family with it. As far as my parents are concerned, they know of my move away from Clifford. There were no upraised hands and shrill screams of horror. Mother wrote sympathetically and with understanding. *You know dear*, she said, *we both happen to have married very boring men. My generation was socialised to hang in but I don't see why you should.* There was an addendum, a post-script as if the matter were worthy only of afterthought! *I think boarding school is the very best thing in the circumstances. They're intelligent youngsters (thank God they don't take after Clifford!) and as long as you see them regularly, Julie, write and so on, I can't think of a more equitable arrangement. You do have yourself to consider. The notion that women must always be the captured skin, cured and turned into a rug on the dining-room floor is so* passé, *isn't it, dear?*

Mother! Mother! Blessings. You are about twenty years ahead of your time.

Actually I had just read that letter before I went into the office carolling 'The Way We Were'.

What was the point of telling Baxter?

He was about fifty years before his.

*   *   *

Today as I pace the fence-lines of a fat cattle salesyard, I find myself thinking warmly of Bodil Kierkegaard. Clifford likes her. The children like her. A long legal screed has arrived from Sugarville assuring me of school holiday access. The kids send minimal protestations of love. They do not ask me to return. Timothy is now doing senior form maths. I imagine everyone in the acne classes hates him. Poor kid. Where did he get his genius?

In the choking dust of the yards I approach auctioneers, graziers, cattle handlers. I complete my assignment in a slap-happy manner, my nasal passages blocked, my throat tormented by a tickling cough as I try to make my questions register against the public address system. Is this what Baxter wants, the hagiography of bulls?

He disliked my article on the government reserves.

'Too sentimental.' He cut it by half. There no longer remained any crackling denunciation of the residues of colonialism; only a soggy pastiche that read, when he had finished with it, more like a travel guide to depressed areas. I think of Tillie Thursday, limp on her hospital bed the morning I called to say goodbye. I held her hand while she talked to me. She was born on the river bank at Coen, rounded up and taken to a boat at Point Stewart and transferred to Yarrabah with a lot of other squawking youngsters. 'Never seen my mother,' she told me. 'Never seen. Not after that. Only small, see. Must be six them white policemen come. I kept saying want to go home and that white man he tell me you not go back, see. You stay here Yarrabah. Can't talk language no more. Only little words. *Buri* like fire you want matches eh?'

I sat on, holding her hand until it was time to leave and she looked at me and said, 'Never get bitter, eh? No matter what they done to us.'

*   *   *

When bougainvillea last in the doorway bloom'd I say as I return each evening to my half house ... but that's the trouble. It can never stop blooming in this climate. Or the hiatus is so brief you could miss it between breakfast and dinner. This particular thorny enemy is the one known as glabra, purple bracts encasing the secret cache of tiny yellow flowers, so small they pass unnoticed. Like me. I need a multi-coloured personality bract. Everything crackles with heat in a world of crisp paper awaiting rupture. I think more and more of the beach at Bukki, hoping to visit again, perhaps offer myself as camp cook, teaching aide, nurse, floor-scrubber.

I confess these flitting missionary ambitions to Flora and there is a silence so prolonged I fear we have been cut off.

'Bullshit!' she says finally with a touch of the feisty teenager who once wanted to upend the sexual system. As if she has plucked my memory from the detritus of our aligned reliquaries she says, 'Remember how we wanted to reshape the world on the feminine principle? Remember how we gave up for lack of numbers?' This phone call is costing me a fortune, I remind her. She presses on. 'And we couldn't get the numbers. We couldn't get the goddam numbers.' It is the first time I have heard Flora blaspheme in years. Have I touched off something, triggered the figurative with the literal? 'Give in,' she advises. 'Come back. You can't change minds of concrete.'

My problem is to jettison all those tribal rules by which I was nurtured. How counter those charges of child-abandonment? I counter with anything I can dredge up. It's better, is it, for the kids to see a weeping, sulking mum? Better for them to be round a constantly resentful jealous bad-tempered unappreciated poor bit of a wife? That's your problem, say the male psychiatrists, looking slyly at wristwatches to see if they're running overtime and out of pocket with you. They must be bored rigid. They must get so much out of this wounded wife bit.

Triangulation. Is there any term for the triangular form where A and B remain constant but B keeps extending the hypotenuse through C to DEFGH etc? 'That's my problem, doctor,' I had tried quietly and calmly to explain to a marriage psychologist in Brisbane, a sneaked appointment Clifford never knew about. He was a pudgy man with a swag of greasy hair, expensive cufflinks and tie and a soiled collar. (So *she* didn't care either!) 'Your problem,' he said, putting fingertips together and fixing me with a doggy and pseudo sympathetic eye, 'is one most women have to endure.'

'Why?' I asked.

He continued as if I had never spoken. 'You have to talk this thing through' (I thought I'd puke at his jargon) 'and try to make him understand how much his behaviour hurts you. Until he realises this there is no opportunity for *rapprochement*.' He smiled at his own nasalised French. 'No possibility at all.'

'I've tried,' I said. 'It makes no difference.'

I discovered the psychologist and I were speaking together, a kind of antithetic duet. He wasn't listening to a thing I said.

'And when you have done that, when he realises—and do give our sex some credit for a little sensitivity—I assure you there are sensitive men—how much his behaviour causes hurt and distress, then I'm sure your relationship will improve.'

'Your shirt's dirty,' I told him.

End of interview.

So I stand for a moment by Walt's doorway plucking at those papery bracts, scrunching them into thin lines of stain that leave my fingers purple with distress. What to do? Should I make some approach to Clifford, ask him to cease proceedings, beg for another attempt at dubious reconciliation? Should I fight to get the children who, I decide, remembering their attitudes at my last visit, their curtailed duty missives of goody-begging, seem to regard me as no more than a presence once surrounded by nourishing meals and a transporter to entertainment, a presence now taken over by a better cook, a jollier transporter who performs all those functions with aplomb.

What's the point?

Conscience nags.

Conscience nags two ways.

I make up a bundle of brightly coloured readers for Sister Luke and at the same time buy a plane ticket south for that Sunday.

Saint Kierkegaard receives me with the smug look of a victor. She is wearing a loosely flowing housecoat that conceals all structural faults and adds a certain element of graciousness. The whole house is fragrant with the scents of cordon bleu baking.

Clifford launches into a mass of consonants and vowels that explicate his venom more than they challenge my intrusion. The children, I gather, are at various joy spots.

'You've made your bed,' Clifford says predictably after the first verbal assault. 'Now lie on it.'

'But you've lain on so many.'

'Oh the cheap crack! Always the cheap crack!'

For privacy we are walking in the back garden where the mango trees are heavy with fruit, sticky with exudations of sap. The ripe smell is overpowering.

'I want the children,' I tell him. 'I have half a house. Plenty of room.'

'They're perfectly happy as they are.'

'How do you know that?'

'Well, look at them. When they come back for lunch you'll see how damn relaxed they are.'

'I don't want them to come home to that housekeeper of yours. I don't want that at all.'

'I'm afraid, my dear,' Clifford says plucking a mango and sucking at it in a lingering sexual way, 'that that is not possible. After all, you were the one who abandoned them. I need some domestic back-up. You're lucky I'm agreeable to holiday visits. Not that the poor little buggers won't be bored stiff.'

Any minute now he will tell me it's a question of logistics.

'It's a question of logistics,' Clifford says, making loathsome sucking sounds on the mango seed. 'First of all there's the expense of getting them up to you every weekend or every second weekend for that matter. Holidays are going to cost enough. And I can tell you right now I'm not having them shift from Sweetgrass to go to some shonky school you've lined up up there. No way. And then there are my rights. I do have some rights. I'm paying the fees.'

My eyes fill with hate. I'm ashamed of this.

I list grievances.

'At Daniel's birth you were away in Melbourne. A conference, you said. At Etta's birth you arrived drunk at the hospital with lipstick all over your collar. At Timothy's you were overseas tickling the business glands of Japanese developers. He was three weeks old before you met. Some concerned father!'

'I think you should leave now,' Clifford says. He pitches the mango seed skyward where it describes a meteor-like arc of ragged yellow and vanishes into the yard next door. That's my Clifford! He's his own noxious waste.

'I want them next weekend,' I state. 'I want them put on a plane on Friday and I want to see them at that damn airport late Friday afternoon.'

Clifford smiles. I can hear the whirr of clockwork brains running
overtime as he mulls this one. 'If they wish it,' he yields. 'A visit only.
And only if they wish it.'

Baxter has given me a rise. He is moving me from stockyards to
general reporting. But what else have I been doing? What is there up
here beside meat and tourists? But 'Thank you, Baxter,' I had replied
dutifully, eyes lowered, prim in my neat skirt and blouse. 'You'll never
know how grateful I am.'

'Get yourself some contact lenses,' he said. 'Granny giglamps went
out ten years ago.'

*   *   *

Monday. Tuesday. Baxter wants me to go away the next weekend to
cover a strike in Mount Isa. I explain that my children will be visiting.
'Christ,' he says. 'You begged me for this job. You went down on your
bloody knees to get it and now you have it you treat it as if it takes
second place. Do you want to be sacked?'

I go down on my knees again. Literally. 'Will you bloody get up?'
Baxter screams as my mock-begging coincides with the entry of his
latest copy-girl, a slumbrous Italian with knowing eyes. Baxter has
more than copy in mind.

I offer to fly out that afternoon. After all, the strike might be settled
by the end of the week. Already one policeman and two pickets have
been nastily injured in skirmishes at the mine gates. A local reporter
has had an arm broken.

'Okay, okay,' Baxter agrees. 'Thank you, dear'—to the copy-girl
who is eyeing me with muted scorn—'that will be all.'

I pick up funds from the front desk, cram a change of clothing into
an overnight bag and fly out across the salt-pans to the walled city.
That is exactly the feeling conveyed by larger inland towns—walled.
Walled by nothing. Nothing is plain and claypan and dried river beds
and thousands of square miles of quietly starving sheep and cattle.
I stare down at a landscape that mirrors my own. Geminate. Flatness.
Dust. The scrubby townships between the coast and my destination lie
gasping for momentousness. It never comes.

I interview eight miners, a foreman, one manager and six strikers'
wives. One of the strikers' wives is a deviationist and inclined to

whimper a little, but mostly she is eaten up with hostility. 'The wages are good,' she says looking round a kitchen packed with electric devices. A deep freeze hums away, the air-conditioning unit keeps itself busy. 'The men drive me crazy with their constant bickering demands. They're like small boys.'

'But surely,' I suggest as mildly as I can, fearing her resentment might explode into rage, 'it's a demanding job. And in this climate. A really unpleasant job.'

Her face takes on a look of total intransigence, an obdurate jaw thrust out above her teacup. 'They know what it's all about before they go in. They don't have to do it. We had a great little mixed goods business going down south before he upped and tossed it in for the money. The money's better, he said. None of this damn clerical work, he said. Just do the job and take the pay. We'll be able to save twice as much. He said. God, they hit the pubs each day and drink half their wages. It's the nature of the town, they say. It's the climate, they say. There's always something. They say.'

I am seduced by the rhythms of her plaint. There's a bardic quality at work.

'You can quote me,' she says. 'But don't use my name. He'll change my face around if you do.'

So there's a species of social union mafia at work all over the country.

Also I interview, just for the record, three stockmen, four graziers, and two graziers' wives. The wives are the most interesting. At least one of them is, a big butch redhead with granite features, a foul tongue and a giant belly laugh. I like her immediately.

'Over here, dear,' she ordered, edging me away from the luncheon room set up in one of the town stockyard sheds. 'I don't want the others to bloody hear.'

Hear what? I am one throbbing ear!

'Don't believe all the guff they've just given you.' (It is a Country Women's Association meeting.) She is dragging on a cigarette and blowing smoke like Etna. 'There's no nobility of service. It's all bloody hard yacker. Got that? Day after dreary bloody mindless day cooking for the hands, helping with the drenching, feeding the work dogs, coping with a dying vegetable garden, driving in for stores, washing endless work clothes. Somewhere later on I make a pass at the floors, or flick a duster. It's a cultural desert. *The* cultural desert. I don't ever want to hear another word about calving, castrating or cattle-ticks again as long as I live. I'm tired of watching the sky for a change of weather. Our youngest was five before he saw rain. Poor little bugger ran inside screaming. Didn't know what was bloody happening. I don't want to talk about it any more. I don't aim to produce the highest sponge known to man or the lightest scones or the crispest brownies. I want to sink into a bubble bath with a good book and maybe submerge. Okay?' She tapped a long sausage of ash from the end of her cigarette and sucked greedily again. 'And on the other hand I don't want to be useless and feminine and by Jesus that's a bloody great myth. The women are the hardest workers of all out here. Take it from me.' I took it. 'From sun-up to sundown and then some. Believe me.' I believed her. 'I just want to do nothing for a change. And listen, I don't mind if you print all that. Just don't give it a name, eh? The great beef baron would have my hide strung up on a barn door.'

I fly back, my report nicely typed up. The depressed cattle market seems to swamp the miners' strike. I head my article 'The Price of Silence', slip it on Baxter's desk and get ready for the children to arrive.

Surprisingly Baxter says, 'Great stuff! Now that's more like it. Gutsy.' He looks at me closely. 'So you got rid of the giglamps. See your eyes now. *Very* pretty.' He leers. On the strength of his pleasure I ask for an extra day off to coincide with the kids' long weekend.

*   *   *

I come from a long line of wife leavers. Great grandpa. Grandpa.

My maternal forebears lived in a world of women.

Great-grandpa returned from France at the end of the First World War, cuddled Great-grandma and Grandma who was then two and left home that morning with only the clothes he was wearing and his deferred pay crammed into his pocket. Great-grandma smiled wryly, took up nursing again and resolutely refused to hunt down her missing spouse. She nursed her hurt and indignation, keeping it quietly on simmer, indoctrinating Grandma against men with the inevitable result that Grandma, an excessively pretty woman, cut a swathe through the next generation of young men our government was sending to be slaughtered in New Guinea and married one of them a week before he was due to embark. Great-grandma sobbed loudly all through the wedding, embarrassing everybody. Nine months later Mother was born. Grandma's first words to the attendant nurse were: 'Not another poor wretch of a female. God help her.' Grandma's delphic proclamations were not wrong. Grandpa returned from New Guinea but not to the family home. He wrote from Melbourne. *Dear Muriel, I'm afraid this may cause you some distress. I feel I married too young and am not yet ready for the responsibility of raising a family. All the best.*

My own father (Mother married twice) dispensed with writing. He was seen boarding the *Sunlander*, friends told Mother who was receiving post-natal care at a Brisbane clinic after a complicated delivery. Other friends told her later that he had gone to Darwin and dropped out. There was a lot of dropping out then. Reports came in from time to time: he was working the prawn boats off Karumba; he was running a charter boat from Broome. He was ... 'When I thought about it,' Mother said, 'I realised how pointless the whole thing would have been.' We stayed with Grandma for some years while Mother put herself through university and teachers college. By the time I was seven Mother had remarried, this time to a radiologist who was wealthy, loyal and dull. They began a new family and later boarding school solved the problems of a mixed brood and honed our independence glands to a very fine point.

At school I met Flora who was a casualty of marriage and fed me highly decorated neglect stories that remained unproven.

I digress. But I feel I must point out that the two of us were oddballs in a school so notorious for its jingoism—England, my England! the flag!—we must have been a burden. The headmistress, Flora swore, was such a regophile she counted corgis to get to sleep. Sometimes the change that overtook Flora leaves me entirely baffled. In her favour I must admit she reads no alleged women's magazines and is not constantly revivifying the old farmhouse. The five of them, Hamilton, Flora, Hengist, Horsa and Chubbsie live in a kind of organised squalor from which they emerge happy, well-adjusted and good-natured. Flora ignores the legislation changes of couturier queens and appears most frequently in oversize pants discarded by her husband, held up by the bowyang of a knotted tie. She favours his old workshirts that flap around her and emphasise the fragility of her body. She looks stunning.

Perhaps I went wrong with yellowing collections of egg-stained recipes and ikebana, constant repaints of living-room walls, reorganised furniture that still looked dreary and kids' rooms refurbished for rites of passage. Oh those rites of passage! All endured while Clifford whored around, was spotted lunching here and there with this nubile blonde or that; while he brought them home for working suppers, careful to prefix their name with 'Miss' across our dinner table; while he vanished for whole weekends and often weeks to conferences at all the most seductive beach resorts from here to Byron Bay. Like a politician, really. I laugh like a drain every time tax-payers fork out for a party conference in the far north at the peak of the winter season!

Who do they think they're kidding, huh? Who?

And who does Clifford think he's kidding?

*   *   *

Will I kidnap them? Will I refuse to return them, as Clifford insists, on the late Sunday afternoon plane?

I am waiting at the terminal building, stuffing myself with nervous coffees, conscious of the poverty of my apartment, the bedrooms lacking posters, tapedecks, expensive gadgets that are the ransom demanded by the young. Blood ties went out the window with the me generation.

They are in for a surprise. I have planned taking them next morning by plane to Charco where a hired campervan awaits, and driving them north to sample the maturing influences of Bukki Beach. Sister Tancred, warned by letter a week ago, has assured me of welcome. I am taking as many books, paint-boxes and bundles of modelling clay as I can lug onto the plane.

Will my over-indulged children resent this or will they regard the whole thing as a freak-out?

*   *   *

Everyone is bedded down, including me. They have inspected the flat, Daniel's and Etta's lips compressed over mother's penury. They have

eaten hugely at the best restaurant I can afford. They have twitched
dials on my rented television set and pronounced they are bored. We
have discussed school and father and Kirky and father and father and
me. They looked at me with a tired despair.

'Dad won't change,' Daniel said like an aged analyst. 'There's no
point really in trying to make it work. He's an utterly selfish man.'

(How old are you, Daniel? Fifteen? Fifty?)

'Agreed.' Etta is running languid fingers through a mane of incred-
ibly bouffant hair. She is not as good-looking as her brother and
already is developing a forceful jaw passed on to her by her grandmother. 'It would simply make things worse. Timothy sees this.'

'Do you, Timothy?' I ask diffidently.

Timothy has been quietly playing himself chess in a corner of the
living-room. 'What?' he asks. 'I'm busy.'

Etta repeats her proposition, edging him towards an affirmative
with a transparency that is unnerving. Timothy puts down his black
knight and looks over at me. There is still the small boy under that
humid sweaty thatch. For a moment our eyes lock. He ignores Etta
and Daniel.

'I'd like you back, Mum,' he says.

In seconds we are scooped up in each other's arms while he blubbers
a little and Etta and Daniel turn their sophisticated older profiles
away. Surprisingly Etta volunteers to make cocoa.

'Me too, me too,' I am sobbing when Timothy straightens up in my
arms, wriggles away from me and says, 'But it's okay. I'll come up every
weekend. I'd still like to go to boarding school. Dad's such a nong.'

I know this is the moment for reproof—never malign the other
parent to a child and again never et cetera et cetera—but it is so funny
and I say, after we have all giggled guiltily, 'Well, I don't know about
every weekend, Tim. It's so expensive. But maybe every two or three,
hey? How would that be?' And he says 'Great!' and goes back to his
chess as if this moment of maternal trauma has been the merest wind-
whiffle on an otherwise bland sea.

*   *   *

When we head out to the airport first thing in the morning they are
stunned. I haven't told them anything. 'It's a surprise,' I say. 'Hang
in there.'

'We're not going back already?' Daniel asks resentfully.

And I reassure them that no, we are going farther north.

The constant passage of money soothes their worry glands. Cash flow reassures the young. Waiting for the plane they wolf down cokes and packets of crisps. They blackmail me for bags of unhealthy sweets. 'It's barely a twenty-minute run,' I tell them. They look at me with wise eyes. The feeder plane to Charco takes longer but when we get off at the airstrip the campervan is waiting. I cannot believe things have gone so smoothly. The kids glare while I sign papers and pass over more wads of notes.

'Roughing it!' Daniel complains, wrenching open the campervan door and peering in at the minuscule kitchen, the bunks, the fold-out table. It is a luxury job. There is a small battery operated television. 'Cosy cosy,' Etta comments enigmatically. I can hear Timothy bouncing on the upper bunk. 'I like it, I like it,' he is yelling. The woman at the car rent desk and I roll eyes at each other in that Esperanto of female exchange. She knows the score. I see the deep groove her wedding ring has cut and she sees me seeing. The ring is missing. 'Hang in there,' she says. And tears prick behind my eyelids.

＊　　＊　　＊

I cannot believe this. The children have actually been enjoying themselves. It is late in the afternoon and they are sleepy, inclined to lounge un-seat-belted on their bunks. Charco had been snoozing in heat when we drove away from the airport, heading into the small township, along Charlotte Street and up Grassy Hill. I did a tour guide spiel for them, pointing out the spot, the very spot, where Cook had fothered the *Endeavour*. I suggested they imagine the township without houses, motels, shops. Across on the northern bank of the estuary mangroves sulked in the afternoon sweat. Behind us locusts screeched unendingly. Somewhere in the streets below a dog yelped once. By the wharf and the old powder station two fishing boats slid in with their engines cut.

Enough. This was terror Australis, the fear of those unending spaces, the wild unenclosures. I found myself shuddering.

We stopped for lunch outside Charco, pulling into a side track near the Kennedy River and grilled sausages on the campervan's barbecue. 'Where are we stopping tonight?' they kept demanding singly and

together. They had drawn closer to each other. Etta's arm was round
Timothy. Daniel had taken Timothy's free hand and was swinging it
to and fro in big brotherly fashion.

'With friends.'

'Up here?'

'Even farther up here.'

'Who?'

'You'll see.'

'We mightn't like them.' Timothy.

'They mightn't like you, stupe.' Daniel.

'They will love you. I love you. They'll love whoever I love.'

We drove on and Etta started us off singing all those foolish and
unforgotten childhood numbers that create the songlines of family
tribes. We yelled rounds. We screamed choruses. Daniel had forgotten
he wanted headbangers on the van tapedeck.

The drive was taking longer than I bargained as the awkwardness of
the camper pitted itself against the gravel of the road. The sun had long
dropped behind us by the time we reached the Bukki Beach turnoff.
One last bloody surge of light and then darkness thick as felt blotting
out landscape and sky. The children slept behind, breathing gently,
giving little murmurs as they pursued dreams. I felt happier than I had
for a year. I feel happier. I am unexpectedly me once more, enrolled as
mother, needed, the tigress protector behind the steering wheel.

The rainforest glitters in the van headlamps, towers, a tunnel of
flashy green into which we plunge, each leaf trapped in the car blaze
delivering itself simply to the flick-flack second as we eat up the last
ten miles or so. I listen to my children sleeping and I urge the van
forward to the lights of my home. To the lights. To the lights.

*   *   *

As we drive in past the car-illuminated tumbledowns of tin and plastic
I am glad I cannot see the kids' faces. Behind me I hear Etta gasp, 'But
this isn't . . .' and sense her nudged into silence by her elder brother. Then
the headlights pick out a sprawl of purple, the white sidewalls and
verandas of the convent, the massed beds of hibiscus and croton clumped
along the far side of the building and I draw into the space where the
nuns' park their own van, switch off the ignition and turn round.

'We're here.' And before they can even voice one comment, Tancred, Aloysius and Luke are clustering at the van door and the children are enveloped in such smiles, such warmth, so many questions about themselves, they don't have time for pouting lower lips, for complaint. They are dazzled by a blaze of welcome and a graciousness of spirit that over-ride surroundings.

The sisters have created high supper. The little sitting-room table is decorated with allamanda. There are bowls of freshwater prawns Billy Thursday nets along the creeks. There are baked bananas and slices of mango drowning in coconut milk. There are freshly baked bread rolls and a jug filled with soursop.

'We've gone native,' Sister Tancred says, her glance moving from dish to dish. 'We thought the children might like to try some very local food.'

'It looks wonderful,' Etta says. She is attempting enthusiasm, pinned in to her best behaviour, but her eyes are curious. I can tell she is alerted by these three women in their simple habit, the cross shining on their breasts, their cosmetic-free faces young-old beneath the calm of years of other-interest.

Afterwards I unload my offerings from the van. They are delighted with everything. Luke exclaims over the books I have brought for her classroom, the boxes of poster paint, the stacks of paper. While I am talking with her my spy ear is cocked to Tancred explaining their work in the settlement, the hospital, the clinic. Aloysius sits listening, her face half in shadow as Tancred bends her smile on the three upturned faces.

'They are very poor,' she is saying. 'They have very little. When you visit them tomorrow, and I know you will want to talk to the children, you must be very careful not to stare too hard. You understand?' I take time off from Sister Luke's delight to observe my three children nod solemnly. It is as if they are mesmerised by the slow deliberate voice, the sweetness of the smile. 'You might have glimpsed their houses as you came in. They aren't like yours, are they? You have only to turn a tap and you get water. You have lovely beds and kitchens. You have radios and television and lots of beautiful clothes. Haven't you?' The children nod again. It is the gentlest of bullyings. 'And you realise how fortunate you are, I'm sure. So you must not do anything at all that shows you are aware of what they haven't got.'

She pauses. 'Of course, Sister,' Daniel says with adult poise. 'Of course. We understand.'

Etta is nodding vigorously. 'Of course we won't.' It is as if they have ripened ten years since the pep talk began.

Timothy says, 'When we get back we'll get the kids at school to take up a collection for them. All the classes have to have a charity, you see. They can be ours.'

'Not charity, dear,' Sister Tancred says very gently. 'Maybe love is a better word, eh? Something to love.' She puts out a hand and rumples Timothy's fair thatch for the smallest moment. 'That would be a wonderful thing to do.' She turns to me and conquers them in one sentence. 'What grown-up children you have, Julie. What a lucky woman.'

* * *

Lucky! The word clipped past the kids but it hung over me with the scaly horror of a snake.

Within the next few months Clifford will formalise his relationship with Saint Kierkegaard. Flora has assured me the rumours are true. It is a celebratory gesture to mark the end of his assault on Hummock Island where, I hear, his resort is complete and throbbing.

I lie on my bunk in the van sleepless, hearing Bodil say, *Är det gott? Är det?* And my mono-non-bilingual husband groans, *Gott! Gott!*

Skulle ni vilja ha lite mera? Saint Kierkegaard asks in the steamy dark. And she is forced to translate for him in his ecstatic moaning, Would you like some more? And he can only cry, *Gott! Gott!*

Ja. Var snäll, Kirky murmurs reprovingly. *Please.*

That wonderful accent, vestigial in private but heavily affected for the crowd. What a come on! *Ja tack. Ja tack.*

I creep out of my bunk and go to the doorway of the van. Palms creak and behind me the children mutter in their sleep. There is no other sound. I go back and fumble in my case for a sleeping pill, hedge my bets, swallow two and eventually, eventually, pass out of imagined erotic stage sets into dream ones where Bodil Kierkegaard asks me my name over and over. *Vad heter ni? Vad heter ni?* Her voice is tinged with arrogance. There is irony everywhere like fog. *Ursäkta,* she says. Excuse me. *Förlåt att jag stör er.* I am sorry to disturb you.

But nothing disturbs the new day cracking its shell, emerging green-fresh, wind-cleaned. The kids stuff themselves with bacon and eggs and pester to go down on the beach.

'Soon,' I tell them.

Timothy bursts through my dream and leaves it around me in musty shards.

'Snart,' he says, sucking on an orange.

'What's that?'

'Swedish for soon. *Så snart som möjligt,*' he says approximating Kirky's voice.

'Don't spoil my day,' I mumble. 'Don't.'

No one hears me. No one has ever heard me. The only time Doctor Glasnost, my Brisbane shrink, heard me, was when I told him he had a dirty shirt.

Sister Aloysius shows the children round the hospital and the school. Tillie Thursday and Glory Fourmile have long gone home and now there is an old man with tropical ulcers, a small boy recovering from an appendectomy and in a screened corner of the room, little Jeannie Thursday, Billy's youngest sister, suffering from measles. Sister Tancred bustles out of the clinic to check on my own children. 'Measles can be a real killer with Aborigines,' she says softly. 'We have to take every care. If you want to say hello, don't go too close. I want to keep her infection from the rest of the community if I can. Though I think by the time we realised what was the matter it was too late.'

Jeannie's face is a muddy ash colour from which her eyes, lit with fever, stare away from us. She lies listlessly, curls damp on the pillow.

'Jeannie,' Sister Tancred says bending over. 'Jeannie, I've brought back your friend.' Carefully she eases the little girl up and helps her sip water. For half a moment Jeannie looks blankly at me then her face splits into a smile. 'I got measles,' she says.

'I know,' I say. 'I saw you catching *wirul*. I've got something for you.' Etta is toting a bag with a collection of jointed dolls that squeak, gurgle or grunt on pressure. She says, 'Hello, Jeannie' and produces a fat rubber clown from the bag. 'Look. See how this works.' She is starting to sound like the totally trustworthy headgirl.

She squeezes the doll and its arms waggle up. She squeezes again and they flop. Yet another press and a bumpkin snigger emerges from the grinning red lips. 'See. It's a clown.' Jeannie keeps her tiny hands in knotted fists, sliding back into the shelter of the bedsheets, her eyes closed tight. Sister Tancred smiles ruefully at both of us. 'Give her time, Etta. It's frightened her. You see, she hasn't seen anything like that before. When you go, then we'll see. Just leave the doll there where she can reach it.'

Outside the day is a juicy fruit, warm, dripping with frangipani and an overlying tang of salt. Tancred steers us towards the settlement's heart, waving, calling greetings, stopping to exchange words with the old people sitting in the sandy road outside their shelters. The children are playing it very cool, with fixed smiles, eyes swerving from the rotting timber, the loose sheets of galvanised iron propped up teepee fashion to form a room. 'We've nearly finished the amenities block,' Tancred is saying, pointing proudly to a concrete block structure at the end of the main track, half concealed by pisonias. 'Mother house relented. They sent a formidable cheque and the place has been crazy with cement mixers and plumbers up from Charco. We've developed two little teams of the younger people to keep it in order. They're growing flowers outside, masses of impatiens, see?'

Their next project, she tells us, will be a meeting hall, something comfortable and functional, where they can hold talks, something to be proud of. Barrages of letters have forced a quasi promise of government aid.

Tancred is ushering the children busily ahead and I cannot help noting how their eyes widen at the heaps of rusty tin, the doors hanging by one hinge, the glassless windows. They are silent, too silent, and I feel more for them than for the inhabitants. My children are catching their first real glimpse of third world living in the lucky country. Timothy runs back and takes my hand. 'Why are they poor?' he whispers. I bend down. 'Because we took everything from them. That's why.' He presses his lips tight and walks steadfastly ahead, clutching my fingers. 'I'm calling on Tommy and Mella,' Tancred announces over her shoulder and leads us off down a side track towards the beach where, beneath chaotic undergrowth, leans a half shed, a three-walled structure inviting the sea in. A grove of black bean trees dangles its foliage onto the rusting roof. The ground is littered with empty pods, the seeds scattered, the pods like toy canoes. An old man is working at the front of the shed mending a broken chair, hammering a leg back, using a log as bench. Beyond him under the comb trees, a woman is hanging washing on a line strung between branches.

Sister Tancred calls gaily, 'Tommy! Tommy! May we visit?'

Tommy is a thickset man, stooped now, his hair almost white. He must be sixty or more, a good age for an Aborigine for their life span is so much less than those of the whites. He puts down his hammer and comes over to us with a smile and I see his features are thickened by the ravages of Hansen's disease. 'Mella!' he calls. 'Sister.' And she comes back through the comb trees, tentative because of strangers, smiling at Tancred, her eyes swerving from the children and me. There are the same tell-tale thickenings on her features.

Tancred introduces us slowly, carefully, one by one.

'Mella and Tommy both came up from Palm fourteen years ago, isn't that so?'

'And before that, Fantome,' Tommy says.

'Tommy,' Sister Tancred says, turning to the children, 'does the most beautiful carvings. I wonder if he might show you some. Would you like that?'

The children are all tense smile and culture shock. Flora's brood could do with a dose of this too, I think. From where we stand outside the shack its interior is pitifully exposed in its emptiness: a table, one other chair, and along the back wall a bench and some shelves with a few groceries, a spirit lamp, a dish for washing and a kettle. On the floor against a side wall is a length of foam mattress and two uncovered pillows, grey now, and flattened from overuse, dark shadows holding the imprint of their heads like a personal history, another version of the Turin shroud, I think, not intending blasphemy.

Tommy's workbench stands under one of the comb trees whose great buttressed bole makes a natural shelter from the sea wind. There are various lengths and chunks of wood. 'Black bean,' he explains. At the far end of the bench are a group of small heads, not rough hewn as I expected, but finely detailed, the wood oiled on some, on others smoothly sanded and worked out of the yellow sapwood. There are faces I know.

'Why!' Etta cries, picking one small carving up. 'It's you, Sister

Tancred. Oh, it's so good!' She holds the tiny carving up to the sun which strikes at the lines of amusement about the steady unblinking gaze of the hollowed orbs, the crinkle at mouth corner. 'And there's Sister Aloysius!' Daniel is working his way along the bench, picking up, putting down. There are a number of whole figures, children playing, their limbs trapped for ever in attitudes more vigorous, more human, than Keats ever dreamed of. A boy about to plunge into space, the twentieth century, the world, from the tip of a rock. 'That's the one,' Daniel says. 'Oh that's the one I love.'

The moment is too fragile to ask if Tommy sells his carvings. Sister Tancred tells me that now and then when he goes to Charco he takes some down and sells them to one of the tourist shops. 'They cheat him, of course. They never give him what they're worth.' Tommy is showing the children his carving knives and whet stone. He tells how he burns out excess wood, how he smooths the pieces, using the coral sand from the beach and rubbing, rubbing. His palms are worn smooth on the inside, the palest beige silk.

'How long does each take?' I ask.

'Depends,' old Tommy says. 'Coupla days, some. Coupla weeks, others. Depends.'

He sucks at a small cut on his thumb, then points to one of the seashore trees, a spreader with great clumpings of leaves along the branches, small fruit dangling, fruit with a soft fleshy outer case and a small hole at the apex. 'Them leaves,' he says and he walks over and grabs a fistful and rubs one of them on the cut. 'Them leaves we put on sores.'

'What's it called?' Daniel is crackling a leaf, sniffing. 'I'll take a bundle back for matron and the football coach.'

'Island people, they call that *napiripiri*. My father, he come Santo long time now, up Big Bay. He tell me. He come trawler, marry girl from Yarrabah.'

Sister Tancred puts out a hand and rests it gently on Tommy's own. 'You come up to the clinic later and I'll give you some other medicine as well. Nearly as good as your medicine, Tommy.' Gravely she thanks him for showing us his carvings. Mella comes out from the shack and offers tea, shyly, anxious to give.

How refuse? Perhaps Tancred senses my caution for she says to me,

'You run along now, Julie. Sister Aloysius was expecting the children back ten minutes ago. She has something for them. You hurry along now. I'll stay for a little with my friends.'

And she puts her arms around the old woman and kisses each diseased cheek in turn.

* * *

Ashamed of my die-hard reactions to the legends of leprosy. Ashamed. I excuse myself on the grounds of concern for the children. They question me as we walk back along the beach, wondering at Tancred's sprightly dismissal. I try to explain as simply as I can, as unemotionally. 'But they're better now,' Daniel argues. 'I've read up about that stuff. Anyway, Sister Aloysius told me they're all cured here. It's just the disease has left a mark.'

Like marriage, I want to say. Like children. Like living.

We are driving back that afternoon and even the kids are sorry to leave what I am now coming to regard as a personal funkhole from the world's weather. A flurry of hugs and kisses before we drive out. Sister Luke organises a little honour guard of school children to wave goodbye. The drive back to Charco uncoils twice as long but just before I return the children to their father by plane from Townsville they assure me it has been the best holiday ever.

Daniel had even taken me to one side for a son-to-mother talk.

'I think it's better this way,' he said, looking far graver than his years. The darling thing was spattered with the beginnings of pimple and fuzz. It just about broke my heart. 'I mean you and Dad. We all know it was impossible. Impossible for you. Dad's a real slag when it comes to women. We've known that for years. And we don't blame you.'

'I want you all to move up with me, though.'

'No, Mum,' Daniel said. 'We do like boarding school. We don't mind old Kirky. But we have the holidays to see you. Anyway the Family Court says we can't.'

'Bloody Family Court. I wonder how Clifford pulled that one.'

'It was a lady judge,' Daniel said smiling with what could only be compassion. 'I guess he laid her.'

We giggled together. And as we giggled I knew I still had them.

'But Timothy. He's so young.'

'Timothy's doing great. He's like you say. Eight going on eighty. He's top of his class and revoltingly superior. He's okay.'

They leave me, mouths crammed with gob-stoppers. So was my own.

* * *

Outside my half house it is raining unseasonally. Real rain. None of that half-hearted drizzle of the south. The rain pounds like faucets opened by a free hand, banging on iron and leaves, cutting its name into the dust, scouring gutters and hill runnels. When it clears everything will return to that unnatural blue. I remain blue all the while. For once, my future stares me bleakly in the face. Here I am, squatting not far from the equator, one failed marriage on my gun handle, three children living away from me, an ill-paid job and no prospects.

Well, there are prospects of a meretricious kind.

Two days ago sitting at my office desk I received a fax from Baxter who works only thirty feet away. He does this as a whimsical comment on late twentieth-century technology. This time the fax reads: Will you marry me you moron or will we live in sin?

I fax back immediately: I have desired to go where springs not fail etc etc. Baxter replies within the minute: Don't give me that Gerard Manley Hopkins bullshit. Answer the question.

I fax back: I can't Baxter. I can't.

'Can't what?' he says poking his head around my door.

'Answer the question.'

'You're fired,' he says.

I begin packing my things immediately and head for the door but he comes after me, stinking of Scotch, needing a shave, his eyes leery.

'Look,' he says. 'I didn't mean that. Take the morning off. I'll handle this garbage.'

We give each other sad lop-sided smiles and I head down the mall to a slum hole-in-the-wall that is still called The River Rose Café and sit there drinking pot after pot of tea and watching the weather change.

There is nothing more drab, I suppose, than having a privileged middle-class background. We wanted for nothing. Now I have it. Nothing. Flora was my one adventurous leap into the sort of bohemianism Brisbane provided in the seventies. I sit on and on, wanting to vomit by this stage and staring at the pay phone near the doorway. I need advice. Not about Baxter. My mind has become the half moon curve of Bukki Bay and festers with notions of service. Eventually I get a handful of change from the girl behind the counter and dial. Flora answers from the depths of midday torpor. There is no news here, she tells me, except that Clifford is reverting to form after a few brief months. Saint Kierkegaard now comes and complains to her.

So what is new?

'I have received an offensive proposal of marriage,' I tell her.

'Don't take it.'

'Why not?'

'You'd have to be crazy.'

I ponder this while the cents tick over. Admissions are forced out of me.

I tell her about the mission at Bukki Bay. She already knows, thanks to the children's fast telegraph and bursts into peals of unbelieving laughter.

'The old missionary urge,' she gurgles over three hundred miles of wire. 'That old chestnut.' I discover unburied fragments of my former brittle pal here, the mini-skirted jezebel who set up her beat in George Street. Hi Flora! Howya doin'? Her tenacious voice digs at my enfeebled spirit that requires transfusions of grace. 'What's up with you?' she demands. But I run out of coins and Flora and her dogmatism are cut off—for ever, I want to say—but know it is only breathing space.

That night (Baxter had left the office on my return and taken his own time off with the hissed words: 'The offer still stands!' as I tottered in in four o'clock heat), I sit hours after supper asking myself whether it would be better for the children were I to accept that offer. Baxter is peripheral. After all, they would have two married parents instead of one wed and another neurotic single. Now I don't believe I'm neurotic but it's a popular misconception of male psychiatrists. Freud, you have a heap to answer for! The original male chauvinist *schwein*! In a world where most infringements of the law are perpetrated by males, why is it the world has to have male judiciaries, synods, colleges of cardinals, all rocking in prejudicial rhythm? I begin to hum 'Rockin' in Rhythm'. It doesn't help. The female hasn't a hope with all this hunk stuff confronting her. They set the rules. We don't get a say, not even on matters that concern us most closely. Oh this tired old stuff, I think, heading inside to reheat the coffee. It's been *thought* by the lesser half for centuries and *uttered* for the last fifty years and the status quo hangs in there. A world run by dickheads, dick being the operative word.

I cannot consult with the children. It is now too late for one thing.

I ring my mother.

'Darling,' she says from a clear eight hundred miles distance, 'I was just thinking of you.'

I outline possibilities.

'You'd be a fool to remarry,' she says. 'And that is my last word on the matter.'

'But the other thing? Working at Bukki? Giving a hand? At least it's a contribution.'

'Would it satisfy you?'

'I believe it would.'

'Money?' demands ever practical mother. 'Your father won't help with anything he regards as harebrained. You know that.'

'I suppose I could go on the dole. After all there isn't much call for journalists in the wilds of the Cape.'

'But would it be enough? There'll be times when you want to fly down to see the children. Birthdays.'

'I know. That worries me.'

'You know I'll help as much as I can, don't you, whatever you decide, even if it's remarriage though you won't have my blessing.'

The blessing is the only thing I want.

Clifford has always been a kind of successful bumbler. I think he regarded the world as a cosmic jumble sale through which he might pick up the most incredible bargains. He's always been like that. I hear Hummock Island is booming. Any moment he will be looking for more coastline to despoil. Weekends in the early days of marriage used to be spent with Clifford scanning the trading post sections of national and local papers. 'How about this?' he would cry. 'Brain surgeon's kit, as new. Only used once.' I swear it is true. 'Or this? Ten thousand unused decals from the Melbourne Games?' I *mean*!

His madcappery was suckled by a clutch of buddies who always managed to side-step regulations including one who connected his house to the water mains by hiring a trench digger and cutting a private pipeline through at night four miles to the main coastal highway. When we visited one weekend I was stunned to see sprinklers in full play over his lawns in Handelian arpeggios of water. 'You're on town water now,' I marvelled scanning other drought-shrunken gardens around us. 'That's so,' he agreed. 'But God, you're miles from the pipeline!' I said. 'Don't tell me they ran it in just for you.' 'Right,' he said. 'I connected up myself. Have another beer, Julie. Have you tried this czabai? Great stuff.' 'Don't be such a noser, Julie,' Clifford reproved, frowning at me. 'Don't needle the man.' Oh God, the breath-taking impudence! On the way home Clifford was to say, 'Great guy, that! He's taught me a lot.'

Enough. Absolutely enough.

*   *   *

The days melt into each other like some over-chewed lump of caramel, a sticky brown mess of work eat sleep through which Baxter, affronted by rejection, looms juggernaut across my daylight hours, rolling ponderous between the milling crowds but managing to crush only me.

In a moment of weakness Clifford had allowed the children to visit for a long weekend. They were moving away from me. Timothy appeared to have grown another foot, his vocabulary increased by several hundred polysyllabic words. If I hadn't been his mother I might have found him obnoxious. He was losing that small boy perfume of sweat and lollies. Etta had begun to varnish her nails and thought only of boys and clothes. Daniel, trembling on the verge of six feet, had commenced shaving and talked only of sport. My timid suggestion that we revisit Bukki Bay was greeted with languid yawns. True, for a term or so they had maintained their school effort and sent off cheques garnered from the sale of stickjaw, recycled paperbacks and tapes. But after a few months their enthusiasm died and my occasional letters to Tancred, Aloysius and Luke held the feeble appeal of the drowning man clutching at straw replies.

I sit down and try sensibly to review my options, to dig up and expose what I want.

I want the peace I had discovered at Bukki Bay.

Am I using the idea of sacrificial service as a crutch?

Am I getting religion? Nothing explained that agreeable calm embracing those three women as they worked, thanklessly, by the world's standards, in the humid bowl of that northern bay.

I write them a long and perhaps foolish letter outlining my confusion.

There are, Sister Tancred replies in a measured sort of way, *many mission orders around the country who could certainly use a lay worker prepared to give up time helping people like ours. You should be warned: There would be no pay, only your board supplied, yet perhaps the pay would come another way in the satisfaction you would get out of helping those less fortunate than yourself. We could,* she adds, *do with such a one here, but we barely have the money to maintain our mission, living as we do on social security. Our work is largely ignored by the diocese. We have no imprimatur from the church. We are regarded as seceders, a splinter group. We are lucky if some sympathetic priest comes through to say Mass occasionally. And I must admit any evangelism comes after*—she had underlined 'after'—*our compulsion to help the sick and elderly and give what schooling we can to the children. We do not run prayer classes. We don't preach religion. Perhaps that is why our presence here has been ignored by the church. Note the small c.*

I'm feeling bitter today. Recently the Bay's population was increased by another dozen aged who had been turned out from a fringe camp near Charco by over-zealous aldermen. We could use someone, I must admit, at least for the little school or as a nursing aide. But I don't want to influence your decision. Think very carefully about this.

I think.

I think.

I think.

Again I plead with Baxter for a long weekend. He grants it sullenly without even raising his eyes. I fly south to the children, hoping for sane discussion or at least expressions of interest. I'm even prepared to discuss my next move with Clifford.

Clifford, Bodil Kierkegaard tells me, is busy at his resort on Hummock Island. 'His secretary he has taken,' Bodil announces with an interested glance into the deeps of my eyes. 'I do not know her name.'

'Mimsie?' I suggest.

'No. She is long gone.' She smiles at the memory. 'Another name. Too boring to remember.'

She has the right attitude.

'He will be back this evening. The children too. Have dinner with us.' Bodil can afford to be generous.

'After,' I say. 'I'll come after. Mustn't frighten the horses.'

'*Ursäkta?*' she says prettily. 'Excuse?'

'Just a phrase. Old English. Don't tell Clifford. I'll just turn up.'

I eat alone in a downmarket greasy spoon. My rapacious motel avoids the ennui of meal-serving. I think briefly of ringing Flora but getting out to see her will involve so much effort I decide against it. Yet while I eat I see one of her twins tooling down the main street on a motorbike, followed seconds later by his brother. To my delight they park outside this terrible eatery and stalk in, helmets dangling from their arms, faces so alike even in late adolescence, I feel I am seeing double. They greet me with bear hugs. Gravy is splashed about. None of us cares. 'Flora will be furious you didn't call,' they admonish. 'We'll run you out now, the moment you've finished whatever it is you're finishing.'

They are gulping milkshakes. Their faces burst outwards with good health and humour. They tell me about Daniel.

'He misses you, you know,' Hengist says. 'Or maybe I shouldn't say that. They all do. But Clifford is a jerk. Sorry, Julie. But he really is. We all know that. Especially Flora.'

'I'll be seeing them later tonight. I'm just giving Saint Kierkegaard time to serve up one of her cordon bleus and then I'll drop in for a civilised coffee.'

'Can you ride pillion?' Horsa asks.

'Never done it.'

'There's always a first time,' Horsa says. 'My bike or his?'

We have tottered into the twilight. I feel ill from badly cooked steak and onions. I wonder at the wisdom of riding pillion and roaring out of town my arms clutching Horsa's waist. I point out that I have no helmet.

'That's cool,' Horsa says. 'Take mine.'

'But you'll be fined.'

'Tough.' Hengist helps the old girl hitch her leg across the saddle, checks the buckle on my helmet and in a moment Horsa has kicked the motor alive and we ride off to the farm at a sedate speed, Hengist following closely.

'To pick up the pieces,' he had warned me.

Flora was all delight, all gladness she.

She was also, considering her juvenescent pranks, all righteousness.

Despite the occasional accusing look, the tightened lips, she felt for me, I was certain. Hamilton sat quietly listening, sheltered by an avocado boom, confident in his bank account, his wife, his children, his bowels.

'It's you we're worried about,' Flora kept insisting. 'You. Hamilton and I feel you are wandering lost out there, cut off from your kids, cut off from your old friends, ready to do the first crazy thing you think of. How can you stand it Julie? We worry.'

Hamilton looked as if he never worried about a thing. His glass of Riesling rested on a heap of *The Farmers Guide*. Beyond the house the acres and acres of Fuerte, Sharwil, Hass and Nabel stretched under the moon behind their barriers of bana grass. The air was fragrant with their growth and near me, through the window open on the side lawn, spilled the scent of lemons. Fruitfulness. That was what Flora had achieved. I uttered the phrase and Flora bounced forward in her chair, tipping Riesling on the coffee table.

'That's it, isn't it?' She appealed to her mildly smiling husband. From the twins' room came the muted racket of a stereo spewing heavy metal. 'It's what we all want.' I appeared to have capped further comment with a wry smirk of havingness.

'I think I've found what I want.'

They waited.

'It's a long story,' I began. 'It started last year just after I moved away.'

Flora refused to prompt. I staggered on with it—there was no Scheherazade principle—with Tancred and Aloysius and Luke and the gentle face of Tillie Thursday.

Silence met my finale, my stammered admission of wanting to live there, to finding a purpose.

'Still the missionary bug,' Flora said. 'Come rather late, though. We all went through that at fourteen just before boys. Well, didn't we?'

'I didn't.'

'Then you're a late developer, Julie. Very late. I think it might be madness. Have you discussed it with the kids?'

'That's what I've come down to do.'

'They won't like it, you know.'

'How do you know? I don't think they'll even care. How can you be so sure?'

'Well, the older two mightn't mind. They'll just think you're crazy. But Timothy will be harder to convince.'

'But he hardly sees me now. It's not as if I'm taking vows for God's sake. I simply want to help in a lay capacity. I'll be able to get away and visit the kids as often as I do now.'

Flora looked thoughtful. Hamilton had resumed reading *The Farmers Guide*. 'I suppose,' she conceded doubtfully. 'Maybe you should just do it and not tell them till it's a *fait accompli*. Give it a try for a few months. It's the money that's the problem. Or the lack of it.'

I think about this as Flora drives me back to my once house and drops me in the night shadow splodge of the poinciana trees.

'Look, I do understand,' she says. 'I do. I do. Clifford ...' and she drops her voice to a whisper, 'always makes me think of a bullock gone mad. He's not Muslim by any chance? He goes on like those crazed guys I'm always seeing on the telly.' And she begins to giggle.

'He's one of nature's Muslims.' I giggle back.

Fortified I re-enter the lights of home.

*   *   *

So long, Baxter. So long, Townsville.

I'm at Bukki Bay, have been for three months, establishing a rhythm of work that takes in nursing at the hospital, home visits to the elderly sick and helping Sister Luke with the older children. I find myself beset by my own plans for the next day and the next and the next. Sometimes, standing on the water-munched sands of the bay in late afternoon I am riven by nostalgia. Why is it that our most emotional high spots concern what is long past or about to come? Is it never possible to trickle tears for the now?

Early days project on the screen of my mind with the clarity of vistavision and songlines so float through my skull which is beautifully voided of Clifford, that colonic money filter, that I am new-peeled to receive other imprints. My mind skitters off in half a dozen arcs of

memory at one and the same time while the kids' voices call Hello
Miss and feet scamper back towards the settlement and I embrace a
wholeness of being never known before. Skinned to receive.

Last week Sister Luke broke an ankle while painting the hospital
ceiling. She fell from a step-ladder and though Tancred re-set the ankle
and encased it in plaster, she is reduced to a crutch-aided hobble.
I have never been busier but the busyness seems constructive. Oh,
I was busy when my own children were small but after Clifford sent
them to their fashionable grammar school, life became a pointless
round of canteen duty and open day cookaways.

Once a month they spare me for a hitched ride to Cairns and
Clifford magnanimously organises the kids' plane fares there. I have
two nights of hotel aridity with them trundling to fast food outlets,
rainforest displays, crocodile parks, butterfly farms. The older ones
manifest boredom. Timothy lusts after his computer. 'That's cool,
Mum,' they say. 'That's a gas. Stay with it. You're doing great work.
Our mother a welfare guru.'

Shee-it!

Months pass. Clifford, having completed the despoliation of Hummock Island is looking for fresh coast to conquer. One weekend when
I am south entertaining the children, he reconnoitres my secret coastline by launch. He puts in at Bukki Bay, so Tancred tells me later, on
the pretence of finding me. He insisted, she relates, on striding through
the settlement like a mobile colossus, insensitive to the niceties of
trespass.

'A rude man,' she describes him.

I fear for them, for the settlers, for the bay, for me. Our days could
be numbered. I want to warn the sisters that the seductions of
commerce, the soft enticements of progress will come and camp by
their very door. He has, I explain, no moral guilt about Aboriginal
owners, no sensitivity for the preservation of cultures, no sympathy
for the disinherited.

'No one can be as bad as all that,' Sister Aloysius says. 'No one.'

I sit there reproved.

Another month goes by.

I am, I suppose, happier than I have ever been. And sadder. Every
action of the sisters is made with tenderness and it is the tenderness
that reduces me to a knowledge of my own unworthiness. On my

stumbling visionary's journey of emulation I write readers for the pupils in Sister Luke's airy classroom. I make up stories about Bukki Bay. The children illustrate the tiny booklets.

I feel useful. I know I contribute something.

The nuns sing their office three times a day. Their voices still sound young. I do not join them, however, but sit outside under the palm trees listening and slowly, ever so slowly sip tea from a large mug. This is a new and mixed version of bliss.

Into which Clifford irrupts.

He drives in unannounced from the coast track in a four-wheel-drive the size of an army tank, flanked by a local councillor and a State member.

'Well,' he comments, eyeing me in my near Mother Hubbard as I bend over the heads of children painfully writing the words *Bukki Bay is my home.*

There has been no warning, no by-your-leave. I shrink into non-action as Tancred sweeps down from the clinic to investigate his invasion. She is cool, aloof, unhelpful.

I take the children down to the beach for a game with a volley-ball. Half an hour passes. There is the sound of the four-wheel-drive grinding away into the curls of the forest and then Sister Tancred comes striding onto the sand, her face plummy with rage.

'That man!' she gasps. Her face is bloated with words she has probably vowed never to utter. 'That terrible man! I'm sorry, Julie, but was he really your husband?'

She shoos the children away into the quickest half holiday they have ever earned. 'Come back to the house,' she says. 'It is dreadful. Really dreadful. There is something we must all discuss.'

On the way she gathers in Aloysius who is sitting by the bed of a baby with croup. For the moment it is asleep, its breathing irregular and harsh.

'Only for a minute,' Aloysius warns. 'I can't leave Tommy for too long. He's nearly over the worst,' she adds to me. 'But I have to keep him under observation for another day or so.'

With all of us there, formally convened, the sitting-room feels crowded, not by our presence but the threat to us Sister Tancred spills out, her calm destroyed for once.

'The land ...' her arm swings out to indicate bay, forest, protecting hills, 'is being rezoned by council. There are plans already under way to move the settlement farther up the coast.'

She sits as if horrified by what she had just told us. She apologises for the brutality of her announcement, her inability to soften facts. (I bet Clifford didn't soften a thing!)

'But why?' Aloysius asks. 'Why?'

'Development.' Sister Tancred manages to give the word the taste of obscenity. 'Development.'

'But our land, the land we have? What about that?'

'As well. I'm sorry. But that as well. The zoning amendments went through council a month ago. There's absolutely nothing we can do. We have a year to resettle. A year to relocate. Can you face that?'

'Of course,' Sister Luke says, her jaw more prominent than ever. 'We must simply start again.'

'But the people,' Aloysius says. Her eyes are wet with tears for them. 'How can they relocate? How will they feel? They love this place.'

All of us see the elemental shelters, the line of shackery fringing the bay. We see smoke rising from small fires, the essential punctuation of the heart.

Sister Tancred rises and moves restlessly about the room. It is the first time I have seen this fracturing of composure. 'Our lease has been rescinded. Just like that. There's a verbal assurance, but verbal only, of relocation expenses and some smidgin of compensation. But it's not that! Not us! It's them! That's what matters. I don't know.' She beats one hand softly again and again on the table. 'They said something about moving most of them back to Yarrabah or up to Lockhart River. They're writing a formal letter to the elders this month. They tell me some government official will be up to explain matters. Oh, it's their home! Their home! How can they do this to them!'

'But what is the development?' Aloysius demands. 'What is it?' She has turned a puffy white colour, half risen to go back to the sick child.

'Another Xanadu,' Sister Tancred says softly. 'That gentleman— forgive me, Julie my dear—was Kublai Khan.'

*   *   *

Perhaps she was more than right.

No perhaps. Delete.

We have all lost energy, enthusiasm.

In three weeks Clifford returns with an architect planner, a young-ish man with feral eyes and an expense account. They have driven in from Charco and stand in the listlessness of midday eyeing the settlement with open distaste.

It is the weekend, the hospital is empty for once and the settlement children are playing on the beach or around their houses. Clifford ignores me as he stalks past to bang on the convent door. What is new? Yet Sister Tancred, taking her time about responding to his vigorous thumping, glides past both men with the smallest of nods and forces them down onto the lawn strip where she tackles them beneath the shade of the jacarandas, demanding to know if they are aware of the penalties of trespass.

I wish I could hear God laughing.

I wish I could glimpse some signal of the Christian charity we are supposed to live by.

Perhaps God has re-invented time into a now so that this fusion of all our past days and all our future—moments of happiness or grief— are absorbed into this appalling present.

I am on the circumference of Clifford's arguments, seated as I am on the convent veranda, and unable to hear what is uttered. Clifford has never dealt before with a woman of such dignity as Tancred's. Eventually I see him pound away to the southern end of the beach while his henchman planner heads off to the hill slopes at the rear of the settlement. But it is not he whom I watch. It is Clifford, stumping stolidly, his gut straining against his shirt, heading unfazed through the rotting village in the direction of the forest hump below the headland where horror lies, reconstructed in leaves and vines.

'He even fights with his colleagues,' Tancred tells me unbelievingly when she joins me on the veranda. 'The architect was all for investigat-ing sites back of here but Mr Truscott insisted he wanted the resort to face north. They argued as if I weren't there. Perhaps I should pray for them both.'

Clifford heads on, unaware of the curious faces of children who tag him for a while then fall back as they understand in what direction he is going. They fear this man will re-invent horror.

He becomes a pip, a seed in my eye.

*   *   *

Even four hours later Sister Tancred refuses to be ruffled, the impatience and agitation of the architect planner who has been gulping tea on the convent veranda, swirling about her temperate centre.

The man is sweating brutally and demanding something be done. He has been to the southern headland himself but the gluttonous thickets kept him at bay and though he roared himself hoarse no answering call from Clifford came to assure him.

'Where is the bloody man?' he keeps demanding. 'Can't a few of those damn boongs go in and haul him out?'

'That would be a waste of time,' Tancred tells him. 'At least trying to persuade them would be. There's not one man in the settlement would go in there.'

'Why not?'

'You wouldn't understand.'

'Try me.'

'There's a radio telephone if you're really worried. You can ring through to the police at Charco. But I'm sure you're worrying about nothing.'

'Look,' the man says, 'it's getting damn near sundown. Where's that bloody phone?'

'The bloody phone,' Sister Tancred says icily, 'is in our sitting-room. You may go through to use it.'

But he had already clambered over her words.

Why is it no former loyalties drive me down from my safe perch to screech and riot through that mesh of lawyer vine, shrieking Clifford's name?

The garden is shadowed as the sun drops behind the coastal range. The blue fades from the sea, a shifting fabric of white tassels right out to the purple line of the deeper water.

I should go after him. I should. I say this aloud and Tancred regards me coolly and directly, saying how purposeless it would be, how I would merely compound the problem. The architect planner has already explained the situation to the police at Charco. Something is bound to happen—a helicopter perhaps, truckloads of able-bodied searchers.

Aloysius keeps making tea. We sit. We sit. Clifford's discomfited colleague tends to wander in and out, hesitating on the veranda, waiting by the radio phone, starting off towards the southern headland, ploughing back again. On his last impatient prowl I run after him, guilt-driven I suppose, and we come up from the beach to the fortress of green now turning to a vast hump of black as the sun finally sets.

The silence is thick, is palpable. The air is heavy with aphony, rotten, putrescent with nothing. It is the thundering emptiness of the void.

'Cliff!' the man beside me shouts. 'Cliff!' I can see his foxy features still against the grainy air. The place blots up his shouts as if they were ink. No answering shout, no echo, no reverberation hits back at us poised in twilight, leaning across the pit, hearing those name-cries roar out and then become deadened as if gagged.

'Useless,' I tell him and turn about, heading to the convent for a flashlight. Why? I ask myself. Why? The man comes pumping after me, bitten by terror.

'Wait!' he is crying. 'Wait!' His voice trembles as he pants in my wake, as I outdistance him running between the quivering spots of light that mark the houses. I am intent only on making a gesture to the moment, the snatched-up torch, the in-passing glimpse of the nuns' faces protesting its uselessness.

A kind of inverted terror drives me on to the site of the old school house, a mechanical absorption in my own fear that forces me through the outer walls of scrub to the entrance I found so many months ago. These walls have closed against me. I see the forest as I play the light of the flash up and down, backwards and forwards seeking the aperture, as an enormous pitcher plant, a monster Venus flytrap that has recently taken a victim and enclosed it with gorging sepals. But I fight my way through gluttonous growth, moving inwards to where I imagine that previous entrance was and am clutched by a thickness of vine and branch that gropes out and about me. I scream Clifford's name over and over and the silence whacks back as if I had never opened my mouth.

*   *   *

Clifford was never found. He had joined that long roll call of trackers who had challenged jungle.

The next morning had brought rescue workers from Charco and a chopper that low-scanned the southern headland and the national park beyond. Nothing. Untroubled by taboos, park rangers hacked their way into the heart of the former tragedy, slashing with cane-knives, to waken the tree-house from its grief and discover it empty. The only trace of human intrusion was a half-smoked cigar—I recognised Clifford's brand—and nothing else.

Nothing.

Had he gone to Hong Kong, Mallorca, Rio?

Why talk about it? It became a five-day wonder in the *Charco Herald* and the *Reeftown Daily*.

Despite my protestations, Baxter, always insensitive, published a series of feature articles and fabricated interviews with the former wife of the missing man.

Please, Baxter! Please.

This germinated spates of letters from people remembering other people who had disappeared in similar circumstances in the Gulf, on the Tableland, at Babinda Falls, the Crater, on offshore islands. Old diggers from the Second World War wrote about vanishings in Santo and Guadalcanal.

Time settled over that week, my week, thick as leaves.

Just as I had believed I had discovered the ripe kernel in the heart of the life-fruit, I realised I must abandon it. But to find another again.

*   *   *

'When you want to stop moving,' Baxter had said to me once, 'you're dead.'

Those had been prognostic words I realise now as I twitter into middle age trailing a litter of incomplete projects stretching back across all those long summers (it's always summer here!) rather like that elephant line trailing deserts in Dali's *Temptations of Saint Anthony*. Ah, horrible! The weather has bitten into my bones.

Or I have lost the weather.

I have lost that storm centre that Clifford created.

I have ceased wanting to move.

I am back with the children. Of course.

Searching persists sporadically.

Nothing. Weeks, months trickle away. Still nothing.

There are alleged sightings in Melbourne, New York, Zurich.

Clifford's passport is missing as well.

There are sightings in Amsterdam, London, Paris.

Where is the *Allegro*? Daniel asks. As well he may.

Flora meets all my attempts at speculation with: 'No comment.'

I am with the children but in a different house. Saint Kierkegaard created no problems even though she had been on the lip of a marriage doomed to failure. She had demanded no favours, moving promptly to a flat in town and then, by grace of Clifford's distraught Board, to the position of supervisory chef on Hummock resort. Clifford's business ventures are failing despite or because of his absence but his partners have made a meagre allocation of share funds to help with the children's school expenses. A receiver will soon be appointed. I refused to take a cent and am scratching out precarious personal maintenance on the *Sugarville Mail*, a position achieved through Baxter's influence.

'*Det är tid att gå*. It is time to go,' Bodil Kierkegaard had said as she left the house. 'In every way.'

Oh yes, I agree. It is time for us all. The children visit her sometimes and eat great for two days. There is strong danger of her becoming my friend.

After their initial shock the children ceased mentioning Clifford. It was as if they agreed on the futility of it all. Unless, as happened only last week, a page three headline says: 'Developer sighted in Buenos Aires' causing a brief domestic frisson, or some thoughtless acquaintance drops his name in a social blunder, we remain uncommunicative about him even with each other.

Lately I have been aware of my own mortality, the sickening thrust of *finis* scribbled across my days. For the time being I tell myself, I shall devote myself to the children and watch them grow away from me, learning to be happy for that.

The little mission at Bukki is still there, development zest having died with Clifford's disappearance. We correspond, the sisters and I, but I have never gone back. Perhaps in time. Perhaps.

For always at the back of my mind, always, I shall keep a memory of Tancred, Aloysius and Luke as talismanic emblems of a future beyond, of something that eventually I can reach out to when my small world has ceased reaching for me.